Alexander the Alabarch, 3

A Toga In The Wind

Kass Evans

An Alexander the Alabarch

Mystery of the Roman Empire

ALEXANDER THE ALABARCH, 3

A Toga in The Wind

Kass Evans

Terra Expressions

Brandon, Florida
2021

Published 2021 by Terra Expressions Publishers, an imprint of Terra Enterprises (Tampa, Florida)
http://TerraExpressions.com ;
copyright: ©2021 by Katherine G. Evans

    ISBN: 978-1-941790-15-1 (pbk.)
    ISBN: 978-1-941790-14-4 (ebook)

The contents of this book are protected by U.S. and international copyright laws. No part of it may be reproduced in print, electronically, or posted online without the written permission of the author. (mail@KassEvans.com)

Evans, Kass.
A Toga in the Wind / Kass Evans.

Brandon, Florida. : Terra Expressions, 2021
295 pages : Illustrations ; 23 cm.

Series: Alexander the Alabarch; 3

DESCRIPTION
Alexandria, Egypt, 12 A.D. Alexander has returned home where he will soon take up the Roman magistracy of the Alabarch. First, he must keep a promise he made to Antonia Minor, niece of Augustus. She has asked him to become procurator for her extensive properties in Egypt. It should have been easy. He just had to assume the duties of Antonia's outgoing land agent. The challenge was the land agent did not want to be relieved of his duties and so he disappeared taking all of Antonia's money and records with him. Next the cattle started to disappear, then a horse, and ... an evil goat. Then the first body is found.

Accompanied by his servant Amarantus, Alexander sets sail up the Nile for Lake Moeris and the many villages where Antonia owns property. He chases the land agent to the desert, the rooftops, the Great Labyrinth, finally getting caught up in a dispute between the crocodile priests. Crocodiles and hippopotami. Could one man in such a foreign land retrieve the goods and stop the killing? 'Good thing Alexander had brought his *xulon* fighting sticks along.

    ISBN: 978-1-941790-15-1 (pbk.)

1. Alexander, Alabarch, active 1st century--Fiction. 2. Egypt--History--Greco-Roman period, 332 B.C.-640 A.D.—Fiction. 3. Jews--Egypt--History--Fiction. 4. Egypt—History--30 B.C.-640 A.D. --Fiction.

PS3605.V367 T645 2021
813.6 EV92

In memory of my father

Frank L. Evans

1932 - 2018

Contents

Prologue 1
1. Homecoming 5
2. The *Epistrategos* 11
3. The *Xulon* Master 27
4. He Said No 39
5. Out of the Deep 51
6. The Beer House 67
7. The Jews of Crocodilopolis 83
8. Philadelphia 95
9. Karanis 113
10. Festival of Petesouchos 125
11. Fowling Things Up 139
12. Pressing Matters 155
13. The Great Labyrinth 181
14. Melee 207
15. An Evil Goat 225
16. Another Corpse 243
17. In the Wind 255
18. The New Alabarch 273
Epilogue 281
Historical Note 285

About this Book

Roman Egypt, 12 AD.

Running, running, panting. Papyrus sandals slapping against his bare soles. Mud everywhere. Then ... *pain.* The great crocodile god Sobek will not be denied.

****

Alexander has returned home where he will soon take up the Roman magistracy of the Alabarch. First, he must keep a promise he made to the Lady Antonia Minor, niece of Augustus and daughter of Mark Antony. She has asked him to become procurator for her extensive properties in Egypt.

It should have been easy. He just had to take over the duties of Antonia's outgoing land agent. Unfortunately, the land agent, Hierax, *did not want to be relieved* of his duties and so he disappeared taking all of Antonia's money and records with him.

Next the cattle start to disappear, then a horse, and ... an evil goat. Then the first body is found.

Accompanied by his servant Amarantus, Alexander sets sail up the Nile for Lake Moeris and the many villages where Antonia owns property. He chases that wretched land agent to the desert, the rooftops, the Great Labyrinth, finally getting caught up in a stick fight between rival crocodile priests.

Crocodiles and hippopotami. Could one man in such a foreign land retrieve the goods and stop the killing?

Good thing Alexander had brought his *xulon* fighting sticks along.

****

Alexander the Alabarch was an historical person, the real life friend of the Emperor Claudius, in-law of King Agrippa of Judea, procurator for Marc Antony's daughter Antonia Minor, and one of the most notable Jews of the early Roman Empire.

What Came Before

A Toga of a Different Color was the first book in the Alexander the Alabarch series and takes place in Rome, 12 A.D. featuring the 22-year old Alexander.

As darkness reigns over the Palatine Hill, a rumbling ox cart stops before the temple of Victory. A man in an *augur's* striped toga removes the famous statue of Victory. He says it is for a procession, but the Victory disappears not to be seen again.

Augustus is furious. Rome wants its Victory back.

At first, Alexander thinks little of it. He's a Jew, so a Roman goddess has nothing to do with him. Then a Jewish art dealer is arrested for the theft. As the man's patron, Alexander decides he must find the Victory if he is to free his client. Seeking the stolen statue, however, soon becomes a very dangerous pursuit.

At Alexander's side are his boyhood friends: Claudius the emperor's ill-loved nephew, Rutilus the poorest patrician in Rome, and Agrippa a Jewish prince and a bit of a rogue.

Standing in their way is an elite group of Praetorian guards who don't want the art dealer freed. In fact, they don't seem to want the Victory to be found. *But why?*

Word of their snooping reaches Augustus who summons Alexander and orders him to find the statue. He is to report back his findings to Tiberius, the adopted son and future emperor.

Time is running short. Alexander's frantic search for answers takes him from the palace of Augustus to the sewer underbelly of Rome. Underneath it all is a sense of urgency for his father has recalled him to Alexandria and Alexander must leave in days -- no matter how much he doesn't want to leave his home, his friends ...or her.

She was beautiful, she was noble, but she was *not* a Jew. And his father had betrothed him to some Jewish girl in Judea. Alexander didn't want her; he wanted to stay in Rome and marry the beautiful Rutilla. But could they find a way to make it work?

Alexander called for Tiberius when he eventually located the statue and the guilty parties. Except the culprits were not who he thought they'd be. In fact, they were people he cared about a great deal. Now he had caused their downfall and exile.

Heartbroken, Alexander boards a ship to return to Alexandria where he will be sworn in as the next Alabarch. He now wears the narrow purple stripes of the *eques* a noble of the equestrian order – his reward from Augustus for finding the statue.

In his pouch is the letter from the Lady Antonia Minor giving him authority over all of her estates in Egypt. His slave secretary, Amarantus, stands by his side. His father and brother Philo await him in Alexandria. Perhaps, it was a time for new beginnings.

****

Alexander the Alabarch was an historical person, the real life friend of the Emperor Claudius, in-law of King Agrippa of Judea, procurator for Marc Antony's daughter Antonia Minor, and one of the most notable Jews of the early Roman Empire.

Major Characters
*denotes historical person

Alexander*	Gaius Julius Alexander
Amarantus*	Slave secretary of Alexander who later became his freedman ; nickname is Ranti [CPJ 420a]
Antonia Minor*	Great lady of Rome. Niece of Augustus, sister-in-law of the future emperor Tiberius, mother or grandmother of the future emperors Claudius, Gaius-Caligula, and Nero.
Claudius*	Tiberius Claudius Nero
Dionysodoros*	*strategos* of Arsinoite Nome 14-15 AD ; nickname: Dion [SB I.5238 ; P. Lond. II. 445]
Hannah	the lady attendant of the teenage Jewish girl Leah
Hierax	Marcus Antonius Hierax – freedman of the Lady Antonia Minor and her land agent in Egypt
Indike	[pronounced In-dee-kay] young woman who lives is Crocodilopolis
Kronion	A priest of Kronos in his aspect as a crocodile god
Leah	Young woman from Judea visiting Egypt as a tourist
Magius Maximus*	Quintus Magius Maximus, Prefect of Egypt, 12-14 AD
Philo*	Alexander's younger brother, philosopher and theologian
Sabinus	A Roman citizen in the Arsinoite nome; good drinking companion
Serenius	Titus Serenius, *epistrategos* of the Heptanomia and the Arsinoite nome
Soknebtunis	Sobek, Souchos, Petesouchos, Kronos – different names of aspects of the crocodile god

Author's Note

The inspiration for this story, at least in part, came from two curious papyri from the village of Tebtunis dating to the early Roman period. The ruins of Tebtunis can still be seen in the area now known as the Fayum around Lake Moeris in Egypt.

The first papyrus is an official petition to the Roman prefect of Egypt from the *"legitimate"* priests of the temple of the crocodile god Soknebtunis.

> *'To ... , the lord prefect, from . . . and the rest of the hereditary priests of the famous temple of Soknebtunis ... in the . . year,*
>
> **when certain bastards from the temple asked for leave to cultivate the land before . . . , late epistrategus of the Heptanomis and Arsinoite nome,** ... *he reserved the land for* **us, the legitimate priests**, *according to the report of the trial in our possession.* (P. Tebt. II.302 - dated 71-72 A.D.)

By **"bastards from the temple,"** the petitioners almost certainly meant persons who could not prove they had a hereditary priestly bloodline. Who were these illegitimate persons from the temple? ... *No one knows. It's a mystery.*

The second papyrus gets into a stick fight at the home of an *exempted* (eg. legitimate, hereditary) priest from the crocodile god temple.

> *To Longinus, decurion of the Arsinoite nome, from Pakebkis* ... **exempted priest of the famous temple in the village [Tebtunis]**. *On the 30th of the month Epeiph, when the hour was late, one Satornilus, with a great many others, ... picked*

a quarrel, going so far as to **rush in with staves [xulons], and seizing my brother Onnophris they wounded him,** *so that his life is endangered in consequence. (PTebt II.304 A.D. 167-8.)*

Who were these men who rushed into the home of a crocodile god priest and started beating his family with sticks? ... *No one knows. It's a mystery.*

This is what I imagine could have happened.

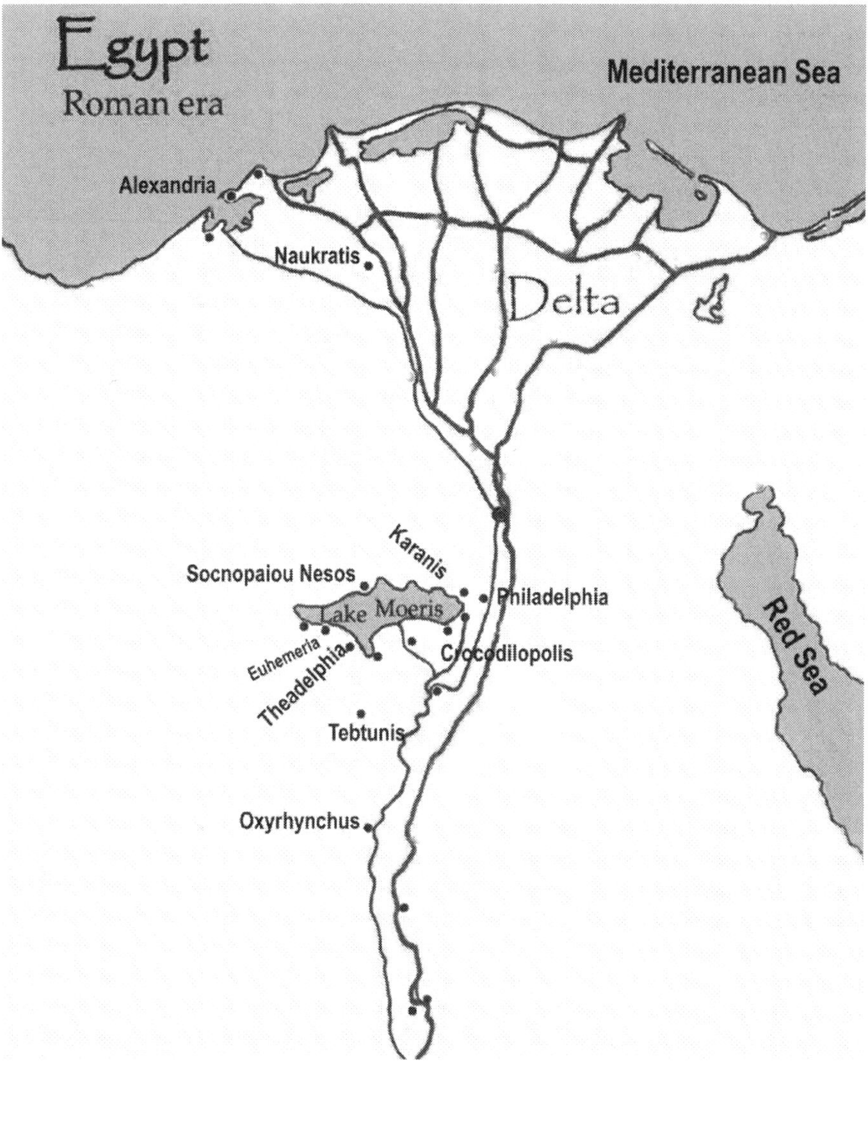
Egypt
Roman era
Mediterranean Sea
Alexandria
Naukratis
Delta
Karanis
Socnopaiou Nesos
Philadelphia
Lake Moeris
Crocodilopolis
Euhemeria
Theadelphia
Tebtunis
Oxyrhynchus
Red Sea

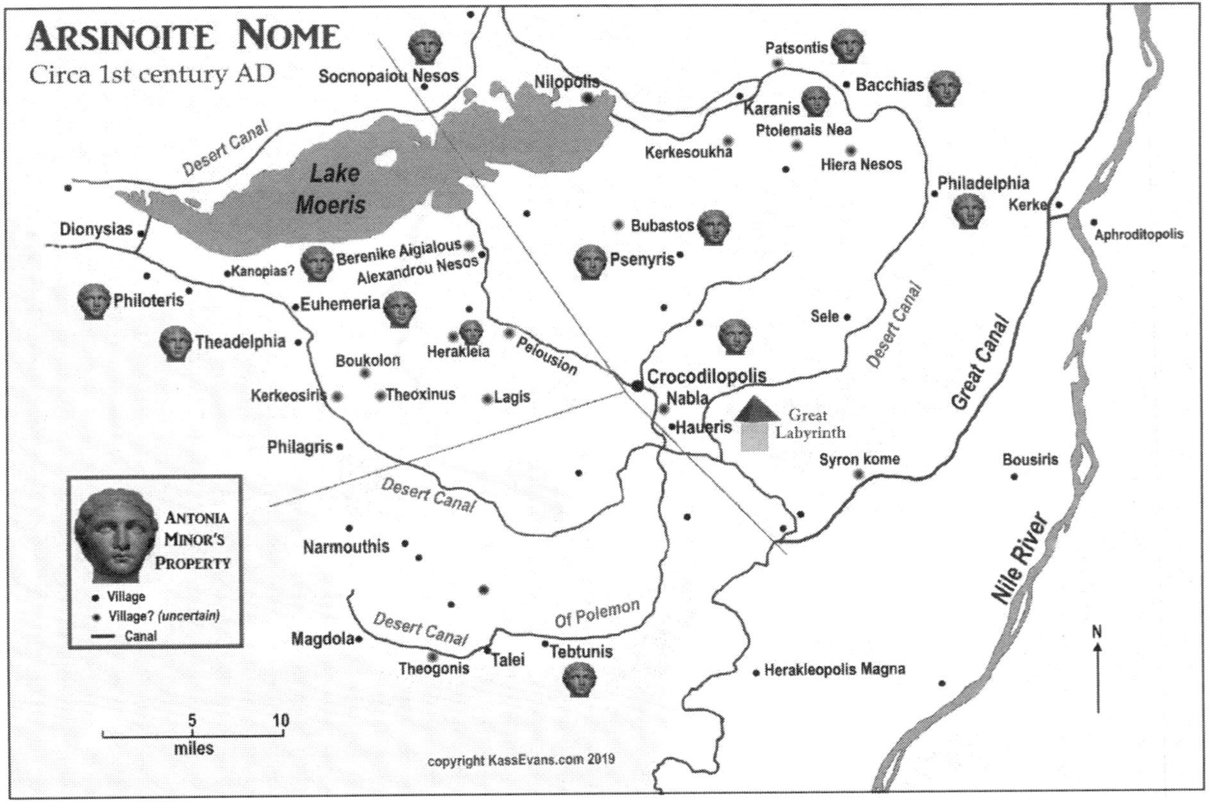
ARSINOITE NOME
Circa 1st century AD
Socnopaiou Nesos
Nilopolis
Patsontis
Bacchias
Karanis
Ptolemais Nea
Kerkesoukha
Hiera Nesos
Desert Canal
Lake Moeris
Philadelphia
Kerke
Aphroditopolis
Dionysias
Bubastos
Psenyris
Berenike Aigialous
Alexandrou Nesos
Kanopias?
Philoteris
Euhemeria
Theadelphia
Herakleia
Pelousion
Sele
Desert Canal
Great Canal
Boukolon
Crocodilopolis
Nabla
Kerkeosiris
Theoxinus
Lagis
Haueris
Great Labyrinth
Philagris
Syron kome
Bousiris
Desert Canal
ANTONIA MINOR'S PROPERTY
Village
Village? (uncertain)
Canal
Narmouthis
Nile River
Of Polemon
Desert Canal
Magdola
Talei
Tebtunis
Theogonis
Herakleopolis Magna
N
5
10
miles
copyright KassEvans.com 2019

Alexandria, Egypt

Late August 12 A.D.
The Annual Inundation of the Nile Reaches its Peak

Year 39 of the
First Citizen

Gaius Julius Caesar Octavianus
Called
Augustus

Adopted son
of the Deified
Gaius Julius Caesar

Conqueror of
Queen Cleopatra VII
and all Egypt
in 30 B.C.

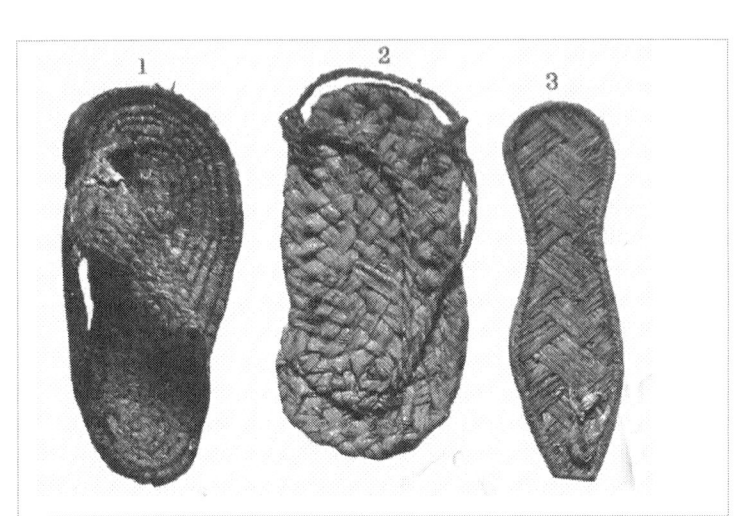

Roman-Egyptian sandals. The remains of (1) rope, (2) rush, and (3) papyrus sandals recovered from villages in the Arsinoite Nome. All date to the Roman period.

Source: Fayum Towns and Their Papyri, B. Grenfell, A. Hunt, D. Hogarth (1900), Plate XVII

Prologue

Running ... running ... panting. The sound of his woven papyrus sandals slapping against the bare soles of his feet.

Not much moonlight. Not sure where to go. He only knew that he had to run. *Run. Escape.*

Ahead. He could smell water. It must be the canal. His foot sank into the mud and he yanked it free. The thong on his right sandal broke, but he didn't dare stop.

Tears filled his eyes. It wasn't supposed to be this way. Had he taken too many risks? Or not enough?

He had thought of it as just a lark, an adventure, a way to make a little money. No one would get hurt. ... But he knew that wasn't true. It had been more than that. His actions had caused harm.

So he had tried to stay quiet, tried to stay away, until now. Tonight, he had come here thinking it would be alright. After all, he had only told one other person about it. Just one. What would happen to him now? Would he have to pay?

Maybe he had done wrong to the villagers, but mostly he had dishonored the Lord, the great, great god. The crocodile god was not known for his forgiveness.

Listen! There was a roar in the distance. Perhaps it was not too late. Perhaps if he prostrated himself before the god and made many vows and offerings, there might be mercy.

He straightened and tried to run again. The broken sandal

strap forced him to stagger. His feet splashed in water and he blindly ran onto the banks of the canal. There, up ahead. He heard a sound. Perhaps if he could approach the god, he could throw himself on his belly and pray.

Then ... No! A vice-like grip clamped down on his leg. There was the feel of teeth biting, rending. He fell. Pain and blood sprang forth. He tried to shout for help, but who was there to hear him, but the god?

He was forsaken and there was no hope for him now. The god had caught him and now he would be judged. The sharp pain in his leg grew greater, and he was being pulled down, down into the deep. Darkness surrounded him. *Breathe.* He couldn't breathe. With a mental sigh, he ceased to struggle and gave himself up to the will of the god. He had run out of time.

Not far away, a large crocodile lay on the bank waiting, watching. As the human creature submerged, it narrowed its eyes and slowly moved its head from side to side. Then he raised his great frame, slid into the water and was gone.

A Crocodile on the sandbank of the Nile River

Source: Photograph taken in circa 1862 by Francis Frith
Library of Congress: https://www.loc.gov/item/2002706151/

Alexander, the future Alabarch
Full Roman name: Gaius Julius Alexander

1. Homecoming

The old man was dead.

Oh, he was still breathing – at least for now. He was still sitting at his desk, still poring through the piles of papyrus scrolls just as he always had. But now there were gray shadows that seemed to contract around his once vigorous frame, a body now grown feeble. Then there were the fits of coughing, gasping, shaking. Oh yes, the old man was dead, or, soon he would be -- this shadow of the man who was ... *his father*.

For Alexander, it explained a lot. --like why his brother Philo had come alone to meet his ship when it had arrived at the port of Alexandria. Or, for that matter, why his father had recalled him from Rome at all – and so suddenly, so unexpectedly. Now he guessed he knew. His father did not expect to be around a lot longer, so he had recalled his oldest son home to ... *to replace* him.

Alexander bit his lower lip as he sat across from his father's desk. He still was not sure what to make of it all. The days preceding his departure from Rome had been a whirlwind of activity ... and emotion. Then the winds had been fair and it had taken the ship just seventeen days to arrive in the port of Alexandria, to arrive at his home.

Home.

Alexandria was his father's home; and, his brother's home. It had not felt like *his home* since his father had taken him to be educated in Rome at age ten. He was now twenty-two. The twelve years he had lived in Rome were practically a lifetime.

His father leaned back in his chair, steepled his fingers under his chin and spoke.

"So the Lady Antonia has asked you to take charge of her estates, then? All of them?"

Alexander startled from his thoughts and looked up. For such a sick man, his father's eyes seemed suddenly intense.

"Yes, *Abba*, all of them. Before I left Rome, Antonia sent a note for me to call upon her. Apparently the accounts being sent to her from Egypt were not adding up and she suspected that her freedman was cheating her."

His father rubbed at the short stubble on his chin. "Did she give you any more detail than that?"

Alexander shook his head and lifted one shoulder in a shrug.

"Not really. She simply asked me to investigate, find the problem, fix it, and then take charge so that it doesn't happen again. I have a letter from her appointing me as administrator for all of her estates in Egypt."

His father shifted back in surprise. "Do you mean the Lady Antonia legally made you her *epitropos*?"

Alexander nodded. "Yes, she did, although in Latin she called it her *procurator*. I'm not completely sure what that will entail." He dipped his head and smiled a bit sheepishly at his father. "I admit that I did not want to appear lacking in front of Antonia, so I may have acted like I understood the responsibilities better than I do. Of course, I have a general idea, but this is not something I ever encountered in Rome."

His father had ceased rubbing at the stubble and now

gripped his chin thoughtfully. "Well, Alexander, in some ways the position will be whatever you make of it. After Augustus and Tiberius, Antonia probably owns more properties in Egypt than anyone else – more even that Augustus's wife Livia. There is not a lot of precedent for exactly what the *uh procurator* should do, especially with her estates being so extensive and scattered. I suppose as long as you show a profit, Antonia will be happy with whatever you make of the position."

Reaching out his father patted a stack of papyrus sheets, shook his head and frowned. "I will need you at the mines soon, my son -- soon to be the Alabarch. There are problems there, I admit; problems that I have not been ... strong enough to deal with myself. However, I think you had best take care of the Lady Antonia's business first."

Alexander nodded. "I agree, *Abba*, although I'm not sure how long this will take. I suppose I'd better start with Antonia's freedman who is currently managing most of her affairs in the Arsinoite nome. His name is Hierax -- Marcus Antonius Hierax. Do you know where I can find him?"

His father shook his head. "No. I don't really know the man and from what little I have seen, I can't say that I particularly like him. Oh, I suppose he was ingratiating enough when the Lady Antonia chose him for this position. Being out here on his own without her supervision must have changed him though."

His father paused to cough and take a sip of fruit juice.

"Honestly, Alexander, this Hierax strikes me as a bit of a predator. You don't want to turn your back on him."

He held his palm up to stop his son's next question. "No, no, I have no evidence that Antonia's freedman land agent has done anything wrong. Before you meet with him, I suggest you talk to Titus Serenius. He is the *epistrategos* of the Heptanomia and the

Arsinoite Nome. That makes him the highest administrator over all of the areas where Hierax is active. He may be able to give you an idea where to find the man and, well, if there's anything more you should know about him."

Alexander knit brows. "Do you think that is necessary? Antonia told me just to relieve him of his duties and send him packing back to Rome."

His father pointed a finger and seemed that he was going say more, but then just gave a non-committal shrug.

"Of course, it will be your decision, Alexander. But, there may be some advantage to acquiring a little bit of information before you face off with the man. *If* the freedman land agent has been involved in anything negative regarding money or property, you may want to find out before he is gone. You are the new man responsible now and it will be up to you to resolve whatever problems he leaves behind."

Alexander curled his lip at the thought of that. If the freedman had been up to something shady – and Antonia thought he had -- it could require a lot of time and money on his part to fix it. He ran a hand through his hair as he took a moment to think of the endless inspections of properties and auditing of accounts ahead of him. *Hmm*, in fact he should probably assume that there *will be* problems with the accounts and properties, issues that will point back to this Hierax the land agent.

His *abba* continued, "I see you understand me. It would be better to have a sense of what you may be dealing with before you dismiss him. ... It may end up being nothing, but I would not be surprised if you find you need to move quickly to seize some of the documents and warehouse goods. Once this Hierax is gone, there won't be much you can do about it. You may get caught out having to cover some of the problems he leaves from your own purse."

Alexander nodded thoughtfully. "You are right, *Abba*. Antonia only mentioned a shortfall in profits that she had been receiving, but a freedman who would cheat his own patron is a man who would not hesitate to cheat others.

"So where can I find this Titus Serenius, the *epistrategos*? Will he be in Crocodilopolis? That is the nome capital isn't it?"

"It is, but, no," his father smiled. "Remember an *epistrategos* is always a Roman and an *eques*, a man of the Equestrian class. He does his duty and visits the nome capitals as required, but most of the time he prefers to stay near civilization. Serenius is here, in Alexandria. I can give you directions."

While Alexander's mind was still busy thinking of what he may do to find and counter any problems created by Hierax, his father rose slowly and stood for a moment wavering and holding onto the side of his desk.

"And now, Alexander, I must rest."

He picked up his cane, and hobbled slowly from the room. But at the door he turned back.

"I am glad you're home, Son. Just having you here, gives me great relief."

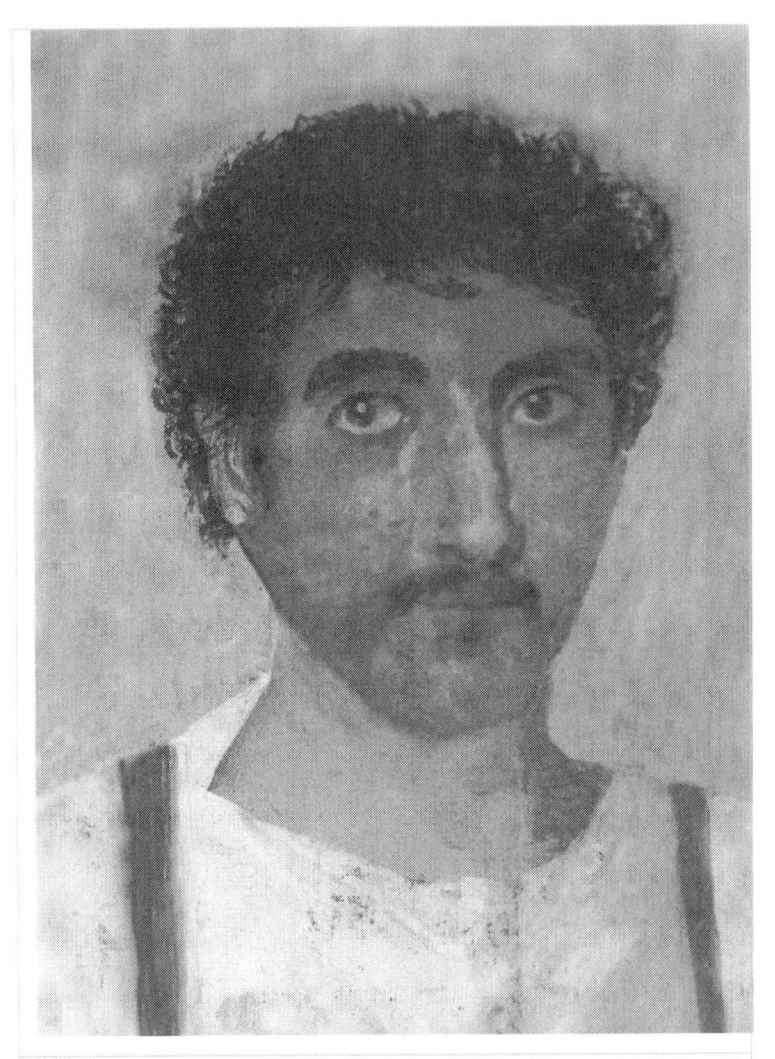

His Excellency Titus Serenius, *epistrategos* for the Heptanomia and the Arsinoite nome, an *eques* or knight of the Roman equestrian order.

2. THE *EPISTRATEGOS*

Much to his surprise, it took very little time for Alexander to get an appointment with Titus Serenius. He had assumed that as one of Egypt's three *epistrategoi* that Titus Serenius would be a busy man. Or, at least, he would perceive himself as such and keep Alexander waiting.

Instead, Alexander's message requesting an interview was returned within an hour with an appointment for the following morning. Alexander had been sitting in his father's study with his slave secretary Amarantus when the small scroll arrived.

Alexander raised his eyebrows, "Well, Ranti. What do you make of this? The *epistrategos* seems almost eager to meet me."

Amarantus returned a knowing nod. "Master, there are two reasons that I can think of for him wanting to meet with you so soon." He held up a finger. "First, he thinks you owe him money."

"No, Ranti," Alexander shook his head smiling. "I have only been back in Alexandria for a couple days now. There has not been time yet for me to get into debt to anyone. Only Agrippa could have accomplished that."

His childhood friend the Jewish prince Marcus Agrippa was known for being perennially in debt.

"So Ranti, debt is out. What is option number two?"

"That should be obvious, Master. He is hoping to transfer some of his workload to you."

Alexander laughed out loud. "While that is most insightful, Ranti, I don't see how that could be likely either. To begin with, I don't have the authority of an *epistrategos* and probably never will. Plus my responsibilities to the Lady Antonia, tending my own family's own properties, and learning to be the next Alabarch should keep me plenty busy. ... No, I certainly won't have time for anything more than that."

If Alexander had been an Egyptian and not a Jew, and if he had been listening, he may have thought that he had just heard the gods laughing.

****

The next morning, Alexander accompanied by Amarantus presented himself at the home of the *epistrategos*. His servant was quickly escorted to the servants' section. So it was by himself that Alexander was ushered somewhat nervously into the office of the *epistrategos* Titus Serenius.

Alexander was clean shaven and wearing his new tunic with the narrow purple stripes that marked his recent rise to the equestrian order. In fact, his elevation to an *eques* had happened only a few weeks earlier. His rank was so new that Alexander did not yet feel confident that he knew how to act now that he was a Roman noble. He wasn't even sure of how to greet others of his same rank.

Indeed, Alexander felt awkward, unsure and he knew it probably showed. That made him start to worry. What if the *epistrategos*, who had been an *eques* from birth, decided not to take this new young Jewish *eques* seriously? What if he looked down on Alexander? What if he scorned him?

It could happen. There were plenty of *equites* in Rome, but in Egypt there were not many at all. The highest administrative positions could be held only by men of equestrian rank and those few were all appointed directly by the Emperor. Would Alexander be accepted among that elite group?

On some level, Alexander realized that he was the source of his own anxiety. There surely was no reason to anticipate some upcoming slight. It was just that this was one of his first formal meetings since becoming an *eques*. He didn't want to make himself look a fool by trying too hard.

Alexander stood as Titus Serenius breezed into the room wearing an almost identical white tunic with the two *clavi*, narrow purple stripes. He was not a big man, probably several inches below Alexander's own six foot height, but he appeared fit. Alexander guessed his age at probably ten years older than himself putting the *epistrategos* in his early to mid thirties. His skin was light, his hair was dark and curly, his nose straight – all as expected of a Roman.

What was startling, however, was the hair above the man's lip. Serenius had *a moustache,* of all things. Why would a man of his rank wear something so very unfashionable? *Hunh.* Then Alexander realized that Serenius must have come from one of the provinces and not Rome itself. He wasn't sure, but he thought that some of the Germanic tribes wore this hair above their upper lip without beards, maybe some of the men from Hispania as well. He wasn't sure and now was not the time to ask the *epistrategos* about his unusual facial hair.

Serenius came to a halt next to his desk. He regarded Alexander with what seemed like a genuine smile and said, "Gaius Julius Alexander, I can't tell you how delighted I am to meet you. Do you go by Gaius?"

"No, by Alexander, your Excellency" he replied somewhat taken aback by the unexpectedly warm welcome.

"Alexander, then. You can call me Serenius. I know your father, of course. How does he fare?"

"He is very ill," Alexander replied, "and, well, the doctors tell him that he is unlikely to recover."

Titus Serenius nodded gravely. "I feared as much after the last time I saw him. ... That would explain your unexpected presence here in Alexandria, then. Your father summoned you home to take over the family affairs?"

Alexander nodded.

"*Ahh*, that makes sense. Honestly, I had barely heard of you, Alexander, until a couple weeks ago. It was a surprise to learn that a new *eques* was coming to Alexandria and would be taking charge of the Lady Antonia's lands. Do I have that right?"

"Yeees," Alexander answered slowly with a nod. To his surprise, Serenius grinned broadly and rubbed his hands together almost gleefully.

"Good. Good. Now that you are here, Alexander, I can safely dispatch a passel of troubles into your newly equestrian hands."

"What? No!"

The *epistrategos* definitely was nodding his head *yes* and grinning as he walked over to his desk and pulled forward a basket filled with papyrus scrolls of different sizes and shapes.

"Do you see these, Alexander? They are all petitions from tenants – even overseers – of Antonia Minor's properties in the Arsinoite nome. Somehow they have all decided that since they are under the *aegis* of Antonia, and since Antonia is such a great Lady and the niece of Augustus, that must mean that each of their problems must be of interest to their *epistrategos* – namely *to me*."

Serenius plucked out a small scroll from the top. "Here, look at this one." He handed the scroll to Alexander. "Go on. Read it. Just read it."

Alexander slowly unrolled the scroll and studied the text. It was worded like a petition and fortunately written in a trained scribal hand so he could read it fairly swiftly which he did aloud.

To his most excellent Titus Serenius, epistrategos of the Heptanomia and the Arsinoite nome, from Ammonios, son of Eirenaios, one of the cultivators of the ousia of the Lady Antonia from Karanis. On the night before the 4th of Mecheir certain persons made an attack on the cattle that I have grazing in the plain of Kerkesoucha, and drove off my red calf. Therefore I ask that you make an investigation so that my red calf will be returned to me. Farewell.

Alexander looked up at the *epistrategos* and raised his eyebrows. "A red calf?"

"Indeed! A cow." Titus Serenius was clearly animated. "For the love of Jupiter, this farmer wants an *epistrategos* to look for his missing cow!"

Alexander glanced at the petition in his hand and then back at the basket that suddenly seemed extremely full of papyrus scrolls and scrunched his eyebrows.

"Are they all like this one?"

Titus Serenius waved a hand dismissively. "Oh, they vary of course. Most seem to involve cases of people infringing on each other's property, but a missing animal is a common complaint. In the basket is one petition where the man assures me that when I find his missing mare, I will recognize it because it is wheat colored.

... Oh, and there is the one with a missing goat named Seth; I gather that's the name of some Egyptian god of evil. That one informs me that his goat can be recognized because it eats everything."

He paused and pointed his index finger at Alexander. "There are different kinds of disputes and problems. But *not a one* of them should require *my* attention. Given the importance of the Lady Antonia, though, I have been reluctant so far to just refuse to consider the petitions from her tenants."

He smiled happily and gestured at Alexander. "I'm sure the Lady Antonia's *new procurator* will sort it all out."

Alexander glanced again at the basket full of petitions. "B-but," Alexander stammered, "Antonia currently has a land agent, one of her freedmen. He has responsibility for her properties in the Arsinoite nome. Yes, I am here to replace him, but surely this was *his job* until I came?"

"*Him?*" Serenius scoffed, "Hierax? He is worthless... lazy. I have tried to get him to take responsibility for some of these petitions, but he keeps sniveling, *'he is just a land agent, he doesn't have the authority, he doesn't have the time, he doesn't have the staff.'* You name it and he doesn't have it. The man will claim anything to get out doing his own work."

Alexander mulled this over for a moment. "Actually, the reason I came here today was to ask you about this man Hierax. I haven't met him yet and Antonia could not tell me much about him. He is her freedman, but she hasn't seen him for years. ... What can you tell me? You say he is lazy, but otherwise is he honest?"

"*Hunh.*" Serenius shook his head. "I doubt it. Not if any of the stories *I* hear are true."

"What kind of stories?" Alexander scrunched his eyebrows.

This was not the description of the man that he had been hoping to hear.

"Well, I don't know for a fact if Hierax has done anything blatantly illegal or fraudulent," the *epistrategos* answered. "But I do know that he swims close to the levees."

Alexander smiled. "Like a crocodile, you mean? My father told me Hierax made him think of a predator."

"That's probably an apt description," Serenius nodded his agreement. "I hear of things like overcharging for the use of the olive press, leaning on the tenants for more rent than was actually due – all off the registers, of course. It may just be a little bit here, a little bit there, but once you add it all up, the man is probably making quite a tidy sum off of graft. My guess is that most of it would be difficult to prove and few of Antonia's tenants would risk coming forward to speak against him."

Serenius chewed his lower lip and gave Alexander a calculating look before continuing.

"Still I would suggest you take a close look at the accounts and inventory what crops are actually in the granaries; also talk to the tenants and those who use the mill or the wine press. Now that *you* are here, Alexander, the tenants may speak more freely. My guess is that the stories you will hear in the villages will not match whatever Hierax has recorded in the estate accounts."

Alexander looked again at the basket of petitions and blew out a long breath.

"You are correct, of course, Serenius. If these petitions are about the Lady Antonia's properties, then they should pass to me. I had hoped to find things in better order, but I suppose that these will help me make some decisions about restructuring how her *ousia,* her collected properties, get managed. Fortunately, I brought my secretary Amarantus here from Rome with me."

"Is that the slave you left out in the atrium?"

"It is. He has a position of complete trust with me. Plus Ranti is pretty good with numbers and accounts. Between us, we'll get it sorted."

Alexander looked at Serenius expecting to see a return of the gleeful smile over having passed on his *"passel of troubles."* The man's thoughts, however, seemed to have already wandered elsewhere.

The *epistrategos* put his fists on his hips and stared – no *glared*-- at another large pile of papyrus scrolls on the other side of desk. He spoke distractedly.

"Would that I could hand off *this* other problem to you – *to anyone*. What is to be done about these battling priests of Tebtunis? I can't imagine what the *Idios Logos* was thinking when he agreed to this one. *Why*, I ask you, would the chief financial officer get involved with priests? I don't know. ... Well, actually I *do* know. The *Idios Logos* has started *selling* priesthood positions. I suppose it's a good source of income."

Serenius pulled out a scroll, grimaced at it, then handed it to Alexander. "Here, look at this one – about half-way down."

Alexander was not getting the impression that Serenius actually wanted *him* to do anything about whatever this was. The man simply seemed to want a sympathetic ear. He could do that, so he accepted the scroll and glanced at the greeting.

> 'To ... his most excellent Titus Serenius, epistrategos of the Heptanomia and the Arsinoite nome, from ... and the rest of the hereditary priests of the famous temple of Soknebtunis also called Kronos, and the associated gods, situated at the village of Tebtunis in the Arsinoite nome.

"No, no, farther down." Serenius walked over and stabbed a finger at a line on the papyrus. "There. Start reading there. Read it aloud."

With a shrug Alexander placed his forefinger in the designated spot and began to read the Greek text as requested.

> *Further in the priestly list which we entered at the village for examination we showed that the cultivation of the aforesaid land was registered in our names, ... when certain **Kronos bastards from the temple** asked for leave to cultivate **our land** before the last epistrategos of the Heptanomia and Arsinoite nome, but he reserved the land for **us, the legitimate priests**, ...*

Alexander looked up puzzled. "*Kronos? Kronos bastards from the temple?* This makes no sense to me."

Titus Serenius raised his eyes upward and shook his head. "I know. Dealing with these Kronos priests can be a challenge; but it is usually not *my* challenge."

He paused as he saw Alexander wasn't following him at all. "You do know about Kronos, yes?"

Alexander shrugged. "Not really." He pointed his thumb at his own chest, "Remember. Jew."

Serenius chuckled. "Well, I suppose Kronos is pretty obscure even for those of us who are not Jews. Still, it appears that Kronos worship has come to Egypt – to the village of Tebtunis in the Arsinoite Nome to be exact." He waved a hand. "Yes, and since it tends to get political, you should probably at least be aware of this.

"Let's have a drink and I'll explain it." Serenius went to a side table and poured some wine into two cups and handed one to Alexander. Then he took a few sips of his own, seemed to consider his words for a moment, then looked back at Alexander and began.

"You see, many years ago, things were different. The temples here in Egypt were rich, funded with lands and offerings. The Egyptian priests, for the most part, were all rich, too ... and they were powerful as well. That was especially true for the priests of the god Amun. It has been said that they were more powerful that the pharaoh himself. *Not anymore.* Augustus changed all that."

Alexander already knew this; of course he did. He was born in Egypt and, Jew or not, one could hardly miss the tug of war between Egyptian religion and Roman politics. Still there were undoubtedly bits and pieces that he did not know, like this *Kronos stuff.* He kept his face composed and listened attentively as Serenius continued.

"Now, under the Romans, the head priest of Egypt is none other than the *Idios Logos,* yes, the chief financial administrator himself. And, yes, that does make sense because all of the temples and their land now belong to the State, meaning to Rome. The priests and temples now have to lease the lands that they had once owned."

The *epistrategos* paused and looked to see if Alexander was following him. Alexander answered noncommittally, "That seems unlikely to have endeared Augustus to the Egyptian priests."

Serenius shrugged. "Well, the priests are not happy about losing ownership of so much property, but in many other ways, nothing has changed for them. They still have their temples, the same gods, the same rites, the same festivals. The priesthood is still hereditary and only those of proven Egyptian descent can become priests."

He paused and held up his forefinger.

"It's true that the more important priestly positions now have to be purchased. But those purchased priesthoods come with their own emoluments – the right to income off of certain lands. Mostly, the system works."

Serenius lowered his finger and pointed it at the papyrus still in Alexander's hand.

"Or it worked until *that* happened. Someone in Tebtunis convinced the *Idios Logos* to declare that the crocodile temple in Tebtunis would now be the joint *Kronos*-Soknebtunis temple with a whole new separate priesthood just for the Kronos aspect."

Alexander shrugged. "Doesn't that sort of thing happen all the time?"

"*Not like this*. The Kronos priesthood does *not* come from the hereditary priestly ranks. They do *not* have to prove their blood lineage. They do *not* have to be circumcised. By Jupiter, they do not even have to be Egyptian and most of them are not."

Alexander understood now. "*Ah*, and that explains why the hereditary priests call them the *Kronos bastards from the temple*. I guess to an Egyptian priest who has proved the proper blood lineage, that is exactly what they are – illegitimate."

The *epistrategos* nodded his agreement. "Indeed, they are all bastards as in not pure in priestly blood. And, apparently, their behavior matches their so-called 'illegitimate' birth, as well. These priests of Kronos have been trying to muscle in on the leases and emoluments already given to the hereditary crocodile priests."

Serenius angrily stabbed his finger again at the papyrus that Alexander was holding. "*For me*, it has just been one petition after another. The *Idios Logos* accepted payment for these so-called Kronos priests, but gave them virtually *no* emolument lands in return. Now they are trying to get the lands that were already parceled out to the legitimate Egyptian priests."

Serenius raised both palms before him. "What am *I* supposed to do about it?"

Alexander smiled sympathetically at the *epistrategos*. He was very glad that this was *not* going to be one of *his* problems to solve; he already had his basketful to deal with. Then he realized uncomfortably that Serenius was giving him a speculative look.

"Say, *uhh* Alexander, does the Lady Antonia have any property in Tebtunis?"

"*Ummm, maaaybe*, a little."

Serenius laughed at Alexander's obviously reluctant tone.

"Don't worry, Alexander. I am not going to ask you to address these petitions against these Kronos priests who have no land. All I'm asking is that you listen to what people are saying about it and pass anything important back to me. I have heard that there have already been incidents where a few men from the temple have gone at each other with sticks. If it gets any more serious, I may need to intervene, bring in a small military presence until I can cool things down. I am just asking *you* to keep me informed of anything you hear.

"Can you do that for me, Alexander?"

Alexander could not see any reason why not. The *epistrategos* was only looking for information, his observations, if indeed he had any. Alexander could certainly do that much.

"Yes, yes, of course Serenius, but I doubt I'll be privy to much of what is being said in Tebtunis. As we have both noted, I need to address all of these petitions associated with Antonia's properties. And that should probably begin with talking to her current land agent, this Hierax. Would you happen to know where

Hierax can be found?"

The *epistrategos* smiled broadly, "Yes, I would know. That would be ... *Tebtunis*."

"*Tebtunis? No?!*"

"Yes, Alexander, I am being serious. From what I understand, the man Hierax does spend part of his time traveling around the Arsinoite nome visiting Antonia's various properties. However, he keeps his own house in Tebtunis. For whatever reason, he finds that particular village more to his taste. His house is near the main causeway. I'll have my secretary give you the street information before you leave."

The two men exchanged a few short pleasantries and Alexander turned to go. Then he had a thought, paused and turned back to the *epistrategos*.

"Tell me, your Excellency, as Antonia's new procurator, do I have the authority to enter this land agent's house in Tebtunis and secure any money and records that I find there? It would be just until I could confirm that all of his accounts are in good order?"

Once again the *epistrategos* gave an almost predatory grin. "I like the way you think, Alexander, but sadly, no, *you* do not have that authority. You probably would if Hierax was living in one of Antonia's properties, but I believe that he either owns or leases the house in his own name. Regardless, of what we may think of him, the man *is* a Roman citizen and his patroness is one of the most eminent women in Rome.

"So, Alexander, no you do not have the authority to enter and search his private home. ... however, *I do*. Bring me something legal I can work with and then you and I both will go take a look at what he may be hiding there. –For example, try to show that he is not paying all of his taxes. That's always a good one."

Once again Alexander took his leave, carrying the basket of petitions from Antonia's tenants and overseers. As he was heading out, the *epistrategos* called after him.

"Welcome back to Alexandria. You know, I think I may like having you here, Alexander. I haven't smiled this much in weeks."

Antonia Minor – reconstructed image of bust from museum on the Capitoline Hill in Rome. The original bust was believed to be sculpted in her lifetime (36 BC to 37 AD), but had survived with the nose broken off. Photo by author.

Amarantus

3. THE *XULON* MASTER

Alexander shifted into the *yawning crocodile* position and raised his fighting sticks as two assailants came at him from the front. His left foot was placed forward, his *xulon* stick pointed straight out from his waist. The *xulon* gripped in his right hand was held above his head. It was a standard defensive position when facing two opponents. Unfortunately, it was also one of the very few defensive positions that he could actually remember. There hadn't been a lot of call for *xulon* stick fight training back in Rome.

He sucked in a quick breath and tried to assess his opponents just as he had once been taught to do. Both men confronting him also fought with *xulons*, but theirs were the traditional four-foot length. Alexander's were barely more than half the length of his opponents'. Sure, Alexander may be taller than either of the men about to fight him, but their longer *xulons* gave them the greater reach. At least each man only wielded one stick, plus each had a short stick in a boiled leather vambrace encasing their opposite forearm. That would be used to block their incoming strikes.

The *xulon* was a highly adaptable weapon. It could serve as a sword, a spear, a quarterstaff, even as a club. Alexander's eyes narrowed. *Hmm*, the four-foot length of their sticks may give them greater reach, but it would make them slower if it came to a sweeping motion. Perhaps he could use that. Alexander's shorter *xulons* should move much faster whether jabbing or sweeping from the side.

That thought passed by in an instant as he focused on the two men. The man on the left was Egyptian, much shorter and older. He held his *xulons* with ease, his face was impassive; he had come here just to fight. Not so for the man to the right. That one was not as tall as Alexander, but broader, more muscular with skin dark like a Nubian's. There was anger in that one's eyes. His aggression felt *personal* -- but why? Alexander was pretty sure he had never seen the man before today. He guessed that this angry one would make the first move, and he was not wrong.

As the man to the right stepped in closer, Alexander shifted to the *reverse yawning crocodile* and moved his right foot forward, *xulon* held outward from his hip, left *xulon* stick held high. If they attacked as one, he should be able to shift to the *rising Nile* position, crossing his sticks into an X at waist height in front him and then sweeping them outward to block both incoming strikes.

... that was how he thought it would work; but that is not what happened.

As the man on his right raised his *xulon* into the *striking asp* position, using it like a spear to strike down at his chest, Alexander swung his stick up and managed to block the blow. He quickly stepped back in time to avoid the body jab from the second man. As he did, he swung his left *xulon* down and out to push away his opponent's weapon.

He barely got his *xulons* up again as the man on the right launched a second attack this time stabbing up at Alexander's throat. Alexander waved his right *xulon* in front of him knocking the attacking stick away. Then, by instinct, Alexander swung his left *xulon* down deflecting a stab at his ribs. He knew he should go on the offensive, or at least, switch to a different defensive position, but the next attack came in faster than he could think. And so did the next one. And the next one.

Alexander forgot all about fighting positions and footwork as he fell back swinging both sticks in arcs in front of him trying to keep his opponents at bay. The man on the right had moved to his side. Not good. Now Alexander had to turn his head to see him and that meant taking his eyes off the second man on his left. He had to correct that, so he fell back a few more steps trying to keep both men in his forward vision.

Unfortunately, his opponents had decided to move, too. The man on the right was holding his *xulon* over his shoulder like a spear again and thrust it down at him. Alexander had to swivel his hips to the right and raise his arms to form an upright X to protect his face. It was enough to save him. He caught and deflected that strike, but...

He was too late to block the man on his left who had bent his knees almost to a crouch, lowered his *xulon,* and swept it low until in connect just behind Alexander's ankles. As his feet were pulled out in front of him, Alexander fell back on the reed mat with a grunt.

For a moment, the only sound came from Alexander's rasping breaths. Then the man who had been his opponent on the right, the aggressive one, walked over and looked down at him, his lip curled with disdain. He said something in Egyptian. Alexander shook his to show he didn't understand. The man switched to an accented Greek.

"You lose because you have a small stick," he said.

In the background, Alexander heard a distinct snicker – it sounded a lot like his servant Amarantus. He groaned as he drew in a deep breath and forced himself to sit up.

"These are the sticks, I used in Rome," Alexander replied. "The city was always crowded with buildings and people. There was no space to wield a long stick like the one you carry."

That much was true. The Egyptians had a long history of fighting with the three- or four-foot *xulons*. Their armies had trained with these along with bows and swords and close quarters grappling. But Egypt was all about wide open spaces, fields, plains, deserts -- even the three Greek cities were laid out with wide, straight streets. It was quite the opposite in Rome with its narrow and twisted streets and alleys. Factor in Rome's million residents and space was limited. It just wasn't practical to walk around the city trying to wield a four foot stick, at least in the traditional Egyptian fashion.

The other man who had been his assailant to the left came over and held out his hand to pull Alexander to his feet.

He shook his head, "Alexander, you have forgotten much that I taught you. You once knew how to place your feet. It should have come to you automatically -- no need for you to think."

Alexander smiled fondly at his old teacher, the Egyptian priest who had taught him to use the *xulons* as a child. "Master, I was but ten years old when my father sent me to Rome and our training ended. I am happy that I can remember anything at all that you taught me. ... but I do plan to work with the *xulons* again, now that I am back in Egypt."

His former master of the *xulon* gave a loud *humph*. He didn't seem impressed with Alexander's excuses. No more, than he seemed impressed with Alexander's unusual *xulons*. He gave them a dismissive wave.

"And what of these, Alexander? They are like the weapons of a child."

Alexander held up his two short *xulons* and looked from one to the other and then gave his *xulon* master a sheepish grin.

"I know this is not the Egyptian style, but it is what I am used to. ... It is how I prefer to wield them for now."

"This is not wise young Alexander," his master responded. "Your sticks do not have the range. You are tall, yes, and your arms are long, but it is not enough to match the reach of a man with a standard sized *xulon*. You will be at a disadvantage."

"Perhaps, you are right," Alexander answered. "No, I mean of course, you are right, master. But, the shorter length does mean that I can get in closer to an opponent. Plus they are faster than the longer *xulon*."

Alexander gave his head a rueful shake. "I am just out of practice since we don't carry *xulons* in Rome. I am sure that if I return to my studies with you I will improve. There were several times in Rome when I was carrying my sticks and they proved quite effective against a knife or a club. Having the shorter length probably saved me more than once."

The older man smiled and shook his head. "You are not in Rome anymore, Alexander. Now, you must think. You are Roman. You are Jew. You are rich. Someday, someone will come after you with normal sized *xulon*. Then what will you do? Tell him he must stop because this is not how you did things in Rome?"

Alexander laughed and bowed.

"I do hear your wisdom Master, but I think that I shall stay with the sticks I have – at least for now. They are what I know. Certainly, the Egyptian *xulon* has a longer reach, but mine will serve me better in close fighting. I don't see myself joining the lines of the ranks of an army, but I can imagine being attacked in a beer house or an alley."

He held up a finger. "I can see that I need more training and practice. That much is obvious. It has been years I have trained with the *xulons* much and I think with a little work some of the old skill will come back to me."

The second man, the angry one, who had sparred with him pointed at Alexander in disbelief. "You say you *like* having a small stick? Other men's sticks will be much bigger than yours."

Again, he heard the soft titter of his servant sitting in the back. Looking over his shoulder, he yelled, "Don't be so quick to laugh, Ranti. I need to practice and *you* will be the one to spar with me until I am good enough to face my *xulon* master again."

As expected, that took the smile right off his servant's face. The *xulon* master smiled and nodded, however. "Then he must learn to fight with the Egyptian style *xulon* for that is what you will be most likely to face."

The Master pointed at Amarantus. "*You*, Alexander's man. Come here."

Amarantus rose and looked at Alexander with wide eyes. Alexander gave him a small nod and tilted his head toward the *xulon* master. Amarantus slowly walked towards him. The *xulon* master looked him up and down, then said,

"I shall loan you a *xulon* that is used by my students. Now stand here. We will go through some basic positions. Your body must learn to do these naturally so that when you are attacked, your heart will not need to stop to think because your body will have already acted."

"And that is for you, too, Alexander," the master held out his palm and curled his fingers towards himself. "Come. You will stand there next to him. This useless scrambling you just showed me was … not commendable. You will learn to do better."

Although a small part of him wanted to be offended, Alexander knew he had performed poorly. When his father had suggested resuming his training, Alexander had been delighted to learn that his childhood *xulon* master was still in Alexandria and teaching. He had agreed immediately to set up an appointment and begin his training.

Yes, it was partly because it is always good to learn a new form of self-defense, but… Alexander knew he needed something more to help him get over the isolation he was feeling. --Not that he would ever admit to that out loud. When his father recalled him from Rome, Alexander had to leave behind his home, his friends, his work, all his favorite places and pastimes. The only one constant in his life that he could still point to was his servant Amarantus who had come to Alexandria with him. Speaking of which…

Thwack.

Alexander grinned as the *xulon* master gave Amarantus a good whack for not completing the form correctly. *Huh,* perhaps this would be a bit of fun after all. He stepped into line and joined as the master drilled them through standard positions and form.

****

"Master, there seems to be a lot of stealing of people's animals."

After cooling down from their morning work-out, Alexander and Amarantus were settled into his temporary office and had begun sorting through the petitions he had received from the *epistrategos*.

Alexander raised his eyebrows. "I take it there is more than just the missing red calf that Serenius told me about?"

"Oh yes, master, there are a lot of cows, some sheep, even a horse."

"Wait, Ranti, I remember Serenius mentioning something about that, but ... *a horse*? There aren't that many horses in Egypt. Most breeds don't do well in a desert environment. The few horses generally belong to the Roman cavalry, or, to a few wealthy families in the major cities."

Amarantus shifted and raised one palm. "Perhaps, that means horse thieves are rare in Egypt. Maybe, that is why this *strategos* who is called Dionysodoros forwarded this petition to the *epistrategos*. The horse is missing from the village of Karanis, the same as the red calf. This is what it says,"

> *To Dionysodoros strategos of the Arsinoite nome, Herakleides division, from Psenamounis, son of Panesis, of the village of Karanis. On the night preceding the 22nd of the present month Phamenoth my mare, wheat-colored, disappeared while being led to water, which I immediately reported to the officials of the village. Since up to the*

present she has not yet appeared, I present this petition and ask that it be entered on the register, so that if she is found, I may retain the right to plead.

"So, master, it appears that besides the red calf that we also will be seeking a wheat-colored mare."

Alexander grunted in return. It was hard to get too exercised over a few missing animals.

Amarantus held up a different sheet of papyrus, "This one is also about a missing animal, but this one is a kind of funny."

At Alexander's nod, Amarantus began to read.

To his most excellent Titus Serenius, epistrategos of the Heptanomia and the Arsinoite nome, from Thonis son of Horion of the village of Karanis. On the 7th day of the month of Phamenoth some unknown person broke down the gate to the pen and took my famous goat. You will recognize him because his name is Seth and he looks evil and he will eat anything he sees in front of him. Please find my goat and return him as soon as you can and hold the one who took him so that I may have justice for myself. Farewell.

Alexander rubbed his forehead and gave his servant an incredulous look. "Hunh. So we have missing a red calf, a wheat-colored mare, and now an ... *evil goat?*"

"Yes, master. It appears that in Egypt, they have evil goats."

Amarantus tried – and failed -- to deliver this last part with a deadpan expression. Alexander shook his head and smiled.

"Well, Ranti, I guess it is easy to see why Titus Serenius was so happy to pass these petitions off to me. These are definitely not like anything we had to deal with back in Rome."

Amarantus hesitated, nodded to himself, and then spoke up.

"Master, it seems *nothing* here is like it was in Rome."

Alexander's smile fell losing all trace of humor. "No, it doesn't does it, Ranti? I never wanted to leave Rome. I never thought we would. ... We ... We really weren't prepared for this, were we?"

He appeared to be about to say something more. Instead, Alexander stopped, shook his head and let out a loud breath.

"Well, Ranti, we already guessed that this was not going to be easy, for either of us. We're just going to have to try to keep going each day. Maybe ... maybe one day we will find that Alexandria will start to feel more like a home to us."

Amarantus tilted his head and seemed to consider for a moment.

"I did like the *xulon* lesson today, master. *That* could not have happened in Rome. In Rome, a slave could carry a club in defense of his master, but there was no training, none of those fancy moves. This Egyptian stick fighting is different. There are so many names and positions and the priests all know how to do it. That priest this morning treated it like it is a ritual."

"That's because it is, Ranti. The *xulon* is the only type of competition that cuts across all areas of Egyptian society. The sticks are used by both the rich and the poor. 'Priest, noble, artisan, farmer – they all train on the *xulon*, just as I did as a boy. And historically, the *xulons* were used by both the Egyptian military and the priesthood. The military had other weapons, of course, but the average soldier was trained with a stick and how to use it as a spear, sword, or club."

Alexander paused for a moment to think, then waved his hand.

"Of course, the military is Roman *now* so all those Egyptian military traditions are gone. But stick fighting has been maintained by the priesthoods and temples. The training of the priests includes the ritualized movements with the *xulon*. Also, I believe that stick fighting competitions are part of many of their festivals."

He chewed his lower lip. "I'm afraid the *xulon* may someday become a lost art in Egypt. With the military gone, the priests have become the last keepers of the traditions."

Amarantus considered for a moment.

"Master, the second man you fought today. Was he a priest?"

"The Nubian?" Alexander shook his head. "No. You could tell he was *not* a priest because his head was not shaved. All Egyptian priests like the *xulon* master have a shaved head. I'm not sure who that man was or why the master brought him to spar with me."

Amarantus gave a wicked smile.

"Yes, but that man the priest brought – his Greek was not very good. He did not realize that his comments about the size of your stick were funny."

"*Huh*," Alexander grunted. "Don't believe it, Ranti. That man knew exactly what he was saying, and the words were intended to insult."

Amarantus looked back in surprise. "But, Master, why? Why would the man that the priest brought wish to insult *you*?"

"I'm not sure," Alexander shook his head and shrugged. "Perhaps, because I'm a Roman. Perhaps, because I'm a Jew. Perhaps, because my family is rich. I suppose any of those might be enough to cause offense to *someone* ... especially if it is someone looking to be offended."

Alexander paused and pointed at his servant. "You, Ranti, have never been to Egypt before now. And *I*, I have not been back often enough to understand the people. I think being subjected to Roman rule is particularly hard for the priests and probably many others as well. That man was well trained on the *xulon* which means he has studied. He may be well educated, possibly from a noble family. ... Well, who knows what his issues are. Maybe we will see him again and maybe we won't."

He pointed at the papyrus scrolls now scattered across his desk.

"Let's continue sorting through these, Ranti. I would like to get a sense of what is here before my messenger returns with that wretched freedman of Antonia's."

"How long will it take him to get here, Master? It is far, is it not?"

"I'm not sure, Ranti. Travel is something we're going to have to learn more about now that we are here. I hope we won't have to leave Alexandria very often, but this time we must. Most of the property owned by both my family and Antonia is down around Lake Moeris."

Alexander paused and rubbed at the stubble on his chin. "I think that it may be close to 150 miles down to Crocodilopolis which is the capital of the Arsinoite nome. Tebtunis is well south of that and accessible only by one canal. Of course, these are not distances as a pigeon would fly."

He smiled ruefully. "There are *no* Roman roads in Egypt, Ranti, not even one. That's going to be another big difference for us. Here, it is all about travelling the Nile, the canals, or, the camel and donkey trails."

"So is that what the messenger you sent to Tebtunis has been doing, master?" Amarantus asked. "He has been traveling on canals and donkey trails?"

Alexander stopped rubbing at his chin and ran a hand through his curls.

"Yes, I think so. My father's steward tells me that my messenger would be able to travel the Nile for most of the way and then cross via a channel to the Great Canal and through smaller linking canals to Tebtunis. Or, he said that from certain villages on the Great Canal, it is only about 20 miles using camel trails. The steward thinks that my messenger should have gotten there in about seven or eight days.

"Then he still had to find this Hierax, deliver my letter summoning him to Alexandria, then another eight to ten days to bring Antonia's land agent Hierax back to me. ... My best guess is that they will both be presenting themselves back here within the next few days."

Alexander stood and pulled another papyrus from the basket of petitions. This hand-off from the land agent was one thing that he thought should go smoothly. Alexander had placed a message for Lady Antonia's land agent on a ship that had sailed a few days earlier for Alexandria than his own ship. That way, Hierax should have received his summons by the time Alexander arrived in Alexandria.

If Alexander's luck held, Antonia's land agent would arrive within the next couple of days, bringing the scrolls relating to Antonia's estates. Hopefully, soon after that the man would board a ship and *leave*. That would be ideal. Alexander certainly didn't need the previous land agent staying around and challenging his own authority.

Fortunately, Antonia had anticipated the problem. She had given Alexander a document signed in her own hand, recalling her freedman to Rome. Then she had directed him to use his own discretion when to produce this document.

Alexander hoped that all would go as he, and the Lady Antonia, had intended. The land agent should arrive here in Alexandria soon and leave without causing him any trouble. He nodded to himself. Yes, quickly getting the man on a ship back to Rome as soon as he delivered Antonia's accounts scrolls would be the best outcome Alexander could hope for. With any luck, this would all be over within a week.

4. HE SAID NO

"He said, 'No'."

Alexander blinked twice. *"No?* He … said … *no?* No *to what?* Are you telling me that Hierax has refused to come here to meet with me?"

The messenger shuffled his feet and stared at the floor.

"He did, *kurie.* … Or, I suppose I should say that his house steward did. Marcus Antonius Hierax refused to even see me. I know your orders were to place the letter into the land agent's hands myself – and I tried. I really did."

The messenger looked up from the floor and gave Alexander an earnest look.

"But, you see, his house steward kept leading me in circles, telling me his lord -- his *kurie* -- was busy and I should come back later. Then when I returned, he said I had to come back the next day. The next day, the steward said his master would not see me until he had read your letter first. There seemed no choice, so I gave him your letter and went back the next day for his master's response."

The messenger paused and looked embarrassed. Alexander spun his hand is a "hurry up" gesture. The messenger sucked in a breath and said,

"I went back the next day and still I did not see the land agent. Nor did I receive any letter in reply. *Kurie,* his house steward told me that Hierax was too *busy* right now and that he would get around to speaking to you when he could find the time."

Alexander rocked back on his feet. He was stunned. His summons to the Lady Antonia's land agent had *not* been a *request*. The letter had clearly informed this land agent that by the order of Lady Antonia Minor, Hierax was to present himself in Alexandria immediately and bring her account scrolls with him.

The messenger was still looking at Alexander apprehensively. "Did I do wrong, *kurie*? For three days, I went to the house and asked for an audience, but I was never even allowed across the threshold."

Alexander was angry. He was very angry, but it was not the *messenger's* fault. He tried to rein in his temper long enough to reply.

"No. No, *you* did not do wrong. Someone has made a very great mistake, but it was not you. It sounds like you did all you could. Indeed, I will reward you for your persistence and I will certainly be having more work for you in the future. For now, though, you may rest."

The messenger bowed and turned to leave when Alexander had another thought.

"Wait. One more thing. Do you think Hierax will be in Tebtunis if I were to go there now?"

"That is one thing that I do know, *kurie*. His house steward said that Hierax is leaving on an inspection tour of the Lady Antonia's properties. I expect he will travel by barge and take the canals through each village; but, the house steward would not tell me his route."

"*Huh*, well can you at least give me a description of this man Hierax? No one back in Rome could remember what he looked like."

"I cannot, *kurie*, though not for lack of trying. As I said, I found his house in Tebtunis and I spoke with the house steward who *said* Hierax was there, but he was too busy to see me. That house steward was *difficult*. He acted like he thought of himself as a very important man. Perhaps he thought that being the steward of Lady Antonia's own freedman gave him status as well."

A slightly turned up lip showed what the messenger thought of the pompous house steward.

"Anyway, when I asked him about Hierax, he would tell me *nothing*. I tried waiting outside his house for hours watching to see if Hierax would come out, but I saw no one, *kurie*, no one except the house steward."

After the messenger left, Alexander turned to his servant Amarantus.

"*That* is ... *unexpected*. I thought that Hierax might do something shady with the accounts. Lots of excuses and ingratiating smiles were expected, but it never occurred to me that he would simply refuse to come."

Amarantus gave him a wry look. "This does fit with the basket of unanswered petitions you received from the *epistrategos*, master. It would appear that Hierax is a man who does not take his responsibilities very seriously."

Alexander threw up his hands in the air. "What could he possibly hope to accomplish by this delay? I have a letter from Antonia. I am her new procurator. *I* am here to *replace* him."

"Yes, master, but it would seem that Hierax does not wish to be replaced."

****

"WAAIIIOOOOO."

Alexander cringed as an ear piercing howl rang through the house. This was not normal, for his father was adamant about his home being a place of peace and quiet. He spun towards Philo for an explanation and saw his brother looking up at the ceiling and shaking his head.

"Philo, w*hat* was that?"

Philo continued to shake his head and replied, "I was expecting that our father would have already explained *this* to you. After all, this was *his* doing."

He blew out a breath. "It appears it has been left up to *me* to tell you. ... It wouldn't surprise me if *Abba* was off somewhere hiding."

Alexander scrunched his brow, "*What?* Tell me what?"

Philo noted his brother's confusion, then gestured with his hand for him to follow. "Come, Alexander. This is something you will have to see for yourself."

The two young men wandered through their home and emerged into the courtyard. Filled with flowers, trees, and sculpted shrubs, the courtyard was designed to be a place of serenity. But not today.

There was another howl and Alexander quickly turned in that direction and blinked. There staggering toward him was a ... filthy creature ... not much more than two feet tall. When it saw them, it changed direction and came their way.

Alexander ran his hand through his hair. "Philo. What. Is. That?"

Philo let out a loud sigh. "*That*, Alexander, is our *new little brother*, Lysimachus. Recently adopted, recently arrived."

At the sound of his name, the child toddled forward and pointed his finger at them. "*Peeloh, Peeloh,*" he shouted.

Alexander rubbed his chin. "Is he trying to say your name?"

"Yes," his brother nodded. "That is his version of *Philo*. *Ahhh*, it will be interesting to hear what he does with *your* name."

Here, I will introduce you and then we will go in. I think this explanation calls for wine."

Philo leaned forward toward to the child, but held his hands behind him, careful not to touch.

"Lysimachus, this is your elder brother. His name is Alexander."

The child looked at him, swung his gaze toward Alexander and then looked back. "Alexander," Philo repeated. "Alexander."

The child just stared. "Maybe your name is too long for him," said Philo. "Let's try your nickname."

Once again Philo leaned down to address the child. "Lysimachus, this is your elder brother. His name is Xander. Xander."

Lysimachus looked up at Alexander and pointed. *"Waander, Waander."*

"Yes, yes, Lysimachus, that is close enough." Then Philo muttered. "Quick, let's get away before he tries to get you to pick him up."

Fortunately, a woman who was probably the nurse appeared to gather up the child hopefully for a bath. A very bemused Alexander followed his brother back inside.

Philo's explanation ended up being much what Alexander had already guessed. A wealthy Jew from a priestly bloodline had died leaving his son an orphan. The boy's father, Lysimachus, had made a dying request that their father adopt and raise the child. Since both families had such prominent lineage, the request was not *that* unusual. Still, Alexander wondered how this would work with his father's age and failing health. *Hmm,* one more thing to worry about in the future.

He did have one question though. "So, Philo, is the boy a Roman?"

His brother made a face that Alexander couldn't quite interpret.

"Oh yes. Our dear *Abba* made a formal Roman adoption. The boy's name is now Gaius Julius Alexander Lysimachus."

Alexander sucked in a long breath. That was also expected. An adopted son took the full name of the father with his own cognomen added at the end. Still, the name was so like hearing his own that it was a little … jarring.

Hmm. So now he had a new brother named Lysimachus. Did it change anything? The boy would not make any difference to Alexander's inheritance. Jews in Alexandria observed the law set forth in the Torah regarding the double share of the firstborn. This young adopted son would not change that.

What about his sense of family? Not really. Because Alexander had lived in Rome, he hadn't been part of the Alexandria household for the past twelve years. The presence of this new child did not make the house feel any more or less familiar to him. That would not be the same for Philo who had grown up here – being the only son living at home. How Philo felt about this new brother, he could not even guess.

Oh well, he thought, let it alone. He didn't need any new emotional pulls on him right now. Plus it didn't really matter what he felt. Apparently, Lysimachus was here to stay.

****

Alexander's father stabbed a piece of spiced lamb in a coconut sauce and looked up at his oldest son.

"So are you going after him?"

Alexander, his father, and his brother Philo were dining on the flat roof of their house in Alexandria. He had just told them about his new challenge with Hierax, Antonia's reluctant land agent.

In response, Alexander held up his palms and shrugged. "I'm not sure what good could come of it if I did go after him. It would seem a bit undignified if the Lady Antonia's new procurator were to be seen chasing around Egypt after some recalcitrant freedman. What do *you* think I should do *Abba*?"

Alexander's father nodded slightly and smiled at his eldest son. *Hunh.* Was that a look of ... *approval, fondness?* Did his father even feel these things for him? Alexander didn't know. Despite his residence in Rome, they *had* seen each occasionally.

It was about a twenty day trip to sail from Rome to Alexandria – and, of course, another twenty day trip to return. Not a quick journey, but if you could spare two or three months from your life, the journey could be done. Either Alexander or his father had made the trip between the two great cities several times. A few weeks every couple years, however, had hardly been enough for the boy Alexander to develop any strong paternal bonds. Filial duty, yes; he definitely felt that. But did any one of them feel more? Did he *love* his family? Did they love *him*? That, he did not know.

His father remained silent as he worked his way through the evening meal. Then he seemed to nod to himself and looked over at his son.

"I agree, Alexander, that there may be little to gain by chasing after the Lady Antonia's freedman. Frankly, if you do run him down somewhere you should consider trussing him up until you can bring him back and toss him on the first boat back to Rome. And don't think that you need be too gentle about it either. This Hierax may not know *you*, but he knows who *this family* is. He should have known very well that his behavior would *not be tolerated*."

Alexander felt surprised. That was some tough talk coming from his father. It almost sounded like his father was in a position to … *sanction* someone who got on his wrong side. But, it was not like his father had some sort of mercenary troop or gang or … or *did he*? Before he could think further on that, his father slapped his palm on the table to change the subject.

"Well, this business with Antonia's freedman will get resolved eventually, but in the meantime, Alexander, I suggest you do your duty to the Lady Antonia. You could make a site visit to as many of her properties as you can manage over the next few weeks. Most of them are in the Arsinoite Nome so that would be a good place to begin. If you could go on site and inspect the properties for yourself, you would not be as reliant on any reports from this Hierax. Plus you could let all the locals know who is in charge now."

Alexander hesitated. He had only been back in Alexandria for a matter of days. He didn't feel ready to take on yet another trip, especially one with so many responsibilities.

To his left, though, he noticed his brother Philo was nodding in agreement with their father before adding his own thoughts. "Now would be the perfect time, Alexander. It is almost September, so the Nile is about to peak. The farmers can't plant until the river recedes in a month or so—sometime in October. That could give you weeks to meet with the various tenants."

Philo gave his brother a firm nod.

"Also, Alexander, if you will stop first at the nome capitol Crocodilopolis, *I* will go with you. There's a large synagogue there and I've been corresponding with several of the Torah scholars. We don't seem to be agreeing on how to interpret some parts of scripture, but if I could talk to them directly I'm sure I could convince them."

Their father nodded agreement. "Yes, I think that is a wise place to start. It is very likely that you will find the *strategos* there -- the local governor, that is. He may be able to tell you more about Antonia's properties, and about that land agent."

Alexander nodded. "Yes, I found speaking with Titus Serenius the *epistrategos* to be very helpful, but he is a bit remote from what is actually happening there. From what I understand, the *strategos* is actually one of them; he lives there in the nome so he would know everyone. You are right, *Abba*, that would be a good place to start."

His father's eyes twinkled. "I know another place you should visit when you get there."

Philo rolled his eyes. "*Abba, not* the beer house."

"*Yes*, Philo, the beer house." His father turned to Alexander. "Your brother may not approve of the place, but it is the local bastion for men's gossip. It will be a good place for you to begin to gather information."

Alexander looked at Philo and hesitated before saying, "*Abba*, I don't think we should *both* leave you. I, at least, may be gone for several weeks."

His father returned a grim smile. "I know what you are thinking, Son, but I'm not done for yet. Yes, I know that I am ill, and based on the look you gave me when you first arrived home, I must look bad. However, the physicians tell me that I have a good many months yet. … And besides, I am not going anywhere until I see you installed as the new Alabarch."

Then his father stood and placed a hand on Alexander's shoulder and gave it a firm squeeze. He walked past Philo and gave his second son's shoulder a squeeze, too. And then their father straightened his shoulders and with his cane tapping, walked proudly from the room.

■ ■

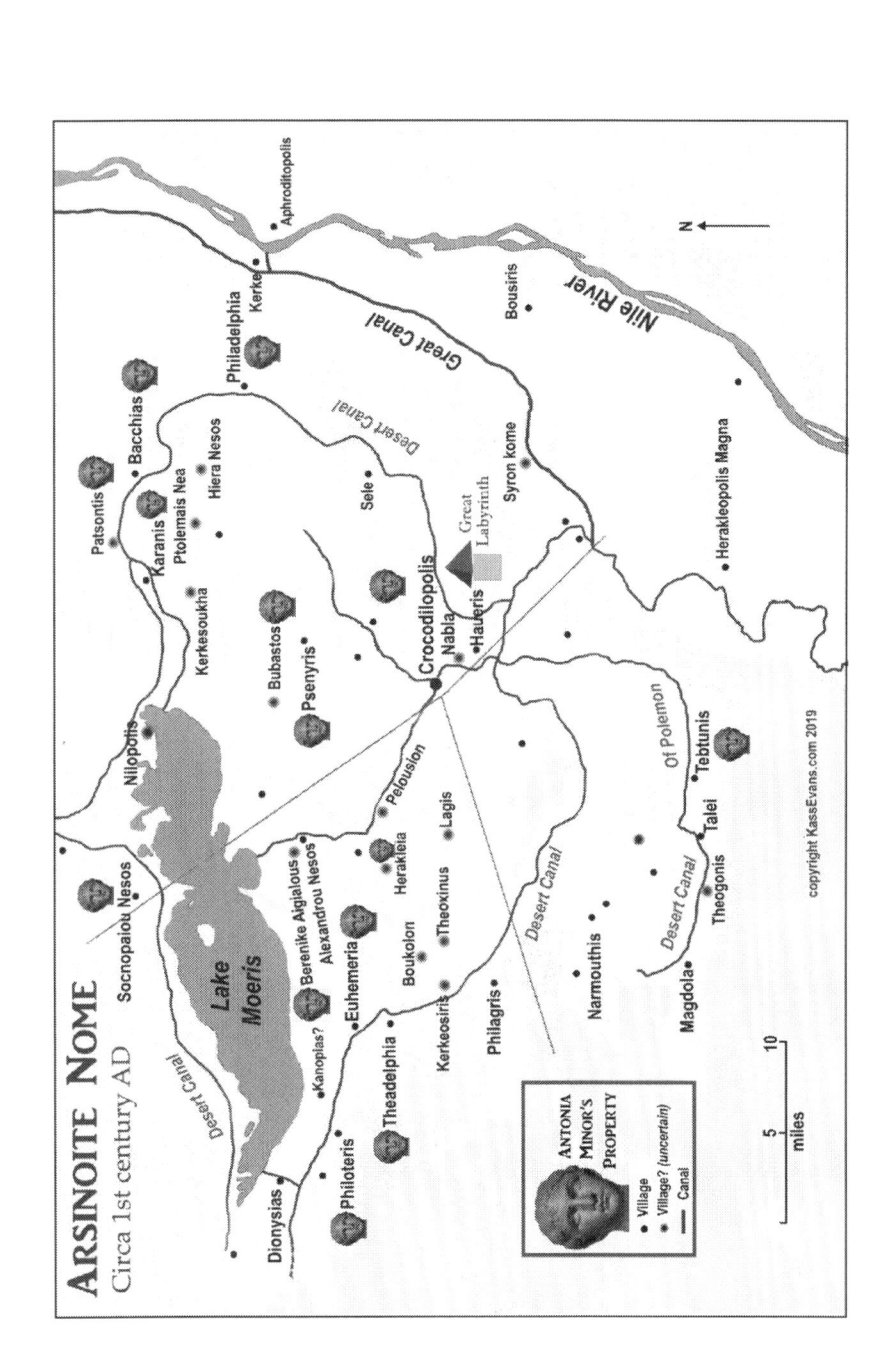

ARSINOITE NOME
Circa 1st century AD

Map showing villages and canals of the Arsinoite Nome, including Lake Moeris, the Nile River, Great Canal, and Desert Canals. Villages marked include: Aphroditopolis, Bousiris, Kerke, Philadelphia, Bacchias, Patsontis, Karanis, Ptolemais Nea, Hiera Nesos, Sele, Syron kome, Herakleopolis Magna, Kerkesoukha, Bubastos, Psenyris, Nabla, Crocodilopolis, Hauberis, Great Labyrinth, Nilopolis, Pelousion, Lagis, Ot Polemon, Tebtunis, Socnopaiou Nesos, Berenike Agialous, Alexandrou Nesos, Herakleia, Theoxinus, Talei, Euhemeria, Boukolon, Theogonis, Kerkeosiris, Philagris, Narmouthis, Magdola, Kanopias?, Theadelphia, Philoteris, Dionysias.

Legend:
- ANTONIA MINOR'S PROPERTY
- • Village
- * Village? (uncertain)
- — Canal

Scale: 0–5–10 miles

copyright KassEvans.com 2019

Kass Evans | Toga in the Wind 49

5. Out of the Deep

Alexander jerked awake as a deep roar split the dawn. It was soon followed by another, and then another.

RAARRRGGH.

The ship master and crew of the bark were up in an instant and launched into frenetic activity.

Alexander and his brother Philo had purchased passage on a boat heading up the Nile destined for Crocodilopolis, the capitol of the Arsinoite Nome. They had made it through the Delta in good time and passed into the Great Canal. At nightfall, the boat had been pulled up onto the bank and reed mats had been spread on the ground for passengers and crew.

The bark's sailing master grabbed Alexander by the upper arm and pulled him to his feet. "Quick, quick, board the boat now."

Alexander glanced sleepily around, "What's happening?"

"No time. Move. Now!" the sailing master shoved hard and he was propelled towards the boat. Philo must have known what was happening because in the early light, Alexander could see his brother scrambling over the side of the boat ahead of him.

"Ranti!" he called, "Where are you?" He tried to turn back to look for his servant, but whoever was pushing him toward the boat had his shoulders pinned.

"I am here, master." Alexander was relieved to hear the

voice immediately behind him. Whatever the current danger was, he knew the ship master would be unlikely to abandon someone of *his* status. As a slave, however, Ranti might be treated as if he were considered expendable.

With a great shove from the ship master, Alexander stumbled the last few steps to the boat. He grasped Philo's outstretched hand and was still breathing hard as his brother hauled him aboard. Once in, Alexander turned and extended his hand to pull in Amarantus. There was no time to reconnoiter though, as one the bark's sailors forcefully guided them to the prow.

"Sit. Sit!" the man barked. "There. Don't move." The crew man grabbed their arms and shoulders and pushed them down to the deck before scurrying off to grab a long pole.

RARRRGGH. Another great roar pierced the air, this one sounding closer than it had before.

"Master, what was that?" Amarantus whispered.

"I don't know," Alexander whispered back then turned to his brother. "Philo, what is happening?" he asked urgently.

Philo pointed over the side of the boat beyond the area where they had camped. "See for yourself."

By squatting on his haunches, Alexander could see over the side of the boat. In the distance the pre-dawn light revealed the tops of a nearby field of crops. He realized that between him and the field he could hear shouting and saw the lights of waving torches. Carrying torches near crops was unusual in itself, but he couldn't guess what was making that roaring sound.

"*Ruuuuunnnn!*" A screaming figure was silhouetted against the dawn running pell-mell towards them with arms pumping wildly.

"*Push off!*" yelled the ship master. Two of his crew standing knee deep in the water shoved the boat back into the Great Canal before scrambling over the side.

At first Alexander wondered if the sailing master was trying to escape the shouting man running towards them. Then the dawn's light reflected on the incomprehensible mounds that were rapidly gaining on the running man. Alexander squinted and peered into the rising sun trying to make out what was happening. The running man was being chased by some type of animal, but what was it? He could tell it had four legs, but it was way too big to be a cow, too stout to be a camel.

The running man was soon overtaken and went down. His shouting ceased. What happened to him? Did he trip? Was he trampled? Alexander couldn't tell. As the first great charging mound moved closer and stopped on the bank, Alexander sucked in a breath.

"Philo," he whispered, "Is that what I think it is?"

Philo bit his lower lip and answered equally softly. "I have never actually seen one before … but I can't imagine what else it could be. That, brother, must be a *hippopotamus*."

"*Merda*, I did not know they could run like that."

Philo looked from the running beasts back at his brother. "I have heard it said that they *can* outrun a man – but only for a short distance. Of course, they are supposed to be much better at swimming."

"But you have never seen one before?"

"No," Philo shook his head. "They have become quite rare now. Father says that when he was young, there were families of hippopotami all up and down the Nile and along the larger canals. But they've been hunted, you know -- mainly because they are crop killers. It is said that at night, these beasts will come ashore to eat and within hours they can consume all the crops in a field. I suppose that was probably the reason for the waving torches we saw; the farmers were trying to chase them away."

As they watched and whispered, the boat was still being rowed quietly away from the bank. They were moving slowly and Alexander suspected the ship master was trying not to antagonize the beasts. ---And beasts they were. They were huge -- bigger than almost anything Alexander had ever seen before, except maybe an elephant. Philo and Alexander pressed shoulder to shoulder and peered over the side of the boat as three of the large beasts came to a stop on the bank and ambled casually towards the water.

"My Lord," Philo breathed. "Look at the size of their heads. It's a third the size of the rest of the body."

Alexander could only nod in awe. "Back in Rome, I saw a mosaic with a hippopotamus, but it was not quite like the animal before us. I think now that the artist must have been working from a vague description and had never actually seen one."

Both brothers continued to peer over the side at the great beasts, while the sailors rowed. Amarantus remained where he sat huddled in the prow. The crew and passengers held their breath as the boat slid away from the bank.

WHAM.

Alexander was knocked to the side as the boat rammed into something solid. Or, had something solid rammed into the boat? He didn't think there would be rocks or sand shoals here to snag their boat – especially not with the Nile flood running so high.

He suppressed the urge to stand and demand what was going on, and instead forced himself to remain silent. No doubt the master of this ship would know what to do; best to let him do it. Unfortunately, his servant Amarantus was feeling a little less ...

stoic.

Too late, Alexander realized that there had been no room where he and Philo had squatted to peer over the side of the boat at the hippopotami. Amarantus who had been sitting in the prow could not have seen them. In fact, coming from Rome, it was likely that his servant had never even heard of such a beast.

Alexander turned to see that Amarantus had pulled himself up and peered over the other side to see what the boat had hit. Then Ranti staggered back two steps blinking in surprise. Then he leaned over and grasped one of the boat's rowing poles, and lunged back towards the side of the ship.

"*Aaiieeee!* Master, arm yourself! Monsters! There are Egyptian monsters in the water. They are surrounding us!"

Ranti's shrill cry was accompanied by him swinging the pole wildly swatting at something in the water. Then … *Wham*. Another jolt rocked them as something rammed their boat again. Ranti continued to lean over the side and scream at the water.

With an angry curse the ship master turned on Alexander and hissed. "*Enough! Control your man.* If he causes us to capsize they will kill us all."

Alexander lunged forward grabbed a wad on his slave's tunic and yanked him back away from the side of the boat. He reached around to put his hand over Ranti's mouth while at the same time, he whispered, "Quiet. Quiet, Ranti."

Amarantus squirmed for a moment. Alexander held his grip until he felt his servant relax. Puzzled, Alexander edged forward to look over the side. If the three hippopotami were behind them on the shore, then what was ramming the boat on this side? He and Amarantus peeked over the side only to see the sight of several beasts, their huge heads not far from the boat.

Alexander turned back to his brother Philo and softly informed him, "It seems we've bumped into the remaining family of those beasts on the shore. The ship master is swinging the ship away from them now. I suppose he is hoping they will cease to attack if they are not further provoked."

Silence fell over the boat that was broken only by the soft murmuring of one sailor who stroked an amulet and softly repeated "Taweret! Taweret!" followed by a string of unintelligible words in Egyptian to the goddess. Soon another sailor followed softly beseeching the crocodile god Sobek.

The boat rocked as it was rammed again. Amarantus's eyes opened so wide that the whites could be seen in the early dawn light. Actually, Alexander was pretty sure his own eyes were opened quite widely as well.

"Master," Amarantus whispered, "Should we not be preparing to do battle with the monsters?"

His servant was right, Alexander thought. They must prepare. He stood and glanced around as he considered defensive positions.

Philo shook his head and snickered softly at Alexander. "What do you plan to do, brother? They are hippopotami. Do you think you can beat them off with your sticks?"

Alexander looked down at his two short *xulons* that he carried in a pouch at his hip. They would not be of much use if the boat capsized. Amarantus gave a panicked jerk; he was breathing hard and his voice was becoming shrill. "Master, how will we fight a monster? I have not purchased any protection magic to guard us against monsters."

Over his shoulder, Alexander could see the ship master angrily jabbing his forefinger at them. Most likely, if he didn't get his servant under control, one or both of them might get tossed over the side.

Alexander grabbed Amarantus by both shoulders and turned him to face him so that he could not see the great beasts in the water.

"Ranti, Ranti, stop. Look at me. That is *not* a monster. That is an animal that lives here in Egypt. It is called a hippopotamus – a river horse."

Amarantus jerked his head back and replaced his panic with a skeptical look. "Master, that is *not a horse.*"

Alexander smiled. "I know, Ranti, but that is what they are called. Many, many years ago when Greeks first came to Egypt and saw this animal they named it the *river horse.* Clearly it is not a horse, but the name hippopotamus has stuck."

"So they are not dangerous, Master?"

"Well, actually that is why we must stay calm and very quiet. I believe they can be dangerous if they feel provoked and threatened. As you have already seen, they could ram the boat until we capsize."

"And then they could snatch us up one by one and snap a man in half in those big jaws they have," Philo added helpfully. "I've heard tell of a hippopotamus snapping a *crocodile* in half with one bite. It would make short work of a man."

Alexander gave his brother one of those *you are not helping* looks and turned back to his servant. "The important thing, Ranti, is that we don't do anything to antagonize the hippopotami. We don't scream. We don't try to hit them with poles in the water. We wait here and we let the ship master move the ship away from them. Do you understand?"

Amarantus hung his head. "I'm sorry, master. I suppose I thought Egypt would be more like Italy. Never did I expect to see such a great *m-mon*... not-a-monster in Egypt."

"Well, perhaps you should become prepared for surprises like this," Philo said. "Think about it -- Herodotus, Strabo, even Caesar. They all describe Egypt as a strange and exotic place. Why do you think that is?"

Amarantus chewed his lower lip. "*Umm*, because *it is* a strange and exotic place?"

"You are right, Philo," Alexander nodded to his brother. Then he added, "When I was a boy, I never really thought about it that way. This was just our home. Plus we rarely left the city and Alexandria, in many ways, is not that different from Athens, or even Rome."

Alexander chewed on his thumbnail and shifted uncomfortably. "Philo, I know this is supposed to be my home now." He hesitated and then corrected himself. "I guess that this *is* my home now. But ... I don't feel like I know this place. ... I'm not sure that I belong here."

Philo didn't answer right away. Instead, he regarded his brother thoughtfully. He had to admit to himself that it was a pleasure to see his older brother looking so uncertain. It had felt that all his life everything had always been about Alexander. Alexander was the clever one. Alexander was the handsome one. And most importantly, Alexander was the *first born son*. That may not have mattered a lot in Roman law, but it sure did in Jewish tradition.

Hmm, perhaps it would be amusing if Philo let his brother flounder a bit, let him find his own way in Alexandrian society. Then everyone who had been comparing the two brothers would see that the eldest wasn't so perfect after all. They would notice which brother was the great thinker, the scholar.

Then, unbidden, other thoughts filled his mind. Memories.

When the boys were very little and sat before their nursemaid hearing stories of magic and evil – didn't Alexander hold his hand when she got to the scary parts? And what about that time they were rough housing and Philo had knocked over the jar of oil splashing it everywhere? Alexander had rescued him from a beating when he had rushed him outside and lifted him up so he could reach the lowest branch and climb the sycamore. The boys had hidden in that tree for hours whispering stories to each other.

Hmm, and even lately... A Jew had come to Alexandria to consult with Philo on interpreting Torah. The man said that back in Rome his brother had recommended *him, Philo,* as one of the leading scholars on scripture. ... which was only right, of course. Alexander was certainly no Torah scholar.

Philo felt torn. Maybe it wouldn't be so bad having his big brother around. After all, Philo was a philosopher now, and a writer. These were things his big brother could not do. Not even close.

Philo looked up and saw that his brother was still looking at him and seemed to be expecting some comment. Well, maybe he would help his older brother a little bit. Not too much. His brother would have to prove himself first for that.

Philo finally replied to Alexander. "Well, maybe you *do* belong here. Maybe you *don't*. In this, you don't have a choice. It is what Father wants and, apparently, it is what Augustus wants. I suggest you concentrate on learning what you need to know. You were always pretty quick as a child; you'll get there."

Alexander blinked. If he had been expecting some warm shower of sympathy from his younger brother, he received nothing back but disappointment. The underlying message there was probably apt, though. Philo seemed to be telling him to toughen up. He would have preferred a little sympathy. Didn't anyone realize that he did not want to be here? Philo was correct. Their father was not going let Alexander go back to Rome. He expected Alexander to become the next Alabarch in Egypt – and soon.

Running a hand through his hair, Alexander's gaze moved from his brother to his servant. Amarantus had been with him for three years now and probably knew him better than just about anyone. He had no doubt that Ranti could tell how much his master hated this new situation – hated to feel helpless and unknowledgeable of what to do.

Seeing his look, Amarantus leaned in towards Alexander and softly said, "Master, I know less about this place than you. I will help you and we will manage just as we did in Rome." His lips quirked into a small smile. "Besides, master, in Egypt we can *both* carry our *xulons*. If anyone insults you, we can beat him with our sticks."

Alexander laughed softly. Even Philo chuckled although he didn't really seem to understand the humor.

The young men mostly tried to stay still as the ship master extricated them from the threat of the hippopotami. After a while they heard the master let out a long breath and then saw his sailors seem to relax. Lifting his chin, the ship master called over to Alexander and Philo.

"All is well now. The beasts are gone. We shall pass out some bread for breakfast, but we will not stop again until we reach the next village."

After the ship master spoke, Alexander observed the two sailors who had been rubbing their amulets and beseeching the Egyptian gods. They both knelt and appeared to offer up a small libation and thanks although he couldn't understand what they were saying. Alexander nudged his brother, and then pointed his chin at the Egyptian sailors.

"So what do you think, Philo? Do you think their pleas to

the crocodile god worked? I'm sure they think it was Sobek who saved us from the hippotomi."

He had only meant to be joking, a little facetious, not set something off. To Alexander's complete surprise, his younger brother Philo stood up in the boat and seemed to strike a pose staring off into the distance as if speaking to an audience. He held up two fingers and began to speak.

"In addition to building wooden and other images, the Egyptians have advanced to divine honors irrational animals, bulls and rams and goats, and invented for each some fabulous legend of wonder. But actually the Egyptians have gone to a further excess and chosen the fiercest and most savage of wild animals, lions and crocodiles and among reptiles the venomous asp, all of which they dignify with temples, sacrifices, processions and the like."

Philo ceased to speak and regarded his brother expectantly.

Alexander was bemused. "Philo, your answer ... it seemed to be a bit *ummm, practiced*."

Philo beamed back in pleasure. "That is because it was. I am writing a *treatise* on this, you know."

"No," Alexander said in surprise. "I did not know. Of course, everyone knows of your mastery of philosophy, but I had not known that you were composing your own treatise. Tell me, what is it about?"

Philo seemed to puff a bit and said grandly. "It is a commentary on the Decalogue."

"The ten commandments that our Lord gave to Moses? You are writing it in Greek, then?"

"It must be," Philo assured him. "Greek is the only natural language that should be used for philosophy."

Alexander decided not to point out that Greek was also the only language in which his brother was fluent. Philo could possibly get by using Latin, but he had not lived in Rome using Latin everyday as Alexander had. Even though both Alexander and Philo had learned to recite the Ten Commandments in Hebrew, neither was fluent. Besides, no one actually *spoke* Hebrew anymore. If a writer wanted his words to be read, Greek was the only real option.

"So, Philo, were you commenting on the commandment against having false idols?"

Again, Philo beamed with pleasure. "Yes indeed, Alexander, you have understood me correctly. This vile practice of worshipping animals is nothing but idolatry of the most despicable nature."

Alexander glanced uncomfortably at the Egyptian crew who were sailing the boat. He and his brother had been speaking in Greek which the crew *may not* have understood – but, then again, they just might.

"But Philo," he protested, "the people who follow the animal gods are not Jews. They are Egyptians, so does it matter what they believe?"

Philo pursed his lips. "It is not just Egyptians of whom I speak. Indeed, some of the greatest proponents of the crocodile god are Greeks – and some Romans, too, from what I hear. When those who should know better choose to honor these irrational animals they deceive the little-wits who do not see through Egyptian godlessness."

Alexander considered this. "Do you speak of the priests of Kronos?"

"Yes, *them*, among others," Philo nodded his head yes. "They are *Greek*, or at least part Greek, every one of them. Yet they worship the crocodile in its animal form. I fear that as you travel the nome you will be exposed to many forms of superstition."

Alexander smiled in return. "Do not worry, my brother. I shall make special effort to stay away from these crocodile gods and all of their priests."

Philo *hmmphed* in reply. "Be wary, brother. These crocodile worshippers can be insidious."

The wind came up from the north, so the ship master set the sail and the boat took off skimming across the water. The passengers and crew stayed mostly silent as the bark sailed down the Great Canal heading for the nome capitol of Crocodilopolis.

An imaginative depiction of a Nile hippopotamus from a mosaic found in Rome. The hippo has a crocodile-like snout and teeth. Edited from a photograph by the author.

Kass Evans | *Toga in the Wind* 65

Photograph of a hippopotamus in the Khartoum Zoo on the Nile River in modern day Sudan, taken 1936.

Hippos haven't been seen in Egypt since the 1800s, but this Nile hippo is probably similar to the ones that lived in Roman Egypt.

Source: Library of Congress https://hdl.loc.gov/loc.pnp/matpc.17313

Sabinus, a Roman citizen of the Arsinoite Nome.

6. The Beer House

"Two purple stripes. Hunh. Just who might *you* be?"

Alexander looked up to see an athletic-looking man with curly hair and an aquiline nose waving a hand obliquely towards his tunic. The twin purple *clavi* that ran vertically down the sides of his white linen tunic announced his rank to any who knew what they meant. Clearly, this man before him had recognized the narrow stripes that proclaimed his status as an *eques*, a Roman noble of the equestrian order.

It had been a relief to finally reach Crocodilopolis after the tiring trip up the Nile and passing through a series of canals. After arriving, Philo had gone on to find the family from the synagogue where they would be staying. Alexander was in no particular hurry to meet up with the Jews from the synagogue because … well, he had his reasons.

Instead, he had sent his servant Amarantus and bags along with his brother, then headed for the local beer house. Alexander blew out a breath. It would be good to get a bit of time to himself, even if it was only a few brief moments. He was used to Rome where he had lived alone in his own apartment with just Ranti there to take care of him. For the past few weeks, personal time had been in short supply.

Well, so much for private time. Alexander scrutinized the man who had just addressed him. As usual, he had to figure out the other man's status, so he would know how to respond properly to him. Acknowledging or asserting one's place was just how society worked – certainly in Rome and probably more so here in Egypt.

But this man was hard to figure. He was clean shaven and his brown curly hair was cut in the Roman fashion. Despite the Egyptian sun, his skin was not very dark so he probably had no Egyptian blood. He wore an embroidered linen tunic and leather boots, both of good quality. Perhaps, he was a well-to-do Greek? Or, there were a lot of men from the legions who had settled in the area. He could be a Roman citizen, perhaps from one of the legions, but Alexander wasn't sure. *Hmm,* best to be non-committal in his reply.

He returned a direct look. "My name is Gaius Julius Alexander."

"*Ahh*, you are the son of the Alabarch?"

"I am. And *you* are?"

"Sabinus. I own a bit of property in the area."

Sabinus. That was a Roman name, but still not quite enough to place the man's social status.

Alexander asked, "Were you in the legions?"

Sabinus waved a negligent hand. "I've done different things. ... But, really everyone *here* is more curious about *you*. Not many *equites* in Egypt and even fewer who would ever show up in a local beer house. What brings you to the capitol of the Arsinoites?"

Alexander considered and mentally shrugged. He couldn't see any reason *not* to state his business, especially to another Roman.

"I'm here at the request of the Lady Antonia, the widow of Drusus. She's made me the *epitropos* – the procurator – for her estates in Egypt."

Sabinus perked up seeming be very interested in that. Well, a lot of people admired the imperials. He pointed at a stool and Alexander nodded for him to join him. Sabinus placed his forearms on the table and leaned forward. "So you've just come from Rome, then?"

Alexander confirmed this.

"And from the Lady Antonia, you say. Do you actually know her? Have you ever met her?"

Alexander laughed and held his palms forward. "Yes, yes. I recently arrived from Rome. Yes, the Lady Antonia did personally ask me to oversee her estates. And yes, I do know her, although not very well. I know her son Claudius much better. *Oh*, and also when I was young, I lived in the house of Antonia's close friend the princess Julia Berenice. Antonia visited her often."

Sabinus rubbed at his chin and seemed to think this over. "So the Lady cares about her properties here in Egypt?"

Alexander blinked. "Well, yes, of course she does. She has been a little worried about their management."

Sabinus leaned forward and gave Alexander a direct look. "So, she will be coming here, then?"

"What? No. Why would Antonia be coming to Egypt?"

Sabinus leaned back and seemed to lose interest. "No particular reason. I just thought that she might be coming to check on her property. You should know that Antonia is quite popular with the locals. It would mean a lot to them if she came for a visit."

"I see," Alexander nodded slowly. He wasn't sure if he bought Sabinus's sudden show of nonchalance, but he couldn't see why it mattered.

"Well, Antonia did not mention coming. ... Although, I suppose it's possible that Germanicus might come sometime if Augustus can spare him. He has property in Egypt, too, so he could check in on both his and his mother's."

That thought caused Sabinus to lean in again.

"Germanicus? *His grandson*? ... I mean, *uhh*, her son? ... *hunh*, he would do, too."

Alexander frowned. "Do what? What do you mean by that?"

Sabinus gave an indifferent shrug.

"*Ah*, nothing much. Like I was saying, the locals love a good celebration and an imperial visit would be about the best reason to have one. They don't get a lot of important guests in this area. A visit from Antonia, or any of her children, would be of great benefit for the community. There would be the public feasts and entertainments. It would be the talk of Egypt for many years to come."

"*Hmm*. I see your point." Alexander nodded slowly. "I guess having been in Rome so long, I forget how remote Augustus and all his family must seem to people in the provinces."

He was distracted as another man walked up to their table and gave a small bow to Alexander. This man was not as cocksure as Sabinus, but he was not too nervous either when he spoke.

"I am sorry to interrupt, but I could not help but overhear what you said. Are you really here to take over management of the Lady Antonia's properties?"

Alexander gave the new man the once over. His clothes were nice enough, but he doubted the man was rich. He was probably Greek, or possibly a Greco-Egyptian. Alexander raised his eyebrows.

"...and *you* are?"

"Oh, I am Dionysodoros. I am the *strategos* for the Arsinoite nome. I apologize that I had no one to formally introduce me to you, but I thought we should meet. If you are here to manage the Lady Antonia's estates, then we may be seeing quite a lot of each other."

Alright, Alexander thought. He actually had wanted to meet the local *strategos*, so this was good. The *strategos* was like a regional governor, but only for his own nome. He had nowhere near the status of an *epistrategos* like Titus Serenius; he didn't even have to be a Roman. Still, as a local magistrate each *strategos* had a lot of influence so Dionysodoros could be a good contact to cultivate.

That gave Alexander an idea. He gestured to a stool inviting Dionysodoros to join them. Sabinus nodded to Dionysodoros as he sat down then he turned to Alexander. "Most of us just call him *Dion* for short. Dionysodoros is just too much to say, especially after you've had a few cups."

The *strategos* smiled. "It is true. You will see my full name Dionysodoros on petitions or other documents, but Dion is just fine for anything that doesn't have to be formal."

Alexander leaned in. "Actually, I was hoping to meet you. I could use a bit of help from you." He waved a hand between Dion and Sabinus. "– from either of you. I need to formally relieve the Lady Antonia's land agent, Hierax, of his duties but he seems to be avoiding me."

Both men laughed as if Alexander had just said something funny. Alexander frowned, but Dion just shook his head and smiled. "It is nothing that you said. It is that Hierax is well known for avoiding anything that involves effort or responsibility. ... Did you try looking in Tebtunis? He has a house there."

"I did," Alexander replied. "Or at least I sent a messenger. My man waited outside his house for three days and never laid eyes on him. Are you sure Hierax spends time in Tebtunis?"

"Oh, definitely," said Dion. "He runs with the bastards."

To Alexander's surprise, the *strategos* jabbed his thumb toward Sabinus. "*His* bastards."

Startled, Alexander started to scoot his stool back out of the way because those sure sounded like fighting words to him. To his surprise, Sabinus just burst out laughing.

"*My bastards*, indeed," Sabinus chuckled. He looked at Alexander's surprised face, "Don't worry. He's just talking about the priests of Kronos. Yeah, I had them created at the crocodile temple there in Tebtunis."

"Huh?" Alexander returned Sabinus's laugh with a puzzled frown. Then a thought occurred to him.

"Wait. Are you saying you had something to do with that new priesthood of Kronos in Tebtunis?"

"Oh yeah, that was me. I started them." Sabinus seemed quite proud of this local accomplishment. The words still made no sense to Alexander.

"You ... *You* started a new *priesthood* here in Egypt? *How? Why*?"

Sabinus gave another one of his dismissive waves.

"The '*why*' was simple enough. You see, I took up with a local woman. She said that she was Greek, but she was not a citizen of one of the Greek cities, so, you know, not much status. I couldn't help there, but she wanted more. She made me promise to do something for her son Kronion. The kid didn't look like much of a soldier so I decided that we would make him a priest."

Alexander was taken aback. "B-, but. How could this be? There are so many laws governing the priesthood. Only pure blood Egyptians can become priests, they have to prove their heritage, apply for circumcision. If this boy was at least part Greek, he could not even qualify."

Sabinus gave an amused nod. "Yes, yes, that's all true. We couldn't make young Kronion a traditional temple priest because he didn't have the right blood or family."

Sabinus rubbed his chinned and nodded. "That's why I had to create a new god for him."

"*What?!*"

"Don't act so surprised, Alexander, you know money can buy just about anything. In fact, Rome had already decided that most of the higher Egyptian priesthoods will have to be purchased now. That's what gave me the idea. I could just *buy* my woman's kid a priesthood.

"Of course, I had to convince the chief finance officer, the *Idios Logos*, that this priesthood was so different that the usual Egyptian inheritance rules would not apply. That meant it couldn't be an Egyptian god, or any Greek or Roman god who had already been associated with an Egyptian god. It took some thought. We had to come up with a god who everyone knew was real, but had never been associated with an Egyptian temple priesthood before."

Sabinus gave a flourish with his hand. "And thus we came up with Kronos. Everyone knows that he's a real god. And Kronos needed his own priests – which I then bought. And since there was no history of Kronos worship in Egypt, there was no hereditary Egyptian priesthood for Kronos. There was nothing standing in the way there. Of course, I wasn't going to pay for a whole temple building. Since her son Kronion was already in Tebtunis, it made sense to just go ahead and use the temple already there and associate Kronos with the crocodile god. That sort of thing happens in Egypt all the time."

Alexander could hardly keep his mouth from falling open as Sabinus bragged about how he had invented and purchased a new priesthood. To Alexander this was *hubris*. Sabinus did not seem to notice his expression and continued with the story.

"Yeah, the temple part was actually easier than inventing the new priesthood – that part got kind of tricky. As you just pointed out, Alexander, there are just so many rules for becoming an Egyptian priest; proving ones blood line was a big one."

Sabinus paused and took a sip of his beer before continuing with a nod.

"But, in the end it just took a little money and a little Roman ingenuity to smooth the way. Of course, the Egyptian priests for the crocodile are still all hereditary. When they refer to the god with the name *'Soknebtunis,'* the priests are pure bloods only. It's when they call the crocodile god *'Kronos,'* is when the priests are not pure blood. In fact, they're mostly Greeks, or part-Greeks."

Sabinus pointed at the *strategos*. "That's why our colleague here calls them *my bastards*. I bought the first few positions for the Kronos priests and they're Greeks, not Egyptian pure bloods."

Alexander shook his head in amazement. "You know that Kronos is being worshipped in Tebtunis as a crocodile god, right? And not just that, do you realize that the people have equated Kronos with a *crocodile* itself? I mean, that is animal worship. That's despicable. That is *not* something we Romans – or the Greeks – can abide."

Sabinus threw back his head and laughed as if Alexander had said something funny.

"Oh Jupiter ... the statues, have you seen *them* yet? -- those little clay models of crocodiles with the name Kronos inscribed across the base? I've seen them. They're hilarious. Well, I can tell you that part was *not* my idea. ... But really, Alexander, who cares? The people seem happy, my woman's boy is happy, the *Idios Logos* got paid for a bunch of new Kronos priesthoods, so he's happy."

Sabinus waved at Dion who lifted one shoulder then said, "It is not like they are really competing with the Egyptians priests. The Kronos priests are not circumcised. Oh, and their heads aren't shaved – well, not really. Only the hereditary Egyptians are allowed to have their heads fully shaved. So, these Kronos priests have a little circle on the top of their heads shaved and let the rest of the hair hang down. It looks a little strange."

Sabinus cut in with a snorted laugh. "Those shaved circles. They are even funnier that their Kronos crocodile statues. You should travel down to Tebtunis and see them just for fun." He raised his hands palms up. *"Huh,* I ask you again, where is the harm?"

Alexander thought for a moment. "I'm not sure that there *is* any harm. At least, I don't see why there should be. But then, I'm a Jew and these various crocodile gods mean nothing to me. But..."

He held up one finger. *"Point.* It may not matter to you or to me, but apparently it does matter to the hereditary priests of Soknebtunis. I heard about this from the *epistrategos,* Titus Serenius. He's been receiving petitions about it. The Egyptians refer to the Kronos priests as *the bastards*. There's been some disputing over land rights – probably nothing new in that – but, apparently it has been escalating into some stick fighting."

Sabinus shrugged these concerns away. "I know nothing of that now. I got bored with my woman and moved on awhile ago. I haven't seen her or her priest son Kronion in a while. As I said, Alexander, who cares? It's none of my affair anymore. Let the priests work it out."

Alexander could only nod reluctantly in agreement. In this, Sabinus, no doubt, was correct. Trouble between priests was none of his business. *And he had Antonia's land agent to find.*

"Actually," Alexander inserted, "this whole conversation started because I was asking about Hierax." He turned to the *strategos*. "When you said that Hierax *ran with the bastards*, did you mean that he associates with these new Kronos priests in Tebtunis?"

Dion glanced at Sabinus before answering. "Yeah, that's what I meant. Hierax spends a lot of his time with *the bastards, umm,* I mean the priests of Kronos in Tebtunis. And, *uh,* well the word is that he's been the one inciting some of the trouble between the hereditary priests and these new Kronos priests – like that stick fighting you mentioned."

"Really?" Alexander asked in surprise. "What could Hierax possibly have to gain by doing that?"

The *strategos* raised both palms upward and shook his head. "I don't know. But from what I do know of the man, he wouldn't be doing much unless there was money involved."

Alexander ran a hand through his short curls and frowned.

"That seems a very strange pastime for the Lady Antonia's freedman and land agent. ... Well, I'm going to be travelling around the lake, visiting as many of Antonia's properties as possible. Hopefully, I'll come across the man soon. I will be *encouraging* him to leave Egypt – and do it sooner rather than later."

The *strategos* scrunched his brows together. "You're visiting *each* of the Lady Antonia's properties? I thought she had quite a few."

Alexander nodded, "Indeed she does, dozens of properties just in the Arsinoite nome alone. Originally, I had thought that she mainly produced wheat for sale in Rome, but I've realized now that she has acquired interests in, well, just about everything. She's got vegetables and orchards in Philadelphia, fishing in Soknopaiou

Nesos, papyrus making in Nilopolis, pastureland in Karanis, vineyards in Theadelphia – not to mention all the warehouses, wheat mills, and the wine and oil presses. I think Antonia owns some property in every large village and many smaller ones, too."

"I knew about some of them," said Dion. "But it sounds like there are even more properties than I realized. How will you ever manage all of them?"

Alexander blew out a long breath, sighed and ran his hand through his hair again. "This will not be easy. Obviously, I'm going to need to work through local overseers. Also, I'll be looking for opportunities to buy and sell."

"Buy and sell?" Dion was clearly puzzled.

"Oh, yes. Only where it makes good business sense, of course. You see, right now, her properties are very scattered due to the way they were bought, or inherited. A lot of her farm and pasture land is not even contiguous. My own family owns land separating parcels of Antonia's wheat crop from each other. It may not matter a lot for some ventures, but I suspect that pastureland and grain fields can be made more productive if they can be joined. That way they can share farm workers, join in crop rotation, or so I believe."

He paused and shrugged his shoulders. "It seems that there will be much more to do than I had originally thought. There won't be time for me to see to it all. I have to return to Alexandria and take up my new duties as Alabarch as well."

Dion gave him a sympathetic smile. "You're a busy man. So what will you do first?"

Alexander waved a hand. "I won't be able to visit every property. So I'll have to try to get an overview, a general sense of how things work. I'll be visiting many of the larger properties and trying to see an assortment of different specializations for food, livestock, and production."

Sabinus had been quiet for awhile but now leaned in. "You'll be leaving soon, then?" he asked.

Alexander nodded back. "Yes, not tomorrow, it is our Sabbath – a holy day, but I'll leave the day after."

Sabinus nodded vaguely. "So, what route will you be taking?"

Alexander bit his lower lip, a habit he had when thinking. "I haven't completely decided yet. I'll probably be taking a barge around the Desert Canal, maybe head north towards Philadelphia and on to Karanis – at least to start. Later, I do plan to go west towards Theadelphia and Euhemeria. My family owns land in Euhemeria, as does Antonia, so I don't want to miss stopping there on this trip. ... Why? Does my route matter?"

Sabinus shook his head. "*Nah, nah,* not at all. 'Just idle curiosity. ... But, *hmm*, if you decide to head north on the canal, then I could travel with you -- at least as far as Philadelphia. I manage some lands in that area and it wouldn't hurt to check up on how they are doing."

Alexander nodded slowly. "Your company would be most welcome. As you can well guess, I am somewhat out of my depth here. Conducting business in Rome – that is something I know. Visiting villages on canals surrounded by desert – that I do not. Having a traveling companion who knows the area, even for part of the way, will help."

The *strategos* Dion thought for a moment and added. "Well, how you plan the rest of your route might matter -- just because of the growing seasons. We're well into August now; the grapes are being harvested and pressed into wine. You may want to choose a route that will allow you to oversee that. In another two or three weeks, the grape season will be over and you won't get another chance until next year's crop."

Alexander rubbed his chin and nodded thoughtfully. "That is an excellent suggestion, Dion. That is one of the things – *huh*, one of the *many* things -- I should understand if I am to be of any use as the new procurator. ... *hmm*, but that does not actually help me to decide my route. I believe the Lady Antonia has vineyards in both Karanis and Theadelphia."

The *strategos* shrugged.

"I can't tell you anything about Karanis, but I can tell you that the vineyards in Theadelphia are quite extensive. There is a wine press there, too – a modern one.

"You see, for the grapes growing around many of the villages, the locals just harvest them and then stomp the grapes in a vat. That works well enough for small gardens, but it's too much labor for a big vineyard like Antonia has in Theadelphia. She has an actual press for her grapes and that's unusual. Since there are only a few wine presses in all Egypt, you might want to see it while it's in use."

Alexander nodded. "I would. Thank you." He looked from Dion to Sabinus and back. "Your advice has helped me to plan. I believe I shall first make a quick trip north to Philadelphia with you if you are still willing to travel with me."

He tilted his head in question at Sabinus who nodded his agreement.

"After Philadelphia, I should make my way to Karanis. I have received a number of petitions from there that I should address – from both tenants and landowners."

Sabinus raised his eyebrows. "Really? Petitions? What troubles do they say they are having in Karanis?"

Alexander waved a hand. "I couldn't say off the top of my

head. My secretary and I will need to review the petitions before each stop. Right now I'm having trouble distinguishing one village from another. *Hmm,* but I seem to recall that Karanis was having a particular issue with missing animals."

Sabinus looked away. "*Hunh,* I had not heard they were having that trouble there, but then I rarely go to Karanis."

Dion appeared to be a bit more engaged. "Will you be heading south of the lake after that? Most of my time is spent in the villages south of Lake Moeris. It's where *I own* land so I only travel north when my *strategos* duties require it. If you are interested I would be happy to meet you and show you around, introduce you to all the people you may need to know."

Alexander was quick to agree. "Your offer is most welcome. I know I will need to learn quickly, but for now I feel at a distinct disadvantage."

"Send word when you're ready," the *strategos* said. "We could meet back here at Crocodilopolis, but I would suggest that you take a boat across the lake to the southern branch of the Desert Canal. If you do that within the next ten-twelve days, you should be in time to see the grapes being harvested and pressed in Theadelphia."

Alexander rubbed his chin and nodded thoughtfully. "We have a rough sketch of the Lady Antonia's properties around the lake. I'll need to study it with my secretary to plan our route after Philadelphia. It is also hard to guess at this point how long my presence will be needed in each village. ... *Hmm.* I will plan to be in Theadelphia before the end of the month."

Sabinus looked up from where he had been studying his beer. "So day after tomorrow, we head for Philadelphia. Then you go on to Karanis. You will need to be south of the lake in Theadelphia less than two weeks after that."

"Yes, yes," Alexander replied. "I think Dion is right that I should be present to observe the wine making since I am already in the area." He blew out a breath. "I will need to develop a schedule of what is happening in each month. From what I can tell, Antonia's properties do everything from wheat to papyrus making to animal herding. It will be hard to keep track of it all."

He stood and glanced around looking for Amarantus and didn't see him. "I had thought my secretary might have joined me by now. I had better go look for him and find the house where I will be staying tonight."

Alexander gave a slight bow of his head to his new acquaintances. "*Kurioi*, lords, it has been a pleasure meeting you. I will look forward to seeing you again soon. For now, farewell."

7. The Jews of Crocodilopolis

Alexander exited the beer house and looked around for Amarantus. His servant had gone ahead with Philo to locate the house where they would be staying that night. Then he was supposed to come to the beer house so he could guide Alexander there.

Hunh. Amarantus was nowhere to be seen. Alexander shrugged. He knew the general direction so he headed that way hoping to meet up with his servant, or even his brother, on the way. It was with surprise that he came to a market square and saw Amarantus standing there and talking animatedly with two women. He squinted his eyes – no, it was *one* woman and one *girl*, not quite a woman yet.

Both of the ladies appeared to be well dressed. Perhaps a mother and daughter? Certainly neither of them could be a slave. Amarantus, however, most definitely *was a slave* and his seeming familiarity with the two ladies was ... unusual. It also was possibly highly inappropriate behavior depending on who the two females were.

As Alexander approached his servant looked up eagerly. "Master, you are here."

Before Alexander could respond, Amarantus gave a sweeping flourish with one arm, bowed to the two females and announced, "This is my master, a noble *eques* of Rome appointed by the First Citizen Augustus himself, and now a leading man of Alexandria."

Alexander blinked. How was one to respond to such a florid introduction? But, once again, Alexander was interrupted before he could say a word. The girl tilted her head and stared at him a bit too boldly for a properly bred young woman.

"So, you're a Jew are you?" she said. "Your man here just told us that his master may be a Roman, but he is also a Jew. Are you a Jew?"

Alexander pulled his head back on his shoulders and simply nodded.

"Well, we're Jews, too," the girl announced waving a hand from her companion to herself and nodding enthusiastically. "But we're not from here."

Alexander took a closer look at the two females. They had light brown skin with dark hair as did most people living in Egypt. But that was also true of other places. As he had already noted, their clothes were of fine quality, Greek in style. The older woman had not spoken yet and seemed to pay deference to the girl. She was probably an attendant, then. Not likely to be the girl's mother as Alexander had originally thought.

The girl, herself looked to be maybe mid-teens. He supposed some would consider her to be of marriageable age, but personally he had always found that age to be too close to being a child. Alexander nodded politely to the two females.

"If you are not from here, then what brings you to Crocodilopolis?"

"Well, the crocodiles, of course," answered the girl. "We came to see the pet crocodiles at the temple."

Amarantus added quickly. "Master, they needed someone to accompany them to the crocodile temple, so I went with them. I knew you would not want them to go to the temple alone."

"I would not have wanted them to have gone to a crocodile god temple *at all*," Alexander retorted. He turned to the Jewish woman. "*What* were you thinking?"

The older woman looked down and said nothing, but the teenager crossed her arms and gave Alexander a defiant look. "*I* wanted to see the crocodiles. And *I* wanted to feed them. And so *I* did."

Alexander gave her an incredulous look. "You *fed* the crocodiles? You should *not* have. To the locals, those animals are considered to be gods. Jews *do not* give offerings to other people's gods. This is the law given to us by the Lord through Moses. Do you *not know* this?"

The girl raised her chin and returned a defiant look.

"*Yes*, I *do* know this. And I did *not* break the law given by the Lord. There was no golden calf. I *did not* pray to the crocodile god."

Alexander thrust a finger at the girl and jabbed it as he made his point. "Yet, you say you went to the temple and you *fed* the crocodile – you gave it offerings. You. Broke. The. Commandment. Tell me, would your father approve of these activities?"

The girl sucked in a breath and looked like she was about to launch into a counter-argument. Then she stopped and hung her head and answered softly.

"No, I do not suppose my father would have approved of my feeding the crocodile. It's just that … I was curious. When I travel, I want to see everything. I want to try everything. If I don't do it now, I may never have another chance."

She hesitated. "I just wanted to see the crocodile. I didn't worship it, really I didn't."

Alexander shook his head. "I *do* understand that Egypt can be a wondrous place. I myself just saw a hippopotamus for the first time a day ago. … But, for Jews there are limits."

He turned his attention to the woman attendant. "It seems

that *you* are supposed to be the responsible one here. You should not have allowed the girl to go to an Egyptian temple and make offerings."

Before the attendant could reply, the girl jumped in.

"She had no choice, you know. I insisted. You see, I am *very headstrong*," the girl announced almost proudly.

"*Hah*," Alexander snorted out a laugh before he could stop himself. He smiled at the girl. "Well, don't brag about it," he said.

He turned back to his servant, "Ranti, did you find the house where we will be staying?"

"I did, master. It is not too far and next to the prayer house that your brother said you will visit tonight."

"Excellent, Ranti, lead on."

Alexander gave a polite bow to take his leave of the females and turned to follow his servant.

"You said it wasn't far, Ranti? I hope to get something to eat before the synagogue meets this evening."

As Alexander walked away the girl called after him. "I'll try to remember what you said. ... Who are you anyway?"

He absently turned and answered the girl over his shoulder. "My name is Alexander ... Gaius Julius Alexander. My family is from Alexandria."

Since he was no longer paying much attention to the girl, he didn't see the startled look she exchanged with her woman attendant.

After they had walked away, it occurred to Alexander that he had neglected to learn the women's names. That had probably been ... inexcusably rude. Briefly, he grimaced at himself. He should have been more attentive to matters of courtesy. ... Oh well, he supposed it didn't matter. It was unlikely that he would ever see them again.

****

That evening, Alexander and his brother Philo accompanied their host, the Archon, to the local Jewish prayer house. Crocodilopolis was the largest city in the Arsinoite nome and had several *synagogues* – or congregations of Jews. Three of them had their own prayer houses with attached *mikvahs* for ritual baths.

As they walked toward the prayer house, other Jews joined their group. Philo appeared to know many of the men. He walked ahead with several of them animatedly discussing ... something. Alexander couldn't tell what they were talking about although it did seem to have something to do with the Torah. He did not share Philo's enthusiasm for debating scripture. Of course, he tried to do all that was expected of him, but Alexander just could not spend his days pondering the mysteries of the Lord's words the way Philo could.

Alexander lengthened his stride and joined the men that were ahead. Like him, each man was wearing a prayer shawl with fringes on the four corners. He soon learned that these Arsinoite men were curious how their synagogue's practices differed from what Alexander had experienced in Rome. He was peppered with questions, but in the end he found that there wasn't that much difference between this synagogue in Egypt and the ones he had attended in Rome. Each meeting revolved around a reading from scripture. There might be some words of interpretation, some chanting, silent or group prayer, but the variations were similar.

In many ways, the Jewish communities in both Rome and Egypt seemed distant from their great Temple in Jerusalem with its high priest and daily sacrifice. The scripture they used in both Egypt and Rome was the Greek translation, not Hebrew. Alexander and Philo were unusual in Egypt in that they used Hebrew to recite their daily prayers but they didn't really know the language. Ironically, the same was also true for many of the Jews in Judea. They knew minimal Hebrew because their spoken language was Aramaic.

But every Jew, wherever they lived, knew how to recite the *Shma*, their most sacred prayer, in Hebrew. Although the prayer meeting they were going to would be held in Greek, at the beginning and the end everyone would recite the *Shma* from memory.

"Shma O Yisrael Adonai elohenu. Adonai echad."

"Hear, O Israel, the Lord our God. The Lord is One."

For Jews, the Lord is *One*. Alexander's mind strayed briefly to thoughts about this new home in Alexandria where he was surrounded by the *many* gods that the Egyptians worshipped. Then his mind wandered to the exchange earlier that day when the Jewish girl admitted she had fed the sacred crocodile. That was an *offering* to a foreign god. How could she not know that was wrong? He smiled as he thought of the girl's pronouncement *"I'm very headstrong."* There could be little doubt about that.

He glanced over at the women's section, but did not see the girl or her attendant. The women here in the prayer house sat in their own section, but they were not screened off – there was no modesty demand on them. Indeed, women in Egypt had more independence than women in Judea or Rome. Even under Roman rule, women in Egypt could own property and had legal protections against bodily harm. Indeed, a woman in Egypt could even sue her own husband just for verbally insulting her.

After the last repetition of the *Shma* the service ended and both men and women began to filter out of the prayer house and into the courtyard. The meeting had not been long, but Alexander found that he felt good, somehow cleansed. He mentally shrugged. Perhaps, it was just the comfort of doing something that felt *familiar* in a world that had seemed to turn sideways since his father had required him to leave Rome a few weeks earlier.

As he exited the prayer house, Alexander saw that his brother seemed to be deep in conversation with yet another small group of men. Not really interested in discussing theology, he looked around and saw their host waving him over. Philo had arranged for them to spend the night with the Archon, the magistrate of the synagogue.

"Alexander," the Archon said, "I thought you might like to meet some of our local men who lease properties from the Lady Antonia Minor."

"Indeed, I would," Alexander perked up. Perhaps he could get some valuable information out of these men.

His new acquaintances greeted his eagerly. One noted, "We were so surprised to learn of your return to Alexandria. The word was that you were pretty well set up in Rome. No one really expected you ever to come back to Egypt to stay. ... You are here to stay aren't you?"

Alexander rubbed his chin. "I suppose I am, although I have to admit that being recalled by my father came as a surprise to me, too."

"A welcome surprise, I hope," remarked one man.

Alexander looked down and bit his lower lip to keep from giving an ungracious reply. No, being recalled to Egypt was *not* a welcome surprise. Instead, he changed the subject. "Apparently, I'll have enough to keep me quite busy. Very soon, I'll start training to replace my father as the Alabarch. But first, I have to get the Lady Antonia's affairs sorted out."

He looked at his new acquaintances, hopefully. "So, has anyone here seen the land agent, Hierax? He seems to be avoiding me for some reason."

The men looked back and forth at one another until one snorted and answered. "Not that he has confided in any of *us*, but it is not too hard to figure out why Hierax would be avoiding *you*."

"Really? I'm listening." Alexander leaned in.

Again, the men looked back and forth at each other before the first man responded again.

"It's the rents, of course. He's been collecting them early."

"*What?* He has already collected *all* the money?" Then, Alexander had another thought. "Wait, aren't a lot of the rents paid in kind, not with coin?"

"Oh, yeah, but Hierax has been taking that, too. ... But nobody knows where he's putting everything, since nothing has been ending up in Lady Antonia's store houses. I'm not saying he's stealing it or anything, but young Alexander, I suggest that you notify all the villages fast that you are the only one who is supposed to be collecting from now on."

Alexander palmed his forehead. "I don't believe this. I don't even have a record of all the contracts and leases."

One of the men patted Alexander on the shoulder. "It could be much worse. You've gotten here at a good time. All that is being harvested now are the grapes and the dates. The wheat, the barley, and the olives all come later. You should have some time to get things in order before they are harvested."

Alexander exhaled a long breath. "Yes, you are correct of course. But *that man* is out there with Antonia's money, crops, and who knows what more. And I can't find him to get it all back."

The men talking to Alexander all nodded sympathetically. Then one added, "You know that he's got our tax money, too, don't you?"

Alexander's shoulders fell as he took several breaths before replying. "No, no. I had no idea that Hierax has been collecting the tax money."

The Archon spoke up. "Well, most of it is not technically money – not bronze and silver coins that is. Remember this is farm country. People pay their taxes with the goods they produce."

Alexander was puzzled. "Wait. Why would *Hierax* have

anyone's tax goods or money? The man is a land agent."

One of the men spoke up. "Because he's a *Toga boy* -- just like them."

"A what?"

"He means a *Roman*," a man responded to Alexander's confused look. *"Toga boys* or *Togas* for short – that's what some people call the Roman citizens in Egypt. It's not meant to be ... complimentary. Hierax is a Roman citizen and one of the Lady Antonia's own freedmen. When he applied for the right to collect the taxes on all of Antonia's properties, the prefect's people in Alexandria were happy to grant him the right. Of course, he collects extra to pay himself, but then all the tax collectors do that."

Another man added. "Yeah, he's one of those *togas* alright – has a pretty high opinion of himself and never lets you forget it. But now, Alexander, are you saying that he's disappeared? He's in the wind, along with our rent and tax money as well?"

Another man added thoughtfully, "Now that you are replacing him, I suppose *you* may be liable for the taxes, Alexander. If you can't get the money already collected by Hierax, you may have to pay it out of your own purse. That's how things are usually done here."

Alexander held up his hand. "No. I'll have to get that straightened out when I get back to Alexandria. I have no interest in becoming a tax collector. I don't have the time, and I don't need the money. Let someone else do it."

The other man was not impressed. "Well, that may be, but we all have *receipts* showing that we paid our taxes to the Lady Antonia's appointed representative. There will be trouble if you don't honor our receipts."

Alexander' brows met. Was that a threat? Seeing Alexander's expression, a man who spoke earlier broke in. "As I already said, it may not be that bad. Most of the rents and taxes are paid after the main crops are in – the wheat, barley, and especially the olives. That won't be done until months from now, so Hierax could not have collected any of that yet. We know he has collected some money and goods from many of us, but he couldn't have gotten most of it yet, not even close."

Alexander nodded slowly. The man was right. This wasn't a disaster ... yet. But he *really* needed to find that freedman before any more harm was done. He was already having trouble controlling his own growing frustration and anger.

In a tight voice he asked, "Does anyone know where I can find Hierax? Since he is refusing to come to me, I am going have to track him down wherever he is."

One man gestured to get his attention. "Actually, Alexander, I may be able to help a little with that. When I heard that you were coming, I asked my barge men if they had seen Hierax. They had not. ... Wait, wait, there is more," he added as he saw Alexander shake his head in frustration. "You see my bargemen have been plying the lower canal – the one that goes south of the lake from here on out to Theadelphia and beyond. ... My point is that if Hierax hasn't been seen on the *south side* of the lake, then he most likely went north on the Desert Canal."

Alexander nodded slowly. "I think I see your point. Hierax wasn't at his home in Tebtunis, but his house steward said that he had headed out on the canals."

"His *house steward*?" the Archon said. "I had not heard that he had acquired his own house steward. My, my, his opinion of his own importance just seems to keep growing."

Alexander chewed his lower lip and swept his across the group of assembled men. "So, what you all are saying is that if Hierax is not at his home in Tebtunis, and he has not been seen in the villages on the southern part of the Desert Canal, then it is likely he is on a barge headed north on the Canal. *Hunh.* That does work for me. After the Sabbath, I will be heading north on the Desert Canal toward Philadelphia, and then I'll travel on to Bacchias, Karanis and beyond. If he's trying to get ahead of me and collect rents and taxes, I should hear of it and hopefully in time to catch up to him."

The men nodded their agreement. "Like my friend just said, he must be up there because the bargemen said they haven't seen him in the nearby villages. In fact, we've been asking around ourselves and we can't find anyone who has actually *seen* him – at least not in a few weeks. If no one has seen Hierax down here, then it just makes sense that he's up there."

Alexander ran a hand through his hair. "I'm sure you all must be right and so it is fortunate that I was already heading north. After that, I plan to come to the villages south of the lake. I want to be in Theadelphia in time to observe the grape pressing."

He gave himself a quick nod. "Yes, yes, that's what I'll do. Thank you -- each of you. But, if you see – or even hear of—the man Hierax, let me know at once."

The Archon had one additional piece of advice. "I suggest you try to find the store house where this land agent has been keeping the goods he has collected for rent and taxes. Even if you don't find him, you'll probably be able to claim back some Antonia's property that he has already collected."

How the village of Philadelphia may have looked when approached by canal.

Adapted from a photo of Philae, Egypt taken in the late 1800s by Antonio Beato

Source: https://www.loc.gov/item/2003690014/

8. Philadelphia

"Master, why are we not stopping at any of these other villages first?"

Amarantus gestured as they slid past a small village a short distance from the shore. They were sitting on a barge as it was part rowed and part poled through the Desert Canal heading north from Crocodilopolis. Sabinus had indeed chosen to accompany him, but at the moment was sitting toward the stern talking with the barge master. Alexander looked up from a papyrus scroll to answer his servant.

"Antonia does have some wheat land in a couple of small villages that we are passing, but I have decided that our first stop is going to be the larger village of Philadelphia."

"Phil-a-del-phi-a," Amarantus slowly sounded out the name and then gave Alexander a puzzled look. "*Sister love*? Master, why would anyone call a village *sister love*?"

Alexander rubbed at his chin in thought, "I suppose that in Greek the name could mean either *sister love* or *brother love*. I think that in this case you had it right. As I understand it, this village was founded by Greeks and named after their king. He was known as King Ptolemy Philadelphos, or Ptolemy the *sister-lover*, because he married his sister."

Amarantus raised an eyebrow. "Master, that is not a pleasant thought. And now we must go to this place named for people who committed incest? To *this city of sisterly love*?"

Sabinus had been listening to the conversation and now he leaned forward and scoffed. "Not *city*. It is better called the *'little village of sisterly love.'* Maybe at one time they thought they were founding a city, but Philadelphia never grew beyond the size of a local village."

Alexander frowned at Sabinus. "Well, no doubt Philadelphia is small by the standard of Alexandria. Back in Crocodilopolis, though, I was told that Philadelphia is one of the largest villages in the Arsinoite nome. Apparently, nearly 3,000 *people* live there."

Sabinus raised his eyebrows and Alexander snorted out a laugh as he realized the humor of his own words. "Alright, it's true. Three thousand people are hardly enough to call it *a city*. *Hmm*, You said you have been there before, didn't you Sabinus?"

In response, Sabinus waved a casual hand. "Many times. But why are *you* going to Philadelphia, Alexander? I thought the biggest property owner in Philadelphia was Livia, the wife of Augustus."

"I think that is so," Alexander agreed, "but the Lady Antonia specifically asked me to visit there. Apparently, Livia showed her some drawing of the layout of her irrigation ditches and Antonia was very interested. Now *I* am supposed to go investigate this irrigation system to see if it should be employed on Antonia's properties."

"Besides," Alexander added, "Antonia *does own* a fair bit of property in Philadelphia. She has wheat fields, pasturelands, and then a building in the village that I think has something to do with weaving." He pressed his lips together and blew out a breath making a sputtering sound.

"This ongoing challenge for me is that I won't know the details of what Antonia owns until I track down Hierax and get the records for her properties."

As they were talking, the barge master called out to attract their attention and pointed ahead of them as the village of Philadelphia came into view. Sabinus watched with a smile as Alexander stood and took in his first sight of the first real Arsinoite village that he would be visiting. The annual inundation of the Nile had recently peaked which meant the rising Desert Canal had left little of the shore line.

The bargemen poled the barge up onto a sandy bank. Not far from the canal were small stands of date palm trees. A dirt road led from the shore straight through the center of the nearby village. Everywhere Alexander looked were shades of golden brown. There were also bits of other colors such as the gardens around the houses, but mostly the vista was of rows of mud brick buildings, each one golden brown like the desert sand.

Some buildings were one story; others were two or three. He could identify a large dove cote, a temple, and what might be a granary. *Huh.* His first Egyptian village and Alexander was struck with how different it looked from anywhere he had lived before.

The buildings in Rome had been made from wood, travertine, or *tufa* stone and many walls were faced with marble. Never the mud brick that Alexander now saw before him in Philadelphia. In Rome, these buildings would hardly last a year. ... Well, Alexander supposed that mud brick could only be used in a place like this where it never rained. He had a momentary image of buildings literally melting as they were pelted by an Italian Spring-time rain storm.

"Master, these are *not* as nice as the buildings in Rome." Apparently Amarantus had been struck with the same contrast Alexander had noted. He had disembarked behind his master and was staring toward Philadelphia with obvious distaste. Indeed, his servant could be a real snob.

Alexander gave a rueful smile back, "Well, it's not the City; that much is certain. But Egypt *is* a Roman province and has been for ... *umm*, forty years. It's as Roman now as any other Roman territory."

He paused at Amarantus's incredulous look. "Well, maybe not *any* other Roman territory. I suppose Egypt is a bit more exotic than some of the other Roman provinces, but we are still part of Rome. There can be little doubt of that."

Amarantus looked like he could doubt Egypt's Roman-ness a great deal, but was interrupted before he could express any of these thoughts for himself.

"Do you wish to give offerings to the crocodile god for your safe journey?"

"Huh?" Alexander startled and spun around to see that a man was standing next to him. He had been so lost in his own thoughts that he had not even noticed the arrival. The man observed his confusion.

"My name is Poudens, chief of the tenant farmers. Your secretary wrote to me from Crocodilopolis and instructed me to meet you when you arrived. At least that is if you are the Lady Antonia's new procurator. Are you this new man Gaius Julius Alexander?"

Alexander swung his gaze toward his secretary Amarantus.

"That is correct, master. The secretary for the Archon had me write a letter which he gave to a bargeman to deliver. This man Poudens is one of the tenant farmers for Antonia's grain fields. In fact, he is the most senior and is called the chief because he can sublet sections of Antonia's property – or so the Archon's secretary explained to me. I wrote to ask him to arrange some accommodation for us since there are no inns or taverns here."

Amarantus looked at Poudens who quickly nodded his agreement. Then he repeated his earlier question. "But first, do you wish to feed the crocodiles? Unfortunately, you just missed the festival for Souchos, but the god will accept your offerings now."

Alexander shook his head. "No, we're Romans. We don't give offerings to animals."

Poudens looked puzzled. "But, *kurie*, they do. Romans, Greeks, Egyptians, they all give offerings to Souchos the great crocodile god. Otherwise, they could not rely on his protection."

Alexander frowned at the man's assertion. Egyptians did worship animals. Everyone knew this. But Greeks did not, and most certainly Romans did not. ... Or, did they? He turned a questioning look at Sabinus who had come walking up the beach behind him.

Sabinus smiled and shrugged. "Yes, I do. I feed the crocodiles. Most of the locals do including the Romans. It is always best to keep the gods on your side, *all* of the gods."

Alexander briefly wondered what his brother Philo would think to learn of Romans giving offerings to crocodiles. Not much, he was sure. He turned back to Poudens.

"No, we will not be making an offering right now. I would rather have something to eat and then see this irrigation system on Livia's estates."

Poudens held up his palms. "As you wish, *kurie*. It may be good for you to do that today since there are many people coming to see you tomorrow. ... You know, to bring you their petitions."

Alexander had not expected that, although he supposed he should have. He turned back to Poudens.

"Any petitions that have been delivered already can be given to my secretary here, Amarantus. I will set aside some time tomorrow to meet with petitioners in person. However, I will not be able to decide on some matters until I get all of the records from Hierax. He should have delivered these to me already, but he has not."

He gave Poudens a hopeful look. "Have you seen him, by the way? Hierax? He is not at his home in Tebtunis or south of the Lake. I was hoping I might find him along this stretch of the Desert Canal."

The tenant farmer shook his head. "No, *I* have not seen him, but there are some who say that he has been here. Goods have gone missing – mostly stuff that was set aside to pay the rents. That is why some people think he must have come to collect them. But if he was here and took our goods, he did not leave receipts like he should have."

Poudens paused and gave Alexander a meaningful look before continuing. "You should know that some of these petitions you will be getting tomorrow will actually be complaints about the Lady Antonia's land agent. There is a lot of hope already that *you* will be a better manager than Hierax."

Alexander curled his lip. "*Petitions against* the land agent? That is not what I was hoping to hear, although at this point I suppose I should not be too surprised. It would seem that this whole transition between his management and mine will be more difficult than I had anticipated."

He shook his head. "This could become a real problem. Antonia never had copies of all of the individual deeds and leases -- there could be hundreds of them. I have got to wrest these documents from that wretched freedman or it could take me years to figure out all of Antonia's properties and contracts."

Alexander wasn't sure if he was addressing Poudens, Amarantus, or himself, so he blew out a long breath before continuing.

"With any luck I will come across this Hierax soon and then I will be able to get Antonia's records. I will also find out if he has been taking products to pay for rent without leaving receipts."

Poudens tried to hide his skeptical look. "Well, I wish you luck with that, *kurie*. I do not think that you will find Hierax to be an easy man."

Sabinus had been uncharacteristically silent, just watching the exchange between Alexander and Poudens. Now he gave an impatient gesture. "Let us go our separate ways and meet up later at the baths."

Alexander perked up. "Baths? There are baths here?"

Sabinus rolled his eyes. "Of course there are baths. These are not nomads living in tents. Plus a lot of Romans live in this area and we like our baths."

Alexander continued to look surprised so Sabinus added, "There is a bath tax. Each person in the village has to pay a small tax and that is used to maintain the baths."

He wagged his forefinger, "But don't be expecting any fancy floor mosaics or wall frescos. Occasionally a local land owner donates a bit of artwork, but mostly, the baths in the villages are pretty plain."

Alexander gave a rueful smile. "I think I will gladly do without a fresco, if there is an opportunity to wash off the travel grime. The sand just seems to be everywhere."

"Perhaps that is because this is the *desert*. There does tend to be a lot of sand there," answered Sabinus with a smirk before striding off on his own to ... well, wherever he was headed. Alexander hadn't thought to ask.

Poudens had duly arranged for Alexander to meet with the overseer of Livia's wheat fields. He learned that the fields had been divided into grids with an irrigation ditch surrounding each grid. Since the Nile inundation had recently crested, each irrigation channel was filled with water, but there was nothing growing yet. The planting season would begin in a few weeks, but for now the fields were empty of any crops.

Alexander supposed that if he had been a farmer, he may have found the whole thing terribly interesting, but ... they were *ditches*. He was taking a tour of lots of rows of *ditches*. *Hmm*, he did not want to appear ignorant in front of Poudens, so he made a mental note to ask Dion to explain the importance of these ditches when he saw the *strategos* again.

****

"Ahhh yeah."

Alexander lay back in the warm water. He had been pleased to find the village had a small but complete Roman-style bath with the separate cold, warm, and hot water basins. At the moment there were only the two of them bathing.

"So Sabinus, while I was visiting the irrigation system, what were you doing?"

Sabinus gave a casual wave. "Oh, I was here and there. Out and about."

Alexander blinked. That was a singularly uninformative answer.

"Sabinus, do you actually *own* any property in Philadelphia?"

Sabinus shook his head *no*.

Alexander continued, "Do you *lease* any property in Philadelphia?"

"In Philadelphia? No," answered Sabinus with another shake of his head.

Alexander laughed. "Then *why* are you here? If you have no business in Philadelphia, then why are you even here?"

Sabinus shrugged. "I didn't say I had *no business* here. I may not be a procurator like you, but I have been asked to keep an eye on the properties of Lucius Annaeus Seneca."

Alexander furrowed his brow. "Seneca? Seneca. *Hmmm.* I think I met a boy back in Rome with the same name. Does *he* own property in Egypt?"

Sabinus smiled. "No, the child in Rome is the *son* of the estate owner although they do have the same name. The father goes by Annaeus and the son by Seneca. A lot of parcels of land around the nome belong to the father – nowhere near as much as you will be managing for the Lady Antonia, of course, but substantial enough."

"That is good to know," Alexander responded. "Does Annaeus live in Alexandria? Or, does he at least visit?"

Sabinus shook his head. "No, he's like most of the big land owners. He's never come to Egypt and probably never will. None of his sons have come either, at least not yet. Lucius Annaeus Seneca has one of his freedmen managing his estates, but I have been asked to keep an eye out and let him know if any problems arise. We don't want to duplicate a situation like *your* current freedman problem."

That last comment felt like a barb, but Alexander decided not to take it personally. He had only returned to Egypt as Antonia's procurator a few weeks ago. It was unlikely anyone would blame him for what looked to be a problem that had been festering for years.

He turned to Sabinus. "The Lady Antonia has placed a great deal of trust in me. I hope I will be able to get any issues resolved quickly, but she has a *lot* of properties. Many of them are here in the Arsinoite nome, of course, but there are others in the Delta and farther south."

Sabinus tried to show at least moderate interest. "Does she really own that many? *Hunh*, I suppose some of those lands must have been inherited from her father, *eh*? ... You know, there are still people around who actually knew him -- Marcus Antonius, I mean. Pretty much everyone in their 50s or older remember him and the Queen Cleopatra, too."

Alexander frowned. For him, Marcus Antonius and Cleopatra were ancient history, but Sabinus was correct. Anyone in Egypt older than forty-two was alive when Marcus Antonius ruled alongside the Queen Cleopatra. Even those people living in Egypt who were too young to remember the time of the Queen and the General, likely had older family who could remember them quite well. But... Antonius and Cleopatra were long dead; so what of it?

"What is your point?"

Sabinus shrugged. "Just that if you are planning to travel

around Egypt as the procurator for the daughter of Marcus Antonius you should know that there are some still around who think that battle should have gone the other way."

"What?" Alexander was genuinely puzzled. What was Sabinus talking about?

Seeing Alexander's scrunched brows, Sabinus added, "If you ask the locals, would they rather have their Egyptian queen and her consort, or, a distant Roman overlord, which do you think they would choose?"

Alexander shook his head and said, "I still don't understand your point. Marcus Antonius has been dead for years. There is no bringing him back."

Sabinus smiled, "No, *not him*, no." Then he turned away and pointed, "But it appears, Alexander, that one or both of us has a lurker in the shadow listening in on our conversation."

Alexander turned and saw that indeed there was a man standing near the doorway watching them. He didn't seem like a threat, but he also had no reason to be staring at them and almost certainly listening in, as well. This was a breach of proper behavior that could not be ignored.

He called out, "You there. Why are you standing there staring at us?"

The man stepped forward. "I apologize for intruding on your bath. I am Tryphon son of Zoilos. I am attempting to determine which of you is the new procurator for the Lady Antonia."

Alexander held up a dripping hand. I am Gaius Julius Alexander, her new procurator. But I am *not* considering petitions while I am visiting the baths."

The man Tryphon did not seem cowed. Instead he held up a papyrus scroll. "I have a letter here," he said. "It is from my brother Nemesion who is the tax collector of Philadelphia."

Alexander quickly shook his head. "No procurator for the Lady Antonia will ever be involved with tax collecting. I do not now nor will I ever have anything to do with tax collecting. Your brother's issue cannot be with me."

"Oh, but it is," Tryphon responded. "I only mentioned that he is the tax collector so that you will know that he is an important man who is trusted by the Romans. Yet he has been treated badly. That is why he asked me to travel to see the *strategos*, but now that you are here, it would be better to ask you."

Again, Tryphon held up the little scroll and waved it back and forth as if it would explain everything.

Alexander said, "Give the papyrus to my secretary Amarantus who is right over there." He turned to his servant. "Ranti take a look and see if this is something that I should address, or, if it should go to the *strategos* as apparently was originally intended."

Amarantus stepped forward and took the papyrus scroll and rolled in open.

"It is not very long," he commented and then scanned the contents. As he read, his mouth quirked into a smile which he tried to hide when he looked up again.

"Master, I believe this *should come to you* because it involves Hierax in his duty as land agent. Apparently, this Nemesion, the tax collector, is also one of the Lady Antonia's tenants and he is *uhh* ... feeling quite put upon."

Huh? Alexander turned a puzzled look at Sabinus who grinned and responded, "*Put upon,* is he? Since your man says it is short, perhaps it would be of interest to hear what would cause a tax collector to feel *quite put upon.*"

Alexander grinned back, then turned to Amarantus. "Go ahead, Ranti, read it to us."

Amarantus first cleared his throat and then read out loud:

> *Nemesion to Tryphon, his brother, greetings. I ask you to go to the officials and inform them that Hierax on account of the land contract is making me disturbed, wearing me down about his rent money; wherefore it is necessary that we appeal to the strategos. I owe nothing, either in arrears or on the current account. If you do not get rid of him, I am going to have no peace. Farewell.*

Alexander turned an astonished look at Sabinus. He in turn laughed and commented, "You may find that the locals here in Egypt tend to be a bit more *uh emotive*, than what you experienced in Rome."

"So, it would appear," Alexander nodded slowly back. Then he turned to Tryphon. "I understand from this letter that there is some dispute over whether rent from a property your brother leased from the Lady Antonia has been paid. Do you have receipts that provide proper proof that payment was made?"

"No, we do not! And that is the problem for four of our cows are gone!" Tryphon was agitated. "Please, lord, let me explain."

Alexander nodded. "Only if you can do so quickly. Otherwise you will need to talk to my secretary to make an appointment."

To his great surprise, Alexander found that Tryphon could indeed provide a quick explanation. It seemed that the terms of the lease were to be paid in cows. Tryphon's brother used his lease for pastureland and raised cows, many of which were eventually sold to the legions for food. Nemesion had placed the cows that would be his rent payment in a separate pen.

One day after a festival, Nemesion returned to his home and found that all of the cows in the pen had disappeared. He had assumed that Hierax had collected them. When he contacted the land agent and asked for his receipt, he was told that his rent was still unpaid and if he no longer had the cows then he must provide coins.

Tryphon gave him a plaintive look. "*Kurie*, we are not the only tenants being deceived in this way. The only ones of us who have suffered are the tenants of the Lady Antonia and none others. For many, what has been taken without our knowledge was exactly what had been set aside for the land agent to collect for rent. No one else would have known what and where it was. We beg you to question the Hierax and learn why he took our goods and did not give us a receipt."

Alexander sucked in a long angry breath. Sabinus gave him a small smile. "You have my sympathies, young procurator. This is not a mess I would want to resolve."

After chewing at his lower lip for a moment, Alexander replied starting with a low voice. "Currently, I have no copies of the individual contracts. I have no financial records of payments. I have no idea where to find these cows or goods of any kind, if indeed they were collected." His voice rose, "And I DO NOT have that *nothus* Hierax to give me these things that I need."

Sabinus gave a snort, "Didn't you say that he refused to come to you? *Huh*, Sounds like *you* had better find *him* before he stirs up a new batch of petitions for you to resolve."

"You are right, of course," Alexander replied. "At first I thought the man just wanted to avoid the unpleasantness of being formally replaced. Having the Lady Antonia reject his service would be embarrassing. Now, I wonder. It seems possible that he is taking this last advantage to enrich himself."

Sabinus answered, "You know that it is also possible, Alexander, that the Lady Antonia's tenants are using this transition to sow a little confusion and keep their rents for themselves."

Alexander nodded unhappily. "You are right again, of course. It could be either way and I can't know for sure until I find that wretched freedman and beat him until I get my hands on every scroll he has."

"I would like to be there to see that," Sabinus replied with a grin. "Hierax is not a popular man. I'm sure a lot of people would like to be there to see that." He rubbed his chin and gazed at Alexander thoughtfully. "*Hmm*, I wonder if it would be possible ..."

Alexander didn't hear the rest as he slowly slid beneath the water and scrubbed his hand through his sand filled hair.

P.Mich.inv. 1638: **Letter from Nemesion to Tryphon his brother**

Provenance: Probably part of the archive of Nemesion, son of Zoilos, tax-collector of Philadelphia, Date: First half of first century A.D.

[*Original text:* Nemesion to Tryphon, his brother, greetings. I ask you to go to the officials and inform them that Papei, on account of the chief of the armed guards, is making me disturbed, wearing me down about his travel money; wherefore it is necessary that they appeal to the *strategos*. I owe nothing, either in arrears or on the current account. If you do not get rid of him, I am going to have no peace. Farewell.]

Source: Advanced Papyrological Information System, University of Michigan   http://quod.lib.umich.edu/a/apis/x-1495/1638r_d.tif

Mockup of a one story, flat-roofed house typical of Roman Egyptian villages.

Fig. 30. Interior view of houses near the North Temple; the house at left preserves a line of beam holes (Kelsey Museum Archives, 1928).

Ruins of Roman era two-story houses in Karanis. The fronts and flat roofs are missing, but note how close they are to each other.

9. Karanis

"Did you find my wheat colored mare?"

"What about my red calf? Do you have it with you?"

"And what will you do about Antas? He grazed his sheep on my fields. We should not have to pay Antonia for the share of the crop that his sheep stole."

Alexander stood in front of the public granary in Karanis surrounded by a crowd of petitioners each wanting to press their claim. In theory, all of these people had a connection with the Lady Antonia's properties. Some were her own workers and others leased her lands. He had a suspicion, however, that many of these villagers surrounding him had no connection with Antonia at all, but were just here out of curiosity.

Once again, Alexander felt the frustration of not having found Antonia's land agent and wrested the account scrolls from him. The few records that Antonia had copied for him in Rome only listed her larger properties with their annual income. This told Alexander nothing about which lands were leased to whom, the rents due – or pretty much anything. Without those records, Alexander had no way of even knowing for which of these people he was even responsible. And he certainly could not let the villagers realize how *little he knew.* If they were aware of how short of evidence Alexander actually was for what monies they owed … *Hmm,* only the Lord knew all the new ways they might find to cheat on their leases and contracts.

Alexander pushed out his palms toward the crowd.

"Wait, wait," Alexander said. "I can only hear one of you at a time. But first, let me explain this to you. I have received and read all of the petitions that were routed through the *epistrategos*, Titus Serenius. You should know that my family owns land in the Arsinoite Nome so the concerns of the nome are also *my* concerns. Even though I am now aware of many of your problems, it will take me some time to address all of your petitions and those I am receiving from the other villages."

He held up his index finger.

"But I assure you that I *will* address *every* petition. You may not like my decisions. I will always be putting Antonia's benefit before all others. I also understand that *your* productivity and well-being may depend on the decisions that *I* make and I will try to keep your best interests in mind second only to Antonia's."

Alexander looked at the faces surrounding him. He saw no evidence of liking for him, but then he also so no open hostility towards him either. The villagers appeared to be withholding judgment for now and that suited Alexander just fine. He raised his voice to address the group again.

"The first thing I need to know from you is whether any of you seen the Lady Antonia's former land agent, Hierax?"

There was some murmuring and then a voice in the crowd called, "Don't you mean Marcus Antonius?"

Alexander moved his head back on his shoulders lowering his chin. *"Huh? Who?"*

The crowd surrounding him tittered and looked amongst themselves before the first man answered.

"Antonia's freedman. Marcus Antonius. That's what Hierax has started calling himself now. He said that everyone had to start using that name for him."

Alexander frowned. That *was* Hierax's real name, at least in part. When Antonia freed him, she also made him a Roman citizen. As prescribed, he took the names – the *praenomen* and *nomen* of her father Marcus Antonius and added his own *cognomen* Hierax at the end. Technically, his legal name was Marcus Antonius Hierax. But for a former slave to use anything but his *cognomen* was *hubris* in the extreme.

Alexander turned back to the crowd of villagers. "I really need to have *a talk* soon with this *freedman*, Hierax. I refuse to call him *Marcus Antonius* and I suggest that you do not call him that either. The Lady Antonia would find that offensive; of that I feel quite certain."

Heads were nodding in the crowd and Alexander realized that while the Lady Antonia indeed had their respect, her freedman Hierax did not. They probably would be very happy to see Hierax gone. Perhaps he could get some useful information out of these villagers. Alexander raised his hands again to claim their attention.

"This Hierax has a house in Tebtunis, but he is not there. People in Crocodilopolis told me that Hierax had probably headed north on the Desert Canal. I asked for him when I passed through Philadelphia and Bacchias. Some people thought he might have passed by, but no one was sure. I ask you now, has anyone seen him? Has anyone here seen Hierax recently?"

The members of the crowd looked back and forth at each other, shrugged, and shook their heads.

Alexander let out a frustrated breath and tried again. "I want each of you to stop and think. Does anyone here know *where* Hierax *might* be? Does he have another house where he might go? Family? A friend? ... Where might he be?"

A few members of the crowd must have decided that it was time to try to be helpful.

"Have you tried Socnopaiou Nesos? He could be there."

"Yeah, or what about Bubastis? He might be there."

Another man chimed in. "Or Herakleia. Try there."

His neighbor turned to him. "Which Herakleia?"

The first man shrugged, "Either of them. He could be at either Herakleia."

His neighbor turned to Alexander. "Well, if you ask me, he's probably gone down south."

Alexander frowned. "Down south? You mean down towards Thebes?"

"*Nah, nah.* 'Don't know where *that* is. I'm talkin' south of the lake. He could be down south of the lake."

Some of the other members of the crowd murmured and nodded knowingly. "Yeah, yeah. Could be. He could be down south. It would explain why he ain't up here."

It now occurred to Alexander that even though the south side of Lake Moeris was no more than a few miles distant, most of these local villagers had probably never travelled that far from home. "*Down south*" of Lake Moeris for them would seem like a distant place. Unfortunately, Alexander had already heard from the barge men in Crocodilopolis that Hierax was *not* down south. No one had seen him on the Desert Canal below the lake.

He took a deep breath to keep from voicing his frustration. These were Antonia's people and he needed them to work with him. It wasn't their fault that Antonia's wretched freedman was causing him so much trouble.

Alexander forced a smile for the villagers and said, "Your advice seems good to me. When I head down south, I will look for Hierax there."

He held up a finger, "But first my secretary and I will hear any new petitions from anyone leasing or working the Lady Antonia's lands. I will resolve what I can today, but some decisions may need to wait until I have toured more of Antonia's properties."

The villagers shuffled around and then pushed one man forward to stand in front of Alexander.

"I say... *uh,* I mean we all say... If you care about us at all, it would be best if you find that evil goat."

Alexander looked blank until Amarantus spoke up from behind him.

"Master, I believe he is referring to that missing goat in the petition I told you about back in Alexandria. The owner's name is Thonis son of Horion and this goat, Seth, has a reputation for eating anything that it sees. I suppose if he is loose, he could be eating up people's valuable crops."

The villagers nodded agreement, but then one of them prodded their 'spokeman' again. *"Go on. Tell him."*

"It's not just that the goat eats everything, you know. That goat is *evil*. I swear to you that goat gave Kephalas the evil eye and within a week his favorite sheep died."

A woman added, "It is true. That goat stared at my cousin and the next day she lost her baby. It is evil for sure. Not one of us is safe with that goat on the loose."

Heads nodded all around. Apparently, there was a universal agreement on the immediate danger of Seth the evil goat.

Alexander really had no idea how to even approach the idea of an *"evil goat,"* so he simply assured the villagers that he would try to locate *all* of their missing animals. He spent a bit more time with the villagers, listening and resolving those issues he could and giving assurances that he would provide the rest of his decisions as soon as possible. It took hours, but he did manage to give each petitioner a hearing. Many of the crowd remained the entire time, even after their own petition had been presented. Curiosity, he assumed.

As Alexander finished and started to walk away, he could hear the villagers murmuring behind him including an overly loud whisper, *"This new man seems like he might be a bit smarter than the last one."*

"And he's much more handsome, too," a woman's whisper added.

"Do you think he'll find the horse thief?" said another.

"I hear in Philadelphia they have cattle thieves. Maybe it's the same ones who are stealing our stock."

"I wonder why he doesn't look for Hierax at the festival tomorrow. He'll likely be there," said yet another voice.

Alexander froze, then turned slowly back to the group of villagers.

"Did someone just say that Hierax may be at a festival tomorrow?"

There was a bit of shuffling then an old man towards the back raised his hand.

"I did. Yeah, tomorrow is the festival for our lord crocodile god Petesouchos. Hierax comes almost every year. Last year he brought one of those Kronos bastards with him. 'Heard they were trying to convince our priests to do something. *Hunh.* Not likely. *Our* priests are all *legitimate.*"

Alexander nodded to himself and turned to Amarantus. "Well, Ranti, I'd say this changes our plans. We need to attend that festival tomorrow and see if Antonia's land agent shows up. Didn't one of the locals agree to put us up for the night?"

"Yes, master. It was the village scribe."

Alexander thought for a moment then gave a quick nod.

"Yes, let's stay there tonight. We will arrange that now and then go exploring. I suppose Karanis isn't a large village, but we should understand the lay-out if we're going to find and trap that wretched freedman tomorrow."

"*Trap*, master?"

"Oh yes, Ranti. I've had just about enough of this elusive freedman. Antonia gave me full authority for dealing with Hierax and he has made the mistake of making me angry – very angry. How am I supposed to deal with these petitions, let alone collect the rents or pay the farmers if I don't even have a record of who they are? Not to mention that Hierax seems to be sitting on months' worth of Antonia's profits and tax money."

Alexander and his servant had been strolling down a road that led through the center of Karanis. On both sides were two and three story mud brick buildings. On this larger road many of them had shops at the ground floor. Most buildings were tightly packed, separated by just a narrow alley that ran between them.

Amarantus paused and pointed up. "Master, look. There are people on almost every roof."

Alexander looked up and saw whole families going about their daily lives on the roofs. It was a lifestyle that he had heard about, but had never seen. Many of the homes in Alexandria also had flat roofs and people did use them, but they didn't *live* on them like the people did here.

"Yes, I see, Ranti. This is just one more thing that is so different from how things were in Rome where we got both rain and occasional snow. Out here so close to the desert, it virtually never rains. There is no need for a sloping roof so the water can run off. For them, it is the heat that matters. It is much cooler for the people to use the roof for cooking, eating, even sleeping.

"Plus, Ranti, the people here are not rich. Usually several families share a single house. They store their belongings in the rooms, but the interiors can get very hot. So they mostly live and sleep on the roof where they can at least get fresh air."

Amarantus looked up and down the length of the street and then pointed at a two-story building before them.

"Master, is that why some of these houses have stairs on the outside leading to the roof? Some of them don't, but I suppose those must have stairs or a ladder on the inside."

Alexander tilted his head and considered. "I'm not sure Ranti, but perhaps it is because they started out as one floor. When the second floor was added, the interior was not designed for a staircase so it had to be added on the outside. I don't know if that's true, but it seems to make sense to me."

"Yes, master, I can see how that would be. But, *I* would not like to live like that. Look. The space between the houses is so narrow that your neighbor would hear everything that you said."

"*Hunh*, you're right about that, Ranti. There doesn't seem to be much privacy here. But I guess they are used to it. It's probably all that most of them have ever known. ... Let's head up this slope that leads to the temple at the top. I want to get a sense for what public buildings are around here."

The two men climbed the path up a small hill and found a medium-sized temple complex at the top. Unlike the surrounding mud brick houses, the temple was made of cut limestone blocks. A set of stone stairs led up to the main entrance and the stairs were flanked by a resting lion on each side. In front of the temple was a large walled-in space that, no doubt, served as the village marketplace as well as festival grounds.

"Master, I spoke with a servant at the house of the village scribe," Amarantus said. "He told me that most of the festival will take place in that market square in front of the temple there. But first, he said, the temple priests and musicians will make a procession and carry a statue of their crocodile god in a little boat."

He gestured towards the temple doors. "They will walk down from the temple and carry the statue to the canal. There is a little pond there with two real crocodiles that they say are sacred. I think then the priests are going to make offerings to the crocodiles so their god will keep the village safe."

Alexander nodded, then pointed his chin toward the top of the path that they had just ascended.

"Well, Ranti, then that is where we will be tomorrow. It seems like it will be a good spot for us to observe the festival since it sounds like everyone will come to see this crocodile god procession."

"Master, in Rome, they sacrificed animals. They did not

pray to them."

"No, Ranti, we definitely did not. – not Jews, not Romans, not Greeks, not anyone. This whole practice of making offerings and petitions to animals is strictly an Egyptian thing – or, maybe not *just* Egyptian. Remember that overseer back in Philadelphia claimed that many Greeks and even Romans make offerings to the crocodiles. The people in Rome would scoff at that, but I guess it is as Sabinus said. They think it is best to be safe and make offerings to all the local gods."

"Master, I think I can understand that. When the hippopotamus attacked our boat I would have been happy to throw it some food if that would have made it stop."

Alexander laughed softly. "We need to be cautious what we say, Ranti. To a Jew, crocodile worship is ridiculous. You heard my brother Philo rant on about it back on the bark. But for these villagers, crocodile worship is very serious and important. This is their god. We must not be heard mocking their beliefs."

"I understand, Master, and I'll be more careful. I do not wish to offend the god. But why are we walking this way? *You* cannot go in that temple."

"Certainly not; that is no place for a Jew. It is also not likely that this Hierax would be inside the temple tomorrow. I think that may be for priests only. So, *hmmm*," Alexander rubbed his chin, "Where will Hierax be? I need to catch him once and for all."

Amarantus scrunched his eyebrows. "Maybe we should not go with the crocodile statue to the pond, Master. If you were to have an angry encounter with the land agent there, it might upset villagers."

"Agreed, Ranti. I think we should wait until after the statue returns from feeding the crocodiles at the pond. After that is when the general festivities will begin – music, dancing, maybe a play or storytelling. Since Hierax is a Roman that seems the most likely time when he will appear in public."

Alexander looked around the big public square. "Yes, that confirms my original idea. We will wait in this area tomorrow, near the head of the path that slopes down the hill. Anyone coming or going will take that path."

Alexander ran a hand through his hair and looked around thoughtfully. "Of course our biggest problem will be that neither of us has ever seen the man. Even my messenger that went to his house in Tebtunis only saw his house steward. Our description of Hierax isn't too helpful, either – He is in his mid-forties, medium height, medium build, dark hair, dark eyes."

"Master, that is like many of the men we see, but I think there may be one particular difference – *his clothes*. If Hierax wants people to call him Marcus Antonius, then I think he must be very arrogant. He will wear the fanciest clothes he can."

"*Hmm*," Alexander slowly nodded. "That is true, Ranti. Still, I'd rather not tackle a man just because he is wearing an expensive tunic."

He smiled. "In fact, accosting any man who is that well-dressed sounds like a particularly bad idea. We must to be sure first. ... Remember that old man among the villagers who said that Hierax comes to these festivals every year? Maybe I can hire him to stand with us and let us know when he sees Hierax. Or, actually the village scribe would probably recognize him, too. I will ask tonight."

Satisfied that they had a plan for the following day, Alexander decided to walk the main causeway and familiarize himself with the village. He hadn't actually planned to purchase anything until he stopped suddenly in front of a particular shop front. Laid out carefully on a reed mat in front were some beautiful pieces of colored hand-blown glass. Alexander had seen lots of glassware back in Rome; everyone had. But these pieces were different, the artisanship was unique.

A young man squatting behind the display noted the well-dressed stranger's interest.

"Karanis is famous for its glassware, *kurie*. Or, I should say *our master* is famous. Perhaps you would like to see some of the larger pieces?"

The young man gestured towards the door just as another apprentice stepped forward holding the most exquisite glass pitcher that Alexander had ever seen. The form and symmetry were perfect, but his eye was particularly caught be the gradations of color as it shaded from a soft lilac at the neck to a deep purple at the base. He wanted it for himself, but Alexander could also see presenting it as a gift to his friend Claudius, or perhaps Agrippa, or his own father.

Alexander nodded his interest and pointed to the purple pitcher. "Do you have more like that one?"

The apprentice shook his head. "We have the same style in a perfume vial, but this pitcher is a sample. Most of our pieces are custom ordered. See, here is another of the Master's unique pieces. No one else makes anything quite like it."

He held up another pitcher where the color transitioned from clear to milky white, but then the added décor on the spout and the bottom were all in the blue of lapis lazuli. In fact, the base looked as if it was set with the gems, although Alexander was sure it must be glass.

Alexander looked at the glassware and thought for a moment. Really, he would be proud to display many of the pieces he saw in the shop, or, to give them as gifts. The work was excellent. He ended up placing a substantial order with the master glass maker as well as leaving the shop with a woven basket filled with many of the smaller glass items wrapped in wool and straw.

There were several small vials for cosmetics, plus small bowls and cups in different designs. *Hunh.* For sure, Alexander had assumed that he would find nothing in Egypt that was as nice as what they had back in Rome. Perhaps there would be a few – just a few – things that he would find to value in this his new homeland.

Samples of hand blown glassware pieces excavated from Karanis dating to the Roman period.

Source: *Roman Glass from Karanis* / Donald B. Harden (Ann Arbor: University of Michigan Press, 1936)

10. Festival of Petesouchos

They spent the night in Karanis with the village scribe, an Egyptian. Alexander usually preferred to stay with a local Jewish family whenever possible. It was simply easier to stay with Jews, than to have to explain one's special dietary needs. However, Egyptians had some similar dietary practices as Jews such as not eating pig so he could make it work.

Alexander was doubly fortunate with his host because the man leased large tracts of land from the Lady Antonia. Plus, as the village scribe he had kept records of harvest totals and tax collection. The scribe was both knowledgeable and eager to share what he knew. In a short time, Alexander learned much about managing properties and marked the village scribe as a man who should be delegated greater responsibility in the future. After all, *Alexander* couldn't spend his time in the nome. He would need the help of a select few men.

The following morning Alexander, Ranti, and the village scribe stood at the top of the slope that led from the main street of the village up to the temple complex on the small hill.

As they waited, the scribe explained what to expect during the festival.

"The great god will emerge from there," he pointed towards the front door of the temple. "He will be riding in his bark – his boat. It is like the one that you would have used to sail up the Nile, but this one, of course, is for the god."

He waited for Alexander to nod his understanding.

"The bark will be carried by the priests of Petesouchos. They will process through this market square, down the hill and to the pond of the sacred crocodiles. There will be prayers and offerings. Then the god and his barge will slowly process back up the hill and return to the temple."

"Are we permitted to observe the procession?" Alexander asked the scribe.

"Oh yes, the deepest mysteries of the gods are performed inside the temple with only the priests present. Having the god come forth on his bark happens just a few times a year. This is the chance for the people to worship the god and ask him their questions. People wait for months for Petesouchos to appear and answer their questions."

Alexander and Amarantus exchanged a puzzled look and returned their attention to the scribe.

"Answer their questions?" Alexander asked. "Are you saying that the statue of the god *talks*?"

The scribe gave a mysterious smile. "You will see. But you must understand, when Petesouchos comes forth, he is *not* a statue. He *is the god* – or the essence of the god."

As they were talking, the procession route was quickly being lined with people from the village. Suddenly, there came the shrill notes of a flute and the murmuring of the crowd all but ceased. Instead they all turned toward the temple and sucked in a collective breath as the doors opened and the bark appeared.

The bark was attached to two long poles which the priests used to hoist it to shoulder level. Standing on the boat was a painted statue with a man's body and above the shoulders was the head of a crocodile. The gathered villagers began a low chant, "Great, great god Petesouchos. Hear me."

Slowly, sedately, the priests and bark moved forward along the procession line. As the god's statue passed his worshippers, they would raise their arms to the level of their heads with palms out and then bowed deeply.

Alexander and Amarantus watched fascinated as the bark advanced to their position. The boat itself was made of wood, much smaller, of course, than one that would ply the Nile. The statue that stood in the middle of the bark was life-size, maybe larger. The body of the man was painted a dark red like the color of clay. He was dressed in a real white linen kilt and a garland of flowers had been placed around his shoulders. The head was painted as well, but Alexander averted his eyes at the very realistic protruding teeth many of which seemed to be coated in bright red – red like new blood.

As the statue passed, Alexander and Amarantus realized that something else was occurring. Periodically, the bark would pause and someone from the crowd would run out and place what looked like a broken piece of pottery into the god's path. Then the bark seemed to wobble a bit, and the priests would resume their procession.

Alexander turned to the village scribe. "Can you tell me what is happening? What are people putting in the bark's path?"

The scribe nodded. "Now you see. Petesouchos answers his worshippers."

"*Uhh*, how?"

The village scribe explained.

"The voice of the god is too great for men and women to hear. We would all die if the god spoke to us directly. Therefore the priests have guided us on how to learn the god's will. The petitioner has a scribe – someone like me -- write their question on a broken pottery shard, an ostracon. Phrasing the question requires skill. Much depends on the proper wording.

"Then the petitioner places his or her question in the path of the god. When the bark gets to the ostracon, the god will cause it to raise or dip in response to the question. If the front of the bark rises, Petesouchos's answer is '*yes*.' If the front dips down then Petesouchos's answer is '*no*.'"

With effort, Alexander held his tongue. For a Jew, this process seemed … well, a little silly.

Amarantus, however, was fascinated. He asked, "But what if it is not a *yes* or *no* question?"

The scribe answered, "It *must* be. No human could bear to hear a more complex answer from the god. That is why a scribe must carefully work with the petitioner to phrase the question just so."

He saw Amarantus's confused face and added, "For example, say a farmer is not sure whether to plant a new plot with wheat or barley. The question may be 'Should I plant more wheat?' If the great god says '*yes*,' that the farmer will plant wheat. If the great god says '*no*,' then the farmer will know to plant barley."

Alexander continued to stifle any comment, but Amarantus was clearly intrigued. "C-c-could *I* ask the god a question? Is that allowed?" he asked.

The village scribe looked Amarantus up and down before answering. "Yeees, but you are not a known worshipper. It will be up to the god if he wishes to answer you or not. Here, I will show you what to do."

The village scribe pulled a broken pottery shard from his belt pouch, and took Amarantus aside. They quietly consulted for a few minutes then Amarantus took off down the hill at a trot to get ahead of the crocodile god towering over his bark.

Alexander turned to his host. "I understand that the Egyptian word for your crocodile god is Sobek and the Greek form of that is Souchos. But why are there so many different crocodile gods? When I was in Crocodilopolis, they called their god Soknopaios. When we passed through Bacchias not far from here, they called their god Soknokonnis. I understand that there is a large temple in Tebtunis for the crocodile god called Soknebtunis and here the god's name is Petesouchos. Why are there so many different crocodile gods, even living just a few miles apart?"

The village scribe shook his head and held up his index finger. "There is only *one* crocodile god. The god may have many manifestations or essences to suit the needs of himself or his worshippers. Even though the great god has two, three, even more essences, he is still only *one*."

Alexander frowned and pondered that for a moment before asking, "So what is the difference between each essence of the god?"

His host merely raised his eyebrows and shook his head. "These mysteries are not for a Jew."

That set Alexander on his back foot as he stammered an

apology which the village scribe accepted graciously. For one thing, he could tell that Alexander had spoken out of curiosity and not malice. Many Romans did openly insult the worship of the crocodile, but he could tell that was not the young man's intent. Plus, he did derive much of his income from his leases on the Lady Antonia's estates. Only a fool would cause strife with her new procurator.

Instead, the village scribe waved a hand in the direction of the downhill path and said, "Look, most of the villagers have gone to see the offerings to the sacred crocodiles. Perhaps, now we should review your plan to trap this former land agent."

Just then, Amarantus trotted back up the hill and rejoined his master. His eyes were shining and he seemed happy.

"Master, it happened! The great god stopped right where I placed my question and he answered me. He said '*yes,*' master. The great god said '*yes*' to me."

The village scribe smiled indulgently and advised, "Remember, you must not reveal your question until the god has acted on it."

Amarantus wagged his head. "I will not. It was amazing. I could feel the god's power. Truly, Petesouchos is a very powerful god."

Alexander was amused as Amarantus enthused over being in the presence of a statue of a crocodile god. Ranti was a good secretary and servant to him, but ultimately Amarantus was a slave. He couldn't help but wonder what kind of a question a slave would ask a statue of a god. Alexander brought his thoughts back to the present and looked around the path now empty of most of the villagers.

"Let's try changing our location," he said. "I wish we knew for certain if Hierax will be here today."

"No, we do not know that," the village scribe replied. "However, he has been here for this festival for the last three years. It is possible that he will come again this year."

"Well, we need to be ready if he does show," Alexander said. "Now, as far as his appearance goes, we will be depending upon you since *we* have never seen him. You say that he is medium height and build with wavy dark hair that is streaked with some gray?"

"Yes," the village scribe agreed. "I realize that description fits many men. I don't know if Hierax has a scar anywhere that would identify him, but we would not see a scar from a distance anyway. Once we were close enough to see a scar, we should be close enough for me to recognize him."

"I agree," Alexander responded. "Now, my servant Ranti here has suggested that Hierax might stand out by wearing particularly expensive tunic and boots."

The village scribe brightened. "Yes, this is true. Hierax always wears a fine tunic with a border or embroidery and boots of the softest leather. He even dresses as such when he has to go out into the fields to inspect the harvest."

"That will help a little, then," Alexander nodded. "Even though Ranti and I have not seen the man, we can at least look for a well-dressed man and point him out to you for confirmation."

The scribe and Amarantus both nodded their agreement. Alexander clapped his hands together and continued.

"This is the plan, then. As soon as the bark returns to the temple, the entertainments in the market square will begin. Most villagers and visitors will wend their way up this hill to the square. Fortunately for us, there is only the one path. *We*," he pointed back and forth to Amarantus, the village scribe and himself, "will position ourselves on the hill right where the path ends and the market square begins. Once our esteemed village scribe here identifies Hierax then, Ranti, you will come with me to accost him. We shall each take one of his arms and pull him off to the side so I can question him."

Amarantus gave him back a skeptical look. "We just stand at the top of the path and watch? Master, this does not seem like a very complex plan."

Alexander laughed. "Because it is *not*. It's not much of a plan at all. Consider, we don't know *if* Hierax is even here. We're not sure exactly what he looks like. And we don't have enough people to surround the area or set up anything like watch points. But if we locate ourselves here at the mouth of the path, then we should be able to see everyone who comes or goes to the market square for the entertainments. I think just being located here we will have the best chance to catch him if he is here."

****

Alexander's simple plan turned out to be quite a dreary one. As he had suggested, the three men had set themselves near the top of the path that went up the small hill from the village to the temple and market square.

They ignored all of the women and children, but carefully eyed every man who came up the path. There were a few well dressed visitors for the festival, but each time the village scribe shook his head that none were the freedman Alexander was seeking. It was hot and dusty and they were all beginning to lose their patience.

Suddenly, Amarantus leaned forward. "Master, what do you think about *him*?"

Alexander followed his servant's gaze. It was not someone coming up the hill to the temple square. Instead it was a man still down in the village among the shops and houses. It was too far to see his face clearly, but even from the top of the hill Alexander could see that the man's tunic was well dyed and had trim along the border.

He turned to the village scribe. "Is that him? Is that Hierax?"

The scribe, squinted and stared down the hill, but he could only shrug. "I cannot tell, Alexander. It is too far for me to see. Perhaps, we should go down and get a closer look?"

Alexander felt too hot and thirsty for subtlety. He had no more patience for waiting and stalking the land agent. Instead, he cupped both hands around his mouth and yelled, "Hey you! Down there! Stand still, I'm coming to you!"

From behind him came a choking sound coming from the

direction of the village scribe, but Alexander had no time to delay. He began trotting down the hill towards the man in the expensive tunic.

Everyone at the bottom of the hill had stopped at the sound of his shout and now was staring at Alexander. They saw a man in the purple striped tunic of a Roman noble yelling and waving his hand at them. As they hesitated, Alexander quickened his pace and pointed in the direction of the man in question, "Wait right there! Don't move!"

But, move they did—all of them. For a few moments the crowd shuffled their feet and looked at each other to see if anyone knew what this strange young Roman wanted. Each one shook their head or shrugged; they didn't know what was going on. When the first man broke, it started a stampede. The crowd decided that, no, they did want to know what was going on that badly. Instead, they scattered. Since most of them were locals, they headed for their shops and homes, most of which were on the main street or just behind it.

As Alexander pounded down the hill, he could see that the well-dressed man in question had stopped and was looking around. He must not be a local since he did not immediately duck into a nearby shop or house. The man lifted a hand to shade his eyes as he stared up at Alexander running towards him. Then he shook his head and seemed to come to a decision.

The man in the fine tunic quickly cast his eyes about until they locked onto what he wanted. Then he headed towards the nearest house that had stairs running up the outside to the flat roof. Alexander was closer now, but could only see the man's back. Without hesitation, he headed for the same stairs so he could follow the fine tunic up to the roof.

Alexander was panting by the time he reached the top of the stairs. Some of the family was at home on the roof and they were shouting, shaking fists, and yelling deprecations. The man in the fancy tunic was running straight through them without slowing. Alexander hesitated, wondering where the man was going at such a speed. He didn't understand until he saw the man jump. Oh Lord, the man had jumped to the roof of the next house. Just yesterday, Alexander had seen that many of the houses were built quite close together, but it had not occurred to him that it would be possible to escape by jumping between them. Oh well, he was young, he was fit, and the freedman – if that was indeed Hierax – was getting away.

Alexander sucked in a breath and took off at a good pace and jumped. With a gasp of relief, he realized that he had successfully cleared the alley and landed on the roof of the next house. There was no time for self-congratulations though because he could see the familiar tunic leaping onto the next house down. Without hesitation, Alexander ran and leaped after him.

This time he came down hard scraping his knees. Alexander stood up and cringed inwardly as he saw the fine tunic make yet another successful leap to the next roof. Alexander wasn't sure if he could follow him. It wasn't that he was getting tired of jumping from roof to roof. He could do that. It was just that, *ahhh ... why now?* When he landed, Alexander felt that the knot on his loin cloth was coming loose. If he tried to jump again, the whole garment could slip down around his knees causing him to trip and fall.

The loincloth was tied around the waist with a cord and, well, sometimes the cord came loose. When that happened there were only two options. One, find a quiet spot where you could hitch up your tunic and re-tie the cord. Or, two, casually let the loose loincloth fall, step out of it and walk away as if nothing had happened. Indeed, back in Rome, abandoned loincloths were not such an unusual sight in the Circus Maximus or around taverns.

Well, neither of those was an option here. Alexander was standing on a family's rooftop surrounded by families on neighboring rooftops – all staring at him. Behind him, he saw Amarantus running to catch up. Way ahead of him, 'fancy tunic' was about to leap onto yet another roof. Alexander knew he could not go after him.

Merda, his temper came up. That wretched freedman was going to elude him for sure.

Angrily, Alexander raised his hand, jabbed his forefinger at the fleeing man's back and shouted, *"Tembel gevohah!"*

"Wooooo," came an unexpected reply.

Alexander looked around. All the people on the rooftops were standing and staring at him with open mouths and large eyes.

Amarantus had caught up behind him, noted all the spectators, and turned back to Alexander.

"Master, what were those words you used? I did not understand them."

Still staring after the disappearing tunic, Alexander shrugged and waved his hand. "Yeah well, that's because they were Hebrew."

"Hebrew?" Amarantus said more loudly. "Master was it a curse? Did you just make a terrible Hebrew curse?"

Alexander frowned. *"What? Oh, uh, uh* … yes, yes. That is *exactly* what it was."

Amarantus turned and nodded knowingly at the watching families on the neighboring rooftops.

"That was a powerful Hebrew curse," he announced. "The running man is in deep trouble now."

The rooftop families *oohed*, murmured, and nodded knowingly at each other. Egyptians knew all about the power of curses. Mostly, they knew about Egyptian curses, of course. Some knew of Greek curses. But that well dressed Roman man in front of them obviously could afford the best curse that money could buy. That, *uh, Hebrew* curse was probably very powerful indeed.

Alexander tried not to look sheepish as the rooftop people looked on in awe. He didn't have the heart to admit that when he had yelled *tembel gevohah*, it was not curse. It had been nothing more than a petty insult. For some reason, being back in Egypt was causing him to recall all the childish taunts that he used to exchange with his younger brother Philo.

Well, the good thing about hearing what they thought was an *exotic curse* was that the rooftop families seemed to have temporarily forgotten about how he had so rudely invaded their homes. Now mindful and embarrassed, Alexander turned and made his apologies to the families. One of them pointed out to the others that Alexander was the new procurator for the Lady Antonia Minor.

This caused Alexander to feel even greater regret for his wild behavior, but it seemed to appease the families. In fact, they called and waved to others to come out on their roofs and check out the new man. Alexander forced himself not to roll his eyes as a number of older women tugged girls of marriageable age to the roof sides and called out introductions.

Alexander and Amarantus took a ladder down the center of a roof and tried to quietly leave the Karanis houses behind.

****

"I can't believe he got away."

Back at the home of the village scribe, Alexander was bemoaning another missed opportunity.

"I'm not sure that he did, *kurie*," the scribe replied.

Alexander looked up. "What do you mean?"

The scribe seemed to hesitate, then bit his lower lip and answered. "I do not think that man was the Lady Antonia's former land agent. I know I was too far away to see his face and granted the style of clothes looked right, but frankly Alexander, the man you chased was *athletic*. Yes, the houses here are close together, but not many could actually jump between them again and again as that man did. Hierax is old, in his forties, and he is lazy. Maybe he could make one jump, even two. I don't think he could have jumped between the houses to escape you the way that man did."

Alexander looked confused. "B-but, if that was not the land agent, then why did he run? There would have been no reason for another man to run from me."

The village scribe and Amarantus shared a look. The scribe seemed reluctant to speak up so Amarantus did. "*Umm*, master, you are a tall man. Six feet is taller than most Egyptian men."

Alexander frowned. "*So?*"

"And, master, you are dressed like a Roman noble."

Alexander shook his head, *"So?"*

"And, master, you were yelling at him in a threatening way."

Amarantus paused and watched until the realization sunk in. "Master, I think almost *any* man would have run from you."

"*Oh.* ... I made a mistake, didn't I?" Alexander looked down and ran a hand through his curly hair. "I should have approached the man quietly, discreetly until I could see for sure who he was."

He looked at the village scribe and then Amarantus and saw they were nodding at him. Alexander hung his head. "You are right. I let my impatience and anger overrule my better judgment. If we had gotten closer, it would have been easier to grab him before he could run."

"If it even *was* Hierax," the village scribe added. "I still have my doubts on that."

They sat in silence for awhile.

"So, what will you do now, *kurie*?" the scribe asked.

Alexander rubbed his chin and thought. "I think I should continue my journey. I have already committed to visiting Soknopaiou Nesos. After that I will head south of the lake. I promised to meet the *strategos* in Theadelphia in time to see the wine pressing. ... Plus, I think I should send word to every village possible and let the people know that they *should not* give any more rents to Hierax. That will have to do until I can catch up with the man."

"What about the taxes he has collected?" the village scribe asked.

Alexander shook his head. "I will retrieve any that I can, but only to give them back to the villagers who were cheated out of it. I doubt Augustus made me a Roman noble so I could run around from house to house in every village collecting chickens and baskets of wheat. The Prefect's men will have to find someone else to collect their taxes. *I won't* and Hierax will *not* be staying in Egypt to do it."

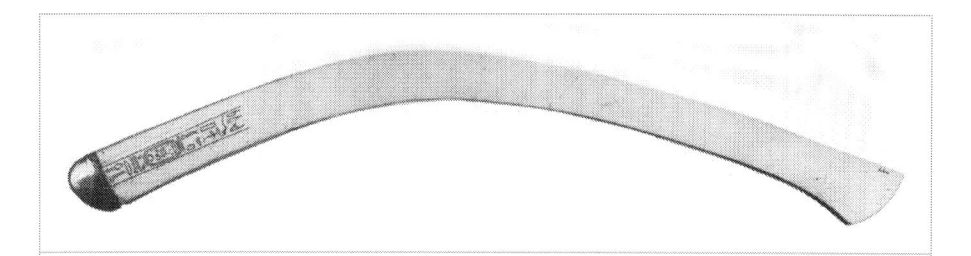

Throw stick from the tomb of the pharaoh Tutankhamen

Throwing or fowling sticks were used to hunt marsh birds. Some styles were flung from the side like a boomerang while others were thrown overhand.

[*Source:* Howard Carter, *The Tomb of of Tut-Ankh-Amen* (London: Cassell, 1923-1933), volume 3, plate XXXI]

11. Fowling Things Up

To Alexander from Philo his brother, very many greetings. You should know that a messenger arrived for you in Crocodilopolis. The epistrategos, Titus Serenius, reminds you that if you go to Tebtunis and if you should hear anything about problems between the hereditary priests and the priests of Kronos that you are to write to him at once. Farewell.

It was a brief missive and its content most unwelcome. Alexander resisted the urge to crush the papyrus in his hand. Of course, his brother was right to pass on the message but... Did Alexander have the slightest care about the problems of crocodile priests in Tebtunis? No, he did not.

Yet, the *epistrategos* seemed to want to pull Alexander into that situation. Alexander could understand somewhat why Titus Serenius had asked for his help. And, he did generally like the man, at least as much as their very brief acquaintance would allow. But the warring crocodile priests of Tebtunis absolutely were *not his* problem to resolve.

Alexander had his own task set trying to track down the Lady Antonia's land agent and retrieve the missing records and rent money. That was not to mention the many petitions he still had to resolve. Just how was he supposed to find missing animals and resolve property border disputes? For certain, Alexander had *no* intention of going to Tebtunis because that was the one place where he was sure the land agent was not.

Before he had left Alexandria to sail for the Arsinoite Nome, Alexander had arranged for the original messenger to set a watch on the house of Hierax in Tebtunis. So far, two messages had arrived from the man – both with the same news. The house steward came and went everyday, but continued to dwell in the house alone. His master, Hierax the Lady Antonia's land agent, had not returned to the house in Tebtunis at all.

This was turning out to be more of a challenge than Alexander had guessed. Everywhere he stopped, Antonia's tenants reported missing items – usually the crops and animals that would have been used to pay the land leases. Missing were the cattle from Philadelphia, the wheat colored mare, red calf and evil goat from Karanis, wheat and barley at every stop. Even at the village of Nilopolis where Antonia had very little property, there were still goods missing.

Yet, not a single villager could confirm that they had seen the land agent Hierax in recent weeks. Most of them *assumed* the land agent was the one who had removed the crops from their barns, but no one could say for sure.

Did that mean that Hierax had *not* come to these villages at all? Could it have been some other person or group taking the goods and animals? In his own mind, Alexander had been accusing the land agent of taking all of the missing items from the villages. But....

Come to think of it though, there had been no evidence at all to prove that Hierax had anything to do with the missing goods. Just because the villagers *thought* the land agent was taking their animals and crops, did not mean he actually was. Of course, who else it might have been, Alexander did not know. So far, everything reported missing came *only* from Antonia's properties or from those of her tenants. Who else but the land agent would have known exactly what kinds of goods would be stored where? Hierax was the one who normally visited the properties to write contracts and collect rents.

The tenants for their part were outwardly concerned that their rent payments had disappeared and they had no receipts to show for it. Over and over again, they expressed their worry that Alexander would try to charge them for the rents that had disappeared. If there had been only one or two, Alexander may have assumed the renter was trying to pull a trick to get out of paying their contractual share. He had heard the story too many times, though, for it to be one farmer's fraud. Villagers from all around the lake were reporting missing goods and animals. Fortunately, not too much actual money in coins was missing, but there was some of that unaccounted for, too.

Yesterday, Alexander and Amarantus had arrived in the village of Soknopaiou Nesos on the northern bank of Lake Moeris. Immediately, Alexander had been greeted with a complaint about a missing boat. Thank the Lord that the missing boat turned out *not* to be *his* concern. It had *not* belonged to Lady Antonia or to any of her tenants. Although Alexander could sympathize with the loss of a valuable boat, there was really no reason for him to give the matter a second thought.

He was also relieved that he could finally welcome a change in scenery. Much of the property that the Lady Antonia owned in the village of Soknopaiou Nesos was quite different from her other holdings around the nome. Alexander had grown bored with seeing every village's variations of wheat fields and animal pens. They were important, of course they were, but after awhile they all started to look alike. Because this village sat on marshland, its economy was built around fishing, fowling, and the collection of papyrus and reed stalks.

For Alexander, this short stay at Soknopaiou Nesos promised to be much more engaging for another reason. The following morning, one of the local magistrates was taking Alexander on a hunt – and not just any hunt. The magistrate said that it would be a traditional style hunt, much the way the old pharaohs used to do it. They would be hunting marsh birds using what was known as fowling sticks or throwing sticks. Later they would be using something called a clap net.

Alexander was genuinely excited. He had always enjoyed

sports and this was certainly something they didn't do in Rome. In fact, he thought, he should make a note to write about it to his friend Claudius and share his experience. As preparation for the hunt, this afternoon the magistrate was teaching Alexander how to use the throwing sticks. At the opposite end of his courtyard, the magistrate had set up a decoy bird made of woven reeds. Before them on the low wall, he laid a series of curved sticks.

The stick was nothing like a *xulon*. It was about the length from Alexander's elbow to his palm and made of some hardwood that had been painted. It wasn't straight either, but was bent or curved in the middle and it was also flat. Alexander picked up one of the throw sticks and gave the magistrate a puzzled look.

The man smiled back. "No these are not used to stab, beat, or hurl like a spear. You fling it from the side. If thrown correctly, one these sticks can go farther and faster than any other wooden weapon. ... well, except for the bow and arrow of course and those aren't used for fowl since they damage the meat too much."

He gave Alexander a shy look. "I have spent many years practicing with the sticks, but I'm still no expert. It is not the most efficient way to hunt water fowl although the sticks can be effective. Think of the throwing sticks as mainly a type of sport where the hunter tests his own strength and coordination. Here I will show you."

The magistrate turned sideways to the woven reed decoy. He held the stick in his right hand out at waist height, swiveled his back beyond his left hip, and then flung the stick forward. Unlike a spear, it did not arc through the air, but actually spun straight out at waist height and hit the decoy duck hard enough to knock it over.

Alexander had never seen a weapon like this, but he had seen something similar. He turned to the magistrate, "I think I have seen a disc held at waist height and it spun like that after it was thrown. *Huh*, is this not just like the discus throw used in athletic competitions?"

The magistrate nodded. "In some ways it is – or least similar. But the discus is actually slower and designed for distance. These throwing sticks move faster and are designed to knock fowl out of flight." He pointed toward a small cloth laid across the wall with additional sticks, each different than the first. The magistrate waved his hand over them.

"As you can see, there are different styles of throwing sticks and each requires a different type of release – different arm and wrist movement. This one, for example, uses an overhand throw." He gestured at a stick with the curve about a third of the way down. "But for *tomorrow's* hunt," he continued, "We will only use one style of throwing stick. Here you try it now."

It soon became apparent that mastering the throwing sticks would take considerably more practice than the brief time that they had to spend. Still, Alexander was intrigued and announced his intention to acquire some throwing sticks and practice using them once he returned to Alexandria. The magistrate seemed pleased at Alexander's interest and selected a bright blue and yellow painted throwing stick and gifted it for him to keep. Curious, Alexander asked why the throw sticks were painted such bright colors.

The magistrate explained, "Tomorrow, we will be using our servants to retrieve the sticks after we throw them. That is why they are each so brightly painted. Otherwise, it would be too easy to lose them in the marsh."

****

The next morning, Alexander waited on the shore between Lake Moeris and the village of Soknopaiou Nesos proper. There was a small delay since today's hunt had not been planned in advance. The magistrate had only suggested it after Alexander had arrived the previous afternoon. So they waited while the magistrate finished organizing the staff for the hunt. They would need the local marsh bird expert and some servants to carry the sticks, nets and baskets for the hunt.

Amarantus was waiting at his side. While Alexander's face showed eager anticipation, Ranti's lip was curled with scorn. Finally, his servant spoke his complaint. "Master, why would the Lady Antonia want to own *a swamp*? It cannot even be cultivated."

Alexander blinked. *"What?"*

Amarantus gestured around him, "Look at this muddle. Her wheat fields were all so neatly laid out, but this place is a mess. Like, *uh,* look over there," he pointed. "That whole area is choked with giant weeds. Why has no one even tried to clear them out so boats can get by?"

Alexander's followed his servant's pointed finger to an area on the edge of the lake that was filled with giant stalks. His servant was correct that there was a haphazard scattering of plants in different heights, but... he smiled with recognition.

"Those are *not weeds*, Ranti, and neither are they worthless. Those are *papyrus* stalks and that is essentially a papyrus farm."

Amarantus peered skeptically at the five to ten foot stalks along the banks. *"That* is what we write on?"

"It is," Alexander nodded, "Although, obviously there is considerable work involved to making the writing sheets. I saw it done once when I was a boy, but I don't remember it very well now. I do remember that it involves stripping off the pithy part of the stalk. These are laid out in rows that are dried and pounded together."

He shrugged. "You know how expensive the writing material made from sheepskin is. Those papyrus stalks represent a lucrative investment for Lady Antonia."

Their attention was caught by the sound of the magistrate arriving with a small team of men and boys. He had brought a local man whom he introduced as their designated huntsman, the fowling expert.

Alexander's anticipation returned as the huntsman explained where they would go to hunt with the throwing sticks. After using the throwing sticks, they would move to an undisturbed area to set up the clap net for catching the local fowl. He explained that the fowling sticks and net were often used for the local breed of goose as well as ducks, but today they would be flushing out a nest of quails.

The local man led them to a place where they could conceal themselves while the birds were flushed out of their nests. Alexander had wondered if they would have to wade into the water or even mount small boats. But no, the huntsman led them to ground that was soft, but firm enough that they would be able to place their feet for the throw.

Alexander crouched near the magistrate and waited quietly for the men to flush out the quail. When it finally did happen, it happened fast. There was the swish and the flap of wings and suddenly a number of birds launched into the air. Fortunately, the huntsman had placed them in the best position and ready. As the birds rose, both the magistrate and Alexander twisted their upper body and arm at waist level, picked out a bird, and then flung their sticks at them. Actually, Alexander just threw his stick in their general direction. It would take a *lot* more practice to be able to aim for a particular bird in flight.

He had originally thought that having only one throwing stick would not be enough. It seemed like he should have been armed with several. Now Alexander saw that the birds moved too quickly for more than one or two throws. He watched as his throwing stick and those of the magistrate and the huntsman slashed the air. Both of the other men hit a quail each and he saw the birds stop in flight and topple to the ground. Immediately, servants were dispatched to collect them.

Alexander's own throwing stick had gone wide of a quail, but he still felt some sense of satisfaction. He had released the stick in time and put enough power into it that the stick did reach the rising marsh birds. Just that much effort had required a fair bit of strength and speed. It was a start. Now that he understood how it worked, he could see how much skill it took to land a bird, but Alexander wasn't deterred at all. Actually he felt that his first effort had gone well enough that some practice would make a difference.

Amarantus sidled up beside him. "Master, that does not seem like a very efficient way to hunt fowl."

Alexander smiled. "No, it does not, does it? This stick throwing is more like an athletic contest than an actual hunt. I suspect that when we get to the clap net part of the hunt, then we'll be catching more birds. ... In the meantime, why don't you go retrieve my throwing stick. You did see where it went, yes?"

Amarantus bit his lower lip and ducked his head. "I am sorry, master. I was watching the throwing stick that actually hit a quail."

Alexander snorted and shook his head. "Well, at least *I saw* where my stick went. Come with me and between the two of us we should find it."

He supposed he might have waited until the magistrate's servants could retrieve his throwing stick, but Alexander didn't mind getting it himself. Despite the bright yellow and blue paint on the throw stick, it turned out to be harder to locate than Alexander expected. He and Amarantus slowly moved near the shoreline pushing reeds apart looking for a flash of color. But when they finally found a spot of color, it was *not* what they were looking for.

"Master, I see a bit of color through there. Maybe it is your throwing stick."

Amarantus edged forward and cautiously moved the reeds aside so he wouldn't dislodge the stick, if indeed it was the throwing stick. ... It was not. He covered his mouth as he started to gag and stepped back quickly.

"Master, there is a man in there. ... a floating man, and he smells bad."

Alexander looked up from where he had parted some reeds and pulled out his throwing stick. He was wiping away some mud on it as he looked at his servant.

"What do mean, Ranti? Are you saying you found a body? a dead body?"

Ranti kept a hand over his mouth as he quickly nodded back. "A very dead body, master."

Alexander squelched over through the marsh, took a quick look for himself and then scanned the area until he saw the magistrate and huntsman standing together. He waved to catch their attention. "There is a dead body here. I think you'd better come take a look."

They did not look happy at the news, but there wasn't much choice about it. The magistrate and huntsman picked their way over and then parted the reeds where he was pointing. Giving a snort of disgust, the huntsman waded into the reeds, grabbed the corpse by the tunic, and dragged it out onto the shore line. The body had been floating face down so he used the toe of his boot to turn it over onto its back.

It was just as disgusting as Alexander expected it to be, but fortunately since he was not the local magistrate, *strategos*, or any other official, the body was not his problem.

The magistrate pulled his tunic up over his face and quickly looked away. He asked the huntsman, "Who is it? Can you tell?"

"Yeah, I know him," the huntsman said and turned toward magistrate. "And so do you."

The magistrate startled, then took a closer look. He sucked in a breath. "Is that Salbios? The boat man?"

"Yeah," the huntsman nodded. "That's him. ... 'Been here awhile I think."

The magistrate took another peek. "Can you tell what killed him? Do you think it was an accident?"

The huntsman pursed his lips and shook his head. "No, I can't tell. The body is a mess – too many wounds on it now to tell much. ... but if you are asking me, my guess is this is a *murder*."

At the pronouncement every head swiveled toward the huntsman with a startled look.

The magistrate knit his brows, "Wh- What make you think it's *murder*?"

The huntsman just shrugged. "The man is a boat man, right? ... so where is his boat? If he had simply fallen out near here, the reeds are too thick for the boat to have floated far. That boat has been missing for several weeks. Now we find a dead boatman who has also been missing for several weeks. ... Seems to me, like his boat must have been taken."

Alexander looked around and said, "But the boat could be around here, couldn't it? Perhaps it's just washed up over there among the stalks of papyri."

"No," the huntsman responded. "It is not that kind of boat."

Alexander glanced at the magistrate who was also shaking his head no.

"You are thinking of the small papyrus skiffs, Alexander. Salbios's boat was special. It was larger, made of wood. It was the only boat in this area that was built to carry livestock although it was used for heavy loads of grain as well."

"Livestock?" Alexander bit his lower lip as he had a thought. "Could it have carried four cows, a golden mare, a red calf and a, *uh*, a goat?"

Both the magistrate and the huntsman turned to look at him as if he had just said something exceedingly odd. Well, perhaps he had. Alexander shrugged back. "Those are the animals that are missing from Philadelphia and Karanis. I have received petitions to find them."

"*Ahh,*" the magistrate nodded knowingly. Missing animals were a common complaint.

"I don't suppose either of you have seen these missing animals have you?" Alexander continued. "Or, perhaps seen Hierax, Lady Antonia's former land agent? He appears to be missing as well. Or perhaps, I should say, that he has been ... difficult to find. ... You must know who I mean. Have you seen him?"

The magistrate shook his head 'no,' but the huntsman tilted his head and pursed his lips in thought. Alexander took that as a good sign. "You *have* seen him? Hierax the land agent? You have seen him, haven't you?"

The huntsman hesitated a moment longer, then shook his head. "No. Well, *maybe*, but I couldn't say for sure," he said.

The magistrate gave him a sharp look. "That is not helpful. Explain."

The huntsman shrugged. "I wasn't paying much attention at the time, but I think I saw Hierax. ... And, if it was him, he was acting a bit strangely."

The magistrate waved a hand for the huntsman to continue, so he did.

"I don't hold any property from Antonia, and her freedman is no friend of mine. I say that to explain that although I saw a man that looked like him, I didn't think much about it. ... and I should also say that I saw the man from behind at a distance. I'm not even sure it *was* Hierax." He shrugged, "but we don't get that many strangers around here and certainly not many wearing fancy embroidered tunics."

The huntsman held up his hand, "I'm coming to the point. It was maybe two or three weeks ago, I saw a man heading into the marsh. I might have assumed the man was going fishing except he wore that fancy tunic ... and it was near sundown. It's a bit dangerous to be walking around the marsh in the dark, unless you're very sure of where you are going."

The huntsman stopped and took a deep breath. Alexander had a feeling those words had been an unusually long speech for the laconic man.

Alexander pressed. "You definitely cannot confirm that the man you saw was the land agent Hierax?"

The huntsman shook his head 'no.'

This time Alexander looked between the huntsman and the magistrate. "But can you at least confirm that you spotted this stranger in the marsh about the same time that the boat man Salbios went missing?"

This time the magistrate answered as the huntsman shook his head. "He cannot. No one can. We *don't know* when Salbios went missing. Obviously, as a boat man, it was his job to come and go. The only reason why we knew he was missing was because apparently he did not make some deliveries as agreed. Messages were sent to the village to find out why he was late. It was only then, that we began a search. Still we were not worried since both the boat and the boat man were missing. I mean… we thought he had to be around, just out somewhere on the lake."

The magistrate looked down at the body. A servant had covered its face with a piece of linen. "We now know that the boat man is here and his boat is gone. … *Ah* well, there is nothing we can do about it today. I'll have my servants remove the body. We should get back to the hunt."

The hunt did continue and Alexander did enjoy himself. Despite the disruption caused by finding of the body, they were able to get in two more tries with the throwing sticks. He did not hit a quail either time they were flushed out of their nest, but Alexander could tell he was picking up the speed and rhythm of the throw. He just needed to work on his accuracy. The magistrate gave him a bit of leather which he used to wrap around the throwing stick and attach it to his belt. Alexander was determined that he would practice until he was good enough to succeed in a hunt.

Later, Alexander and Ranti learned how to set up and close the clap net. As predicted, the clap net was more successful at capturing various marsh birds. Alexander could see that considerable skill was needed to use the nets effectively, but they just didn't appeal to him the way the throwing stick did.

That evening, Alexander's thoughts returned to the boat man and his own problems as he and Ranti relaxed in the magistrate's courtyard. What had he learned? *Hunh.* Antonia's land agent may – or may not – have been seen here by the huntsman. A wooden boat big enough to hold livestock and bags of grain was missing. He supposed the boat man's death might have been an accident. Still, Alexander could not help but think about how the boat would have been well suited for carrying away the many purloined items the villagers had petitioned him about.

And the huntsman said that Hierax *might* have been here, so perhaps the land agent *may have taken* the missing crops and animals ... and *he may have* used that boat to remove them. But why?

Perhaps, the land agent had no intention of turning over the rents collected to Lady Antonia. Perhaps he was *stealing* goods so there would be no receipt to connect him to what was owed to Antonia. Could Hierax actually be taking the items and hiding them?

But again, not a single person had definitely seen Hierax here or in any of the villages Alexander had already passed. Could Hierax be responsible and yet remain completely unseen?

Frustrated, Alexander banged a fist on his knee and turned to Amarantus.

"Where is that *nothus?* His house steward in Tebtunis says he is not there. The bargemen on the south canal say he is not there. We have stopped in Philadelphia, Bacchias, Karanis and heard from almost every other small village along the way. Every where they say that he *might* have stopped by, but they really can't say for sure."

"It cannot be coincidence anymore, Ranti. *That man is hiding from me.* Wherever I go, he runs ahead and hides. He is like a child playing games."

Alexander stood and punched the air with his fist. Amarantus covered his mouth and snorted. Alexander turned angrily towards him.

"You think this is amusing, Ranti? That I can't find this man, you think that is amusing?"

"No, master, no … well …," Amarantus tilted his head. "… *perhaps a little?*"

He held up his hands as he saw Alexander losing patience.

"Master, it is like that story they tell in Rome, the one about the bedridden old lady who had but one bad manservant. I'm sure you must have heard it before.

"The old lady became angry with the manservant and dismissed him, but he did not go. She ordered him to hire another manservant thinking that this second man could throw the first one out. Her manservant did not hire another servant. So she ordered him to bring her lawyer, but he did not summon him. She gave him a letter and he did not deliver it. And on, and so on it went until the old lady finally died. The stubborn manservant inherited her house, where he lived happily for the rest of his life."

Amarantus nodded cheerfully. "It is a good story, master, because it proves that a clever servant should always delay because then they will win in the end."

Alexander smiled. "That is *not* a true story, Ranti, and that is *not* supposed the lesson learned. It is called *The Tale of the Recalcitrant Servant* and it is a morality tale. It is told to masters to remind them that they should never allow their servants to gain too much power over them."

He blew out a long breath. "Well, *I am not* a helpless old

lady and Hierax is *not* going to out-survive *me*. If he does not cease making me angry, I will not hold back when I get my hands on him. I will tie him up and drag him myself onto the next ship heading for Rome. I *will* have that man out of Egypt."

Amarantus just shrugged. "Yes, master, but you will have to find him first."

Reconstruction of an ancient olive press *[by author]*

12. Pressing Matters

"It is good that you came today, *kurie*, for all of the workers will be away tomorrow to attend the festival."

Alexander blinked at the overseer of the wine press. "A festival? Is this one to the crocodile god as well?"

The overseer shrugged. "Of course."

Alexander said, "But how can that be? I was just at the big festival for the crocodile god a few days ago while I was in Karanis. Is it not too soon to have another?"

The overseer gave him a puzzled look. "No. That festival was for Petesouchos. He protects Karanis. This is *Theadelphia*. Our great god is Souchos. It is he who we will honor tomorrow."

One of the men standing with the overseer gave them an encouraging smile. "You should come celebrate the festival with us," he said. "There will be music, dancing, storytelling, probably much more."

Alexander was intrigued. "Will there be a *xulon* competition?"

The man held up his palms. "I do not know, but there are usually athletic contests. The young people particularly look forward to those."

Amarantus edged up to Alexander's side and murmured, "Master, perhaps you have discovered why the Greeks and Romans who have settled here have not built temples to their own gods. It seems the crocodile god has better entertainment."

"*SSsss*, quiet, Ranti. Don't let the locals hear you. ... but, candidly, I think you may be onto something there. It has often puzzled the people in Alexandria how there could be dozens of villages settled by Greeks and then Romans in the Arsinoite nome, and almost none of these villages have erected a temple to any of their traditional gods. Yes, Crocodilopolis does have a temple to Jupiter and there are some small shrines, but for the most part neither the Greeks nor the Romans seem to be honoring their own gods – at least not in their settlements in the Arsinoite Nome."

Alexander had arrived in Theadelphia in time to get a good sense of how the grapes were being harvested and processed. He had arranged to meet the *strategos* Dion here, but had only received a message saying that the *strategos* had been delayed and would arrive late – or possibly not at all.

Although, Alexander was disappointed at not having Dion as a traveling companion, he and Amarantus threw themselves into learning the business of the grape harvest. The previous day he had watched as the grapes were cut from the vines in bunches. Some grapes were spread out on papyrus mats in the sun to be dried into raisins. Dried grapes, dates, and figs would supplement the villagers' staple diet of grains and beans. They were also a lucrative side crop since raisins were eaten throughout Egypt.

Today, Alexander was an observer at the Lady Antonia's wine press in Theadelphia. Alexander had watched the village workers turn a capstan that forced a large screw down onto the grapes squeezing the juice out into a little runnel and then into a vat. The overseer had been justifiably proud of having such a modern invention, a true rarity in a land where most grape juice was still acquired by stomping feet.

Alexander had been impressed and said so as they exited the warehouse that stored the amphoras of grape juice for fermentation. Of course, it would be many days yet until this year's vintage would be ready, but the overseer expressed his confidence that it would prove to be a very good year.

"I feel certain that there will be more than enough to fulfill all of the orders that will come from Alexandria," the overseer said with a sharp nod. "Once I know the total production, I can speak with you to decide where to sell the excess. Having the wine press means that we can make wine in greater quantity and more cheaply than the other vineyards around the nome. I have always thought that there might be a way to leverage that into greater profits for the Lady Antonia."

Alexander nodded and was lost in thought for a moment pondering whether it would be better to export to external markets or sell to the southern areas of Egypt, even Nubia, that were not lush enough to produce grapes of their own.

The overseer nudged him and pointed at a circular stone device on the other side of the courtyard from where they were standing.

"The Lady Antonia has an olive press here, too."

"You mean that round structure over there?" Alexander pointed.

"Yes, that's it. It is just a small one. As you can see the handle on the grinding stone is only long enough for one or two people to push. The big ones, of course, have a longer pole that is turned by a donkey or an ox."

Curious, Alexander wandered over to the low stone wall that surrounded a shallow well that formed the olive press. The overseer was right that it wasn't large, but it certainly appeared big enough to suit a village's needs, maybe more. He would have to learn about how much oil could be squeezed for how many bushels of olives. The well of the olive press came up almost to Alexander's waist, but he could see that it had only a shallow basin, not deep like the grape vats.

"How does this work?" he asked. "Do you just place bunches of the olives into the well as you do the grapes in the wine press?"

The overseer shook his head. "No, it is a little different because the olives have pits and they are harder. We take a basket of olives at a time, slice them in half to remove the pit and then they're strewn evenly over the well bottom. That way the grinding wheel can keep moving while the next batch of olives is prepared. You don't want to fill the well area too full or else the stone wheel will become hard to turn."

"Yes, I think I see how it works," Alexander nodded. "It is not in use today?"

"Oh no," the overseer replied. "It has not been used in months since olives have been out of season. The grinding wheel would be difficult to turn now since it isn't maintained between harvests. That will change soon enough. We'll start gathering the ripe olives next month. Then we'll be pressing olives into oil for the next three months after that. The olive season lasts that long."

Alexander rubbed his chin thoughtfully. "I am glad that Dionysodoros, your *strategos*, suggested that I come to Theadelphia at this time. If I am to be of any use as Antonia's procurator, I need to understand how her properties function. Just today alone, I have already learned so much."

The overseer gave him a begrudging smile. "Don't try running your own farm just yet."

Alexander laughed. "Indeed, I will not. Soon I will be assuming my new duties as the Alabarch in Alexandria. At this point, I'm not sure how much time I will be able to spend personally overseeing Antonia's properties. ... Most likely, I'll be relying heavily on my secretary here, Amarantus. You can always contact him directly. He has my complete trust."

Alexander had turned away and did not see the resentful look that the overseer gave Amarantus.

There came shouts from the other side of the courtyard by the wine press. The overseer threw up his hands, "What is it now? I'll be back as soon as I check on that, *kurie*."

Alexander stayed behind for a closer look at the olive press. It was easy to see how a single person could use the wooden stave to turn the grinding wheel for crushing the olives. But he couldn't see how the oil itself was collected as the olives were crushed.

There had been an obvious runnel and vat on the wine press, but it was not so obvious how the oil was collected on this olive press. Curiously, Alexander bent over the basin looking for a trough or hole where the pressed oil would collect. At first he couldn't see anything. Perhaps there was a hole and a runnel on the other side? He bent lower and leaned to the side to see around the fulcrum stone in the center of the well.

"*Ooof.*" Suddenly, Alexander was grabbed from behind and squeezed into a tight bear hug. Someone lifted him up so that only the toes of his boots touched the ground.

Beyond him he heard the cry of *"Masteeerr...!"*

Alexander tried to twist toward the sound of his servant's shout as it was cut off, but his body was held fast. Whoever was behind holding him must have been very large and very strong. Alexander was a tall man himself at six feet, but he could sense that whoever held him was probably at least as tall and broader – and stronger, too. Alexander instinctively began to shuffle his feet and squirm in an effort to free himself, but for all that effort he barely moved.

Frustrated, Alexander stopped struggling, took a breath and tried to let his mind catch up with his rapidly beating heart. His left arm was completely pinned to his side. His right arm was only partially pinned near the shoulder since Alexander had been reaching out to touch the olive press wheel when he was grabbed from behind. He thought he *might* be able to free his right arm, but made himself wait until he knew what he could accomplish with one free arm.

Alexander and Amarantus had been alone in the courtyard when the overseer and his man left to answer the workers' calls from the wine press. From where their assailants had come, he could not guess, but there were plenty of places around the mud brick walls and buildings where men could have hidden. And 'men' in the plural was the correct term. There was the bear of a man behind Alexander who had him pinned. It probably had taken at least two men to overpower Amarantus. His servant was not particularly big or strong, but he was wiry and they were accustomed to fighting off petty thieves and gang thugs back in Rome.

Both Alexander and Ranti had cried out at the onset of the attack, but apparently the creaking of the wine press on the other side of the courtyard had drowned out their voices. The overseer did not appear to investigate. The wine press workers must not have been able to hear their shouts.

"What do you want?" Alexander demanded out loud. "Money?"

He had expected the man holding him to answer, but the reply came from another man standing out of sight farther behind his left shoulder.

"*Huh*, I'll tell you what we want. We want *you gone*. As far away as possible. You don't belong here."

The words were in an uncultured Greek and the voice was a

little raspy like the man was trying to disguise it. Alexander didn't think he recognized the speaker, but couldn't be sure. At least their attackers were talking.

"What about what *the Lady Antonia wants*?" Alexander countered. "This is *her* property and *she is* the one who asked me to be here."

"*Hah.* I doubt that," the voice rasped back. "Things were going fine here. There was no call for complaint. We don't need you here to try to change everything."

A light went on in Alexander's head. *Hmm,* Just who would be so intent on having him leave the management of Antonia's properties as they were? Could that be her former land agent that was standing behind him? Who else would possibly care if Alexander was inspecting Antonia's estates? He decided to test his guess.

"You're Hierax, aren't you?" he called over his shoulder. "I suppose *you* were happy with things the way they were, but *the Lady Antonia was not*. It is too late for you to try to fix things now. Lady Antonia wants you gone. If she had not sent *me* to do it, it would have been someone else -- and soon."

There was a long silence after he spoke. Since Alexander was still pinned in a way that blocked his view of their assailants, he couldn't tell what was going on with them. He had a sense that the attackers were communicating, perhaps through looks and gestures, but he really wasn't sure. He decided to press his point.

"This is enough, Hierax. There is no use in hiding from me any longer. You are in disgrace. The Lady Antonia has ordered you back to Rome and you must go."

No response.

"*I am* Gaius Julius Alexander and *I am* Antonia's procurator, her *epitropos* – her *only* legal representative in Egypt. It is in your interest to turn over all her accounts and any rents you have already collected. You cannot keep them, Hierax. *I will not allow it*, and if you force the issue I will bring in *the prefect*. The prefect will *not* stand by while someone steals from Augustus's beloved niece."

Again his words were met with silence. If that was indeed the land agent standing behind Alexander faking the raspy voice, he chose not to reply – no excuses, no taunts and certainly no confessions. Perhaps Hierax had been convinced to cooperate?

A few moments passed, then the raspy voiced man who still was not visible let out an ugly expletive.

"*You are lying,*" he rasped. "*We* would have heard from Lady Antonia herself if she wanted us to change anything. …*You*. You mouth nothing but lies. We'll show you what we do with liars."

The raspy voiced man behind reached out and grabbed a handful of Alexander's hair and yanked. "Turn him this way," he ordered.

The bear hug remained tight, but Alexander could feel himself being shifted until he was facing the olive press. Three men stood before him with linen bags over their heads. The one in the middle was clearly his servant Amarantus and he was being held fast with a man on each arm. The other two were his attackers and also wore linen bags to disguise their faces, only theirs had eye slits so they could see. The raspy voiced man was still out of his line of sight.

"I do *not* lie," Alexander retorted. "Lady Antonia gave me letters signed in her own hand and sealed with own seal. I am Gaius Julius Alexander her chosen legal representative in Egypt. One of the letters was delivered to the prefect and another to the house of her former land agent in Tebtunis – *your* house Hierax. There should be *no doubt* of the Lady's intentions."

Some soft murmuring started up behind him. Alexander couldn't understand it since they were probably speaking in Egyptian. It sounded like they might be arguing.

"*Enough!*" the raspy voice from behind Alexander's shoulder shouted. "We are committed."

The man leaned into Alexander's ear again hissing a new warning.

"Yeah, we hear who you *claim* you are, Roman, so *maybe* we won't kill you. That depends on if you stay out of our business. You leave today and you don't come around here again -- ever."

The man paused and spoke to the attackers in what must have been Egyptian. They responded with angry mutters. Since Alexander had been speaking to their leader in Greek, he suddenly realized that most of their attackers probably had no idea what he had been saying – no idea that he was *Lady Antonia's only legal representative*. … and Alexander spoke *no* Egyptian. He could not tell them.

Their speaker began to rasp again.

"So *you* will get to live another day. But your slave, here, he's no Roman and I think he can be used to make sure you get our message."

The leader barked some words in Egyptian. Of the two men holding Amarantus the bigger one grabbed him pinning Ranti's arms to his side. But that wasn't all. He had wrapped his arms in a curious counter position opposite the way Alexander was being held. Suddenly, Alexander understood why as his slave was bodily lifted and turned upside down.

"*Masteeer!*" Amarantus screamed.

Alexander tried to surge forward, but was still held fast by the large man behind him.

"What are you doing?!" he yelled out. "Put him down!"

"You will see," their rasping leader said then spoke more words in Egyptian to the men holding Ranti.

Alexander could hear the smirk in the man's voice as he switched back to Greek. "I told them to push his arm in the olive well. A scribe won't do you much good without his hand, now will he?"

With growing horror, Alexander watched as the two men forced the upside down Amarantus into the well of the olive press. They banged his head down on the stones lining the bottom of the well. Amarantus still had the linen bag over his head covering his eyes so he couldn't see. Somehow he had freed his right arm, or maybe the attackers had allowed that because Ranti now had his right hand pressed to the bottom of the well of the olive press. He was pushing hard and it was all he could do to keep from having his head smashed down into the well again.

As Alexander watched stunned, the second man went to the fulcrum pole that would push the grinding wheel around the bottom of the well. If Ranti kept his hand down on the well bed to protect his head, his hand would be utterly crushed under the stone wheel.

There was a rough scraping sound as the second man pushed hard on the stick that turned the grinding wheel. The overseer had been right. The olive press had not been serviced in months. The capstan in the center had not been oiled and was probably filled sand and other debris. It was keeping the grinding wheel from turning for now, but probably not for long. Alexander saw another man moving toward the stick to help turn the wheel. With two men at it, the grinding wheel would not be stuck for long.

Whoever the big man was behind him, had wrapped his left arm around Alexander's waist and the right was above wrapped around his chest. This meant that Alexander's left arm was tightly pinned to his side ... but only his *right shoulder* was pinned immobile.

He was sure that he could squirm out of it. And Alexander's *xulon* sticks were attached to his belt on his left hip. If he could just free his right arm, he could reach down and grab one. Alexander gazed desperately at his servant Ranti. They were outnumbered, but he did not think they would have a better chance. If they were going to fight, it had to be now.

Fortunately, everyone's attention was on the olive press and watching the two men try to turn the stone wheel toward Ranti's helpless hand.

Alexander took a breath and then shoved his body downward as hard as he could at an angle that would allow him to reach a *xulon*. The attacker's grip slipped up over Alexander's right upper arm and was resting on his shoulder. The attacker probably would have tried to squeeze Alexander's neck, but the man had been caught by surprise and did not react fast enough.

Alexander slid the *xulon* out of its case then turned it jabbed it over his shoulder as hard as could. There was a yelp of pain and Alexander was released from the hold. He wasn't sure what the *xulon* had struck, but it was probably the man's cheek, maybe his neck.

"Ranti, fight. Now!" he shouted as he pivoted on his right foot and swung his *xulon* into the head of the large man who had been holding him. It was a hard hit, but the man didn't go down. He was staggering, but Alexander knew he did not have the time to finish him off. He began to scream mindless obscenities as he drew his second *xulon* and sprinted towards the olive press.

"*Asinus mentulae! Nothus! Merda caput!*"

In the meantime, Ranti had heard his shout to fight and had begun kicking and squirming with all his might. As Alexander ran up, he pulled back his right arm and struck the man holding Amarantus hard across his back with the full length of his *xulon*. The man gave a cry of pain and lost his grip on Amarantus as he fell to his knees. Fortunately, Ranti still had his right palm on the well bed of the olive press and was able to catch himself as he fell.

Alexander placed a boot on the assailant's back and shoved him prostrate into the dirt, then cracked him on the head to ensure he stayed there. Then Alexander spun and quickly assumed the *baled wheat* position since he expected to find several thugs gathering at his back. It was a standard defensive position with his left foot slightly forward, arms in front at chest height and the *xulons* held horizontally in front of him one slight higher than the other.

In fact, as he turned, he found just two men had been behind him. Despite the linen bags over their heads, Alexander guessed that they were probably the ones he had identified as the bear hugger and raspy voice. Fortunately, having assumed the defensive position had enabled him to quickly strike out and force aside a knife that was already coming at his side. As he swung his left arm to deflect the knife strike from Raspy voice, he jabbed his right *xulon* forward to strike the other bigger man. That man jumped backward, however, and Alexander's stick passed through the air unchallenged.

As both of his opponents were moving, Alexander returned to the *baled wheat* defensive position until he could assume a more aggressive approach. The men stayed a few feet out of his *xulon* range and they were far enough apart that he had to constantly shift his head and shoulders to keep both in view. Alexander remained in his position shuffling slightly as needed to keep watch.

He wanted to strike out at the men who had attacked him from behind and he felt confident that he could score well against either opponent. Since they both still wore the ridiculous linen bags with eye holes over their heads, neither would be able to respond well in a real fight – but there were still *two* of them. Plus there were *at least two more* men, the ones who had been handling the stick for the grinding wheel and they were mostly out of Alexander's line of sight.

Behind him, at the olive press, Amarantus had not remained idle. He had lowered his upside down body into the olive well bed until he could right himself and remove the linen sack from his head. His earlier attackers were momentarily distracted as they watched the fight between Alexander and the two others. Amarantus could see another ruffian hovering not far out of Alexander's sight. If that man joined the two already engaged, then his master would be hard pressed to defend himself, let alone win.

When he was first grabbed, Amarantus had been disarmed, but he didn't hesitate. He jumped up and stood erect in the well of the olive press. Then he placed his left foot up on the rim and the other a stride back and drew his hand back to his shoulder. For a flash of a moment Alexander saw his slave at the edge of his sight in the familiar stance of Zeus about to hurl a lightning bolt. Then Ranti flung his arm forward and jabbed his forefinger at the first man who had been trying to turn the grinding wheel to crush him.

"*Tembel gvohah!*" he screamed.

There was a gasping of breath and the man seemed to freeze in place.

Without hesitation, Amarantus again drew back his hand and then it shot forward with forefinger pointing at the second man.

"*Tembel gvohah!*" he screamed again.

The second man clasped his chest and staggered backwards in shock. The first man looked wildly from side to side as he started to edge away. After taking two steps, he let out a whimper, grabbed his companion, and they took off at a run. Neither man knew what the Roman's slave had just shouted at them, but they were pretty sure they knew a bad curse when they heard one. And clearly that slave knew his dark magic. He had hurled that evil curse at them with the same confidence as any Egyptian magician.

Alexander used the distraction to close in on his attackers. Since they had positioned themselves on either side of him, he had shifted to the *floating lotus* position that would allow him to swing to either side. He kept sweeping the *xulons* back and forth at waist height as he closed in on them.

The big man who had pinned him earlier stepped forward. In a flash, Alexander shifted to a *reverse yawning crocodile* with his left *xulon* raised to form the upper jaw and the right arm the lower jaw. As hoped, the sudden movement directed the big man's attention toward the upper stick. Then Alexander surged forward and brought his right *xulon* up into the groin of the big man. That man let out a high pitched shriek and clutched at himself.

"Master, duck!"

Alexander didn't hesitate at his servant's cry, but threw himself down on one knee with his head and shoulders bowed. He was just in time as a knife spun through the air just above him and embedded itself into the chest of the man he had dubbed bear hugger. In order to deal with the big man, Alexander had momentarily turned his back on the other – Raspy voice, the one with the knife. That had almost been a fatal mistake.

Alexander regained his feet and turned to charge after the knife thrower, but that man was already disappearing around a building. In fact, all of their assailants were gone, except the man who now had a knife protruding from his chest. If they had been in the countryside, then pursuit may have been worthwhile. The location of this wine press, however, was part of Theadelphia and there were just too many places in the village for their attackers hide.

"What is this?! What has happened?!"

The overseer and his workers in the wine press appeared to have finally heard the noise from the fight and had rushed out to see what was happening. --Now that the fight was over. --Now that Alexander no longer needed their help. Their curious timing was not lost on Amarantus either, and Alexander saw his servant raise his eyebrows at him.

Alexander pointedly ignored the overseer and squatted next to the big man on the ground and removed the linen sack that had covered his head. The thrown knife had pierced the man's heart and his sightless eyes were open to the sky. His cheek was torn and had been bleeding, probably where Alexander had jabbed his *xulon* into it. Other than his size, there was nothing else to distinguish him from dozens of other village workers. Alexander felt certain he had never seen this man before. So why would a stranger attack him?

"Who is this man?" Alexander demanded of the overseer.

"Well, *uh, uh,* I'm not sure," the overseer stammered back.

Alexander stood and strode over to the overseer and stared at him angrily. "I think you know *exactly* who this is." He spoke softly and somehow that made his voice sound even more menacing. Alexander was furious and the overseer could tell.

Amarantus sidled up and pointed at the overseer. "Master, shall I curse him, too?"

The overseer gave Amarantus a frightened look, but continued to stall. "Well *uh, uh,* I may have seen that big man before. Maybe."

That was all Alexander was willing to take. He reached out and grabbed the front of the overseer's tunic and dragged him forward until the man's face was scant inches from Alexander's own.

"*Explain. This. Now.* Which of your people just attacked me and why."

The overseer wagged his head. "They weren't *my* people. I can account for every one of mine."

"Who then?" Alexander demanded.

The overseer just shrugged. "I don't know. Their faces were all covered. Could have been anyone." He gave Alexander a sly look. "Could have been Antonia's missing land agent I suppose."

Alexander was not impressed. Still clutching a wad of fabric from the overseer's tunic, he said, "Then let's try this again." He pointed at the man lying dead on the ground. "Who is he?"

"He's not one of mine," the overseer answered.

Alexander shook him hard. "That is *not* what I asked you. Who. Is. This. Man?"

The overseer licked his lips. "His name is Ox," he finally said. "At least that is what people call him because he's so big." Alexander gave the overseer another shake. "I did not lie; he's not one of mine. He's not even from Theadelphia."

"From where then?" asked Alexander.

The overseer hesitated. "From Euhemeria," he finally said. "He's from the Lady Antonia's property in Euhemeria."

Alexander let go of the overseer's tunic and ran a hand through his hair.

"But why?" he asked. "Why would Lady Antonia's people attack her own chosen representative? ... and why would they particularly target my servant and try to maim him? Amarantus has done nothing. He is innocent in all this."

"*Huh,*" the overseer scoffed. "So *you* say."

Alexander pulled back and knitted his brows. "Well, *yes*. Yes, *I do* say. We only arrived in Alexandria a few weeks ago. And Ranti and I have only been in the Arsinoite nome for a few days now. I haven't had time to do anything yet that would cause this sort of revenge action."

He shook his head. "While I can imagine that Hierax may not be too happy to have me here, I cannot imagine why *anyone else* would have a problem with me, or my servant."

The overseer curled his lip in disagreement. "Well, that is *not* what is being said about you. Word has reached us from Crocodilopolis, and other places, too. It is said that you are planning to turn us all out of our homes. --all of us who manage or lease properties of the Lady Antonia. Yeah, we know what you are going to try to do to us. We have been informed."

Now Alexander was truly puzzled. "But why would anyone tell you that? I have not said or done anything to cause someone to spread such rumors."

The overseer did not look placated at all. In fact, when he answered, his voice sounded even more belligerent.

"You should know, *toga boy*, there are quite a few of us who have been looking after the Lady Antonia's properties for a long time. Do you really think that you can just come here and replace all of us?"

Alexander started to argue that he had no intention of replacing anyone, that he was innocent of these rumors that he was there to force people from his homes. ... Then he stopped. He may not be familiar with these properties in Egypt, but he had run his family's business in Rome for several years. And he could tell when he was being manipulated. This manager of a wine press *worked for him* – not the other way around. He had no need to explain or convince such a man of *anything*. Alexander had let the overseer put him on his back foot and he did not like it. It was time he took back control; *hmm* but how?

He pointedly looked at the dead attacker on the ground, then at the overseer. Without a word, he stalked over to stand next to the olive press. Not that he was looking at the olive press, but instead Alexander stared into the distance over the rooftops of the village of Theadelphia. He remembered once hearing Augustus's adopted son Tiberius speak in judgment. Tiberius's voice had been chilling with a total lack of emotion – and a great deal of authority. Alexander strode back over to face the overseer and tried to imitate that voice now.

"I shall have to inform the Lady Antonia immediately of your *betrayal*." He looked at each of the workers who were now loitering around the courtyard. "Of *all* of your betrayals. The Lady Antonia deserved *better* from you."

The overseer began to sputter, "That is not true. We are very loyal to the Lady. It is *you*…"

"No," Alexander cut across the overseer's defense. "*You* are *not loyal* to her. The Lady Antonia chose *me* to be her procurator in Egypt. *Me*, who she has known since childhood. *Me*, who has been entertained in her home many times. *Me*, who is friends with both of her sons Germanicus and Claudius. *Me*, who she trusts to act honorably in her name.

"Yet *you hid* behind the wine press when you knew there was an attack on me. An attack on *me* is an attack against the person and *dignitas* of that very great lady. Did you come to defend the honor of your Lady? Any of you? … *No, you did not.*"

Alexander shook his head sadly. "Antonia will be grievously disappointed to learn how you turned your back and dishonored her. … but I fear more what *Augustus* will do when he hears how you have betrayed his most beloved niece."

The overseer's face went through a series of contortions as different emotions passed through his thoughts. Finally, he reached a decision and threw himself on his knees before Alexander. "It is not true," he cried. "We have always been loyal to our Lady. … It is just that we were told what we must do by the people in Crocodilopolis."

"No," Alexander cut him off again. "You were not; you were not loyal to Antonia at all. Maybe it is true that others have been rumor mongering, but it does not matter what anyone else says. *I –and I alone* -- am the procurator for the Lady Antonia's properties. All of them. *I – and I alone* – will make the decisions about her managers and leases."

Alexander looked around the gathering trying to meet each man's eyes and continued. "I am *not* afraid of you and will not hesitate to replace anyone who I think needs replacing – especially those of you who have proven your disloyalty to Antonia. But until this attack on us today, I had seen no one that I had wanted to replace."

He looked down at the kneeling overseer and shook his head in disappointment. "Now I shall have to write to Lady Antonia and I will have to give her your name as the man who betrayed her in Egypt, and she will curse your name."

"No, no," the overseer moaned. "Do not name me to her as disloyal. I would not have the Lady think that because I am her man heart and soul. Do not write to her my name yet. Please, *kurie*, let me prove myself to her. I swear on her good name, she will never find me lacking."

Alexander was a bit taken aback at how quickly the overseer had turned from belligerent to practically blubbering. *Hmm*, he could work with that.

Alexander squinted his eyes and tilted his head as if considering and then addressed the overseer.

"*One year.* I will give you *one year* to prove your loyalty as one of the Lady Antonia's trusted overseers in Egypt. If you fail her, being dismissed and exiled will be the least of your worries."

Alexander cast his eyes around the courtyard giving each worker a pointed look. Then he turned on his heel and strode away.

Amarantus joined him at his side and they walked in silence back to the house where they were staying in Theadelphia.

"Master," Amarantus finally asked, "do you really think the Lady Antonia would want to know the name of this man who runs her wine press?"

Alexander smiled. "No, of course not. But the overseer doesn't know that and I doubt it would occur to him that his role is too minor for his name ever to be brought to her attention. ... You see, in Theadelphia, he is considered a very important man. That is how he sees himself. Since he rarely leaves his own village, the overseer cannot conceive of how *little* he is the scope of Antonia's vast properties throughout Egypt, Syria, Italy, Greece."

"So, master, you tricked him."

"Yes, Ranti, I suppose I did, but much less than how he tried to trick us by hiding behind the wine press while we were being attacked. This way he gets to keep his job. That is good for him and it is good for me, too, since I don't have the time now to start replacing managers on Antonia's properties. I just hope that my threat of his being exposed to her will cause him to stop listening to rumors and concentrate on doing his job for Antonia."

"So, master, who do you think started these rumors that you are here to take everyone's lands and jobs away?"

Alexander rubbed his chin. "I don't know, but it seems likely that it must have been Hierax. Who else could possibly benefit from it? -- and no, I do not believe that Hierax was one our attackers back at the olive press. I know that I thought so at first, but it's a question of language, or lack of language I should say. Only one of our attackers appeared to speak Greek and his lack of fluency was excruciating. Hierax could not have faked that dreadful accent even if he had tried. Plus the man's clothes were wrong, not fine enough for the land agent."

"But the overseer specifically said the rumor came from *Crocodilopolis*. Master, can you guess who there might have spoken out against you?"

Alexander blew out a breath.

"I don't know, Ranti. We were only there for two days. I met the *strategos* Dion and that Roman, Sabinus, in the beerhouse. There were also the Jews I met outside the prayer house. Of course, they all knew that I was Antonia's new procurator, but I certainly said nothing to imply that I was here to challenge their leases."

They walked on in silence for a few minutes, then Amarantus gave him a sly look.

"Master, that Hebrew curse that you taught me in Karanis; it is very effective. I don't think we could have won that fight without it. What do you think will become of those men now that I have cursed them?"

Alexander pressed his lips together and covered his mouth with his hand while he thought about what to say. The words *tembel gvohah* were *not* a powerful Hebrew curse. Yet Amarantus had wielded those words to great effect. Alexander doubted that his servant could have frightened their attackers with such conviction if Amarantus had been aware that he was actually screaming at them that they were all *big dummies*.

Perhaps he should wait a little before telling Ranti what the Hebrew words really meant. With their luck so far there could be more danger to come and a convincing sounding curse could come in handy.

"You are right," Alexander said to Amarantus. "Your quick action may have saved us. But you must be careful to use that *uh* Hebrew curse very rarely. *Oh, uh,* and you must never, never scream those words at a Jew."

These small clay oil lamps date to the Roman period. An oil, such as olive oil, was poured into the center hole and then a wick made from a material such as woven reed was placed in the outer hole and lit. [image by author]

Indike *[In dee kay]* of Crocodilopolis

Leah of Judea

13. The Great Labyrinth

"You appear to be a man with some deep concerns."

"Huh?"

After returning to Crocodilopolis, Alexander had decided to stop for a day or two to decide where to travel next. If Antonia's former land agent was causing the kind of problems he appeared to be, then Alexander did not have the luxury of waiting to find him.

At the moment, he was sitting on a low wall surrounding the market square with an elbow on his knee, chin on his fist frowning at ... well, nothing. Alexander had been so lost in his thoughts that he visibly started when he realized that the words had been meant for him. Looking up, he realized the speaker had been the teenage Jewish girl that he had encountered in Crocodilopolis on his last visit – the one who had fed the crocodiles and informed him that she was very headstrong.

He smiled at her. "Hello, little one."

At that she pulled her shoulders back and frowned.

"If you want my help, you will need to be more respectful," she said.

"If *I* want *your* help?" was Alexander's puzzled reply.

The girl gave a firm nod. "Just as I thought. You are sitting there wondering what to do about something and you are not sure who to turn to for help. So, tell me your problem and I will help you figure out what to do."

She gave him a direct look. "I am *very clever*, you know."

Alexander blurted out a surprised laugh as she had parroted the line she had spoken when he had first met her. Except that time she had said, "I'm very headstrong, you know." He smiled and repeated the same response he had given her then. "Well, don't brag about it," he said.

Then Alexander stood up and gave the girl a formal bow. "I regret that the first time we met, I was completely remiss in my manners. Let me try to introduce myself properly." He gave another slight bow, "My name is Gaius Julius Alexander, but most call me simply Alexander. I am the eldest son of Gaius Julius Alexander who lives in Alexandria where he holds the position of the Alabarch."

He shrugged. "Since the Alabarch only exists in Egypt, you probably do not know what that is."

"Actually, I *do know* what the Alabarch is," the girl replied archly. "I *am* very educated, you know."

Alexander smiled. "And does such a headstrong, clever, educated girl have a name?"

She tossed her head. "Of course I do. My name is ... *uh* ... is ... Leah."

"Why the hesitation?" Alexander asked. "Leah is a strong name from scripture. In fact, Leah was the matriarch of my own ancestral tribe, the Levites."

The girl hung her head. "But, Leah ... she was supposed to have been ugly."

Alexander tilted his head and gave the girl a mock appraising look. "And you are not, so I would not put much stock in stories about the appearance of a woman who lived generations ago."

Leah chewed her lower lip, and seemed to decide that his answer was good enough. She leaned back on the low wall and then pulled herself up to sit on the mud brick wall a few feet from Alexander.

"Then it is time for you to tell me what is puzzling you. It was obvious from the way you were sitting there staring that you were trying to solve some problem. If you tell me the problem, I will help you find a solution. After all, I am..."

Alexander held up a hand and laughed. "I know. You are *very clever* – or so you say. Well, little one, let us see what you have to say about this. ... First, you should know that I arrived from Rome just a few weeks ago. Before I left, the Lady Antonia Minor, Augustus's niece, asked me to become her *epitropos* in Egypt. In Latin, that would be called a procurator although that is a pretty broad translation. The point is Antonia asked me to relieve and replace her current land agent whom she suspects has been cheating her."

The girl nodded that she was following so far and responded, "So, I assume Antonia gave you some sort of official document stating that she has given you this authority?" Alexander nodded 'yes' and she continued, "Then where is the problem?"

Alexander shrugged. "The problem is the land agent does not want to be relieved of his authority. That man is nothing more than a jumped up freedman, but he flat out refused my summons to come see me in Alexandria. Now he appears to be hiding from me while spreading ugly rumors. It would not matter so much except that this man -- Hierax is his name -- has all of the records for Antonia's estates – everything like contracts, leases, rents paid and owed. I *need* those records."

He made a fist and shook it in frustration.

Leah seemed to consider, then asked, "So, this Hierax is *hiding* everything from you? ... not just himself, but also the records you need?"

Alexander nodded his head and added, "Not only that, he started collecting Antonia's rent money early and now he has all of that money and goods stashed somewhere that only he knows. I will have to find all of that, too."

"I see," the girl continued. "And, I assume you have asked around for him?"

Alexander held up his hands palms up. "Yes, of course I have. He is not in his house in Tebtunis. I have traveled north of the Lake and no one has seen him up there. Then I traveled south of the Lake and no one has seen him down there. I don't think he has headed for Alexandria, or left the province, but ... *where* is he? And where has he hidden Antonia's money?"

Leah nodded knowingly. "You have a *mystery* to solve."

Alexander frowned. "Yes, I suppose I do, although I guess I did not realize it at first. I just thought Antonia's land agent was being annoying, but now I realize it is something more. He has disappeared and so have all her records, the wheat, the money, even animals have gone missing."

"*Uh huh,*" Leah continued, "You are telling me the man is not just avoiding you, but he seems to have found a really good *hiding place*. *Hmmm*, a hiding place. ... Have you considered the Great Labyrinth?"

"The what?" Alexander asked.

The girl was warming to her topic. "The Great Labyrinth of Egypt. I thought that everybody had heard of it. You do realize that it is not much more than five miles from where we are sitting right now? Really, when you think about it, what better place to hide than in a labyrinth?"

She paused and nodded vigorously. "... and *I* will tell you what else. *I am* going there tomorrow to see it. *You* may come along with us and then we can look for your missing land agent when we get there."

Alexander raised his eyebrows. "I *know* what the Great Labyrinth is. It is an Egyptian temple and *not* a place for young Jewish ladies."

Leah quickly interrupted. "*I know* that, I know. I will *not* be trying to feed crocodiles again or anything like that. But the Great Labyrinth is supposed to be worth seeing even if you never enter the main temple building, and most people don't. There's a pyramid there, and decorative columns and statues. And there's a whole underground cemetery, too, just beyond the pyramid. There are supposed to be lots of carvings and paintings and things to see."

Alexander leaned back and rubbed at his chin. "Actually, I did not know all of that," he responded.

It was interesting, but Alexander wasn't sure what to think about making a trip to this Great Labyrinth. He should get more information before deciding if it would be worth his time. Since, Alexander would be meeting up later with the nome *strategos*, he decided to solicit Dion's opinion on whether the short trip could be helpful. Even though it wasn't far, it would take up another day of his itinerary. Alexander was starting to feel the pressure to get his business done and return to his father in Alexandria.

He told Leah that he wasn't sure if he would go yet, but that he would have his servant Amarantus deliver a message later to let her know for sure.

"That will be fine," Leah replied. "But I will probably be busy, so have him ask for my lady companion, the one you saw with me before. Her name is Hannah."

Alexander agreed he would. Then with a polite farewell, he left to meet up with Dion who was fast becoming a new friend -- his first in Egypt.

Since the *strategos* wasn't Jewish, Alexander had declined

his invitation to dinner. When he lived in Rome, Alexander had learned how to follow a somewhat looser version of the dietary laws by avoiding shellfish and pork, or not eating milk and meat together. It took effort, but it still wasn't the same as being fully observant. Since that night Alexander was staying again with the Archon of the local synagogue, there was no reason for him to compromise on the dietary laws at meals.

Instead of dinner, he arranged to meet Dion at the same beer house where they had first met.

****

"What about this Labyrinth?" Alexander asked the *strategos* that evening as they sat on stools in the beer house. "It's been suggested to me that Hierax could be hiding there. Would that be possible?"

With elbow on the table, Dion placed on palm on his cheek and considered. "The Great Labyrinth? *Weeell*, it is not too far from here, just a few miles. Since you are in the area already you should consider a visit. The Great Labyrinth is famous all around the world. ... but, could Hierax be hiding, there? *Ennnh*, I don't think so."

Alexander raised his eyebrows. "Why not? It seems to me that a huge maze would be a good place to hide."

The *strategos* was already shaking his head. "No. The Great Labyrinth is *not* a maze. –well, it is, but not in the way you are thinking."

Alexander held out his hands, palms up. "*Well yeeees*, I am assuming it is some type of maze. That's usually what a labyrinth is, is it not?"

Dion sort of wagged his head back and forth. "It is confusing to me, too. I myself have only seen a small part of it once. ... Let me tell you what I know. You see, the Great Labyrinth in Haueris is actually a building; a really large temple. It is said that it consists of 3,000 rooms, half are above ground and half exist below ground. Of course, we have cellars in Egypt, but to have such a huge structure below ground is quite unique."

"Even if only half –1,500 you say? – rooms are on the surface that must still be huge. So how big is this place?" Alexander asked.

The *strategos* scratched the back of his neck. "Well, I'm not exactly sure, but I think I have heard that it is around a thousand feet long. There's a pyramid on one end, and beyond that is a necropolis – two actually. There is one for the mummified crocodiles and one for the people."

"So the Labyrinth is a temple to the crocodile god, then?"

Dion shrugged. "That is another thing that no one knows, well no one who hasn't been initiated. There are a lot of mysteries and secrets at the Labyrinth. For sure, Sobek is worshipped there. There are paintings and carvings of him all over. But most people think the temple is dedicated to another god. Some say it is even more important than the Apis Bull at Memphis, so it could be a sun god like Amen-Re."

Alexander considered for a moment then said, "I understand that the Labyrinth is a building, a temple, and it is big and mysterious, but *why* is it called a labyrinth if it is not a maze?"

"That much I do know," Dion smiled. "It is because of the layout and design of the interior of the building. Apparently, there is no symmetry, no known logic, no geometric consistency. As I noted there are a lot rooms -- offices, storage rooms, galleries, audience chambers and so on."

He held up his index finger to stop Alexander from

interrupting. "Every room is unique both in its size and shape, but especially in the way that all of the rooms are connected. There are no straight hallways or direct ways to get from one room to another. Sometimes to get to one room, you have to follow a circular, or maybe a zig-zag pattern through several others. The floor plan is so complex that no normal person can find their way through the structure. Once inside, one loses all sense of direction. Thus it is called the Great Labyrinth. Only the initiated can find their way around inside the building."

Alexander scrunched his eyebrows, "Why design a building that would be almost unusable?"

The *strategos* held up his palms. "Well, *I* don't know. I suppose if I thought about it, I would guess something about symbolism, maybe mystical shapes. Remember that the Egyptians were probably using geometry long before the Romans, or even the Greeks were. I'm not much with mathematics, but someone told that their pyramids had something to do with special geometry ratios, and those have something to do with astronomy, and especially the sun. And the sun was the most important god to the pharaohs and …. I don't know what else."

Dion gave Alexander a rueful smile. "I think I have already exceeded my limited knowledge on this topic. I guess I could just say that the strange design of the temple at Haueris may have something to do with geometry, and symbolism, and astronomy, and the Egyptian gods." He threw his hands up in the air. "Anything more is way beyond me."

Alexander returned his smile and nodded. "I understand – or at least understand that I will *never* understand. Fortunately, I don't think I have any interest in the temple itself. However, I have heard that the grounds outside the temple have many structures. Is that so?"

"Yes, that is so, both above ground and underground," Dion

replied.

Alexander continued. "And would it be worth my time to see if Hierax is hiding there? He doesn't appear to be north or south of the Lake. He's also not east of the Lake. I have checked in Philadelphia, Bacchias, Karanis, Socnopaiou Nesos, and I've sent word at every stop along the Desert Canal. He is not going to be west of the Lake since that is a desert." Alexander shook his head and raised his shoulders. "He must be somewhere."

The *strategos* nodded slowly. "I see your point. Hierax may be a Roman citizen, but he is just a freedman. I think his status would be too low for him to get an appointment to be taken inside the main temple itself. And, of course, no one goes into the pyramid because that is a tomb and it is sealed. ...

"... But you are correct that there are many exterior structures. There are all types of artisans and other services. ... Also many of the people in Crocodilopolis are entombed at the necropolis and the families often go there and spend the day visiting the tombs. It is such a common practice that Hierax would certainly know about the Labyrinth, the necropolis, and all the out buildings."

Dion frowned, "I don't know, Alexander. I suppose Hierax could be there."

Alexander tapped at his chin with his forefinger in thought. "It is not like I currently have any other leads. Plus, I know of a group traveling to visit the Great Labyrinth tomorrow. ... I think I will accompany them. *Hmm*, Antonia doesn't own any land around Haueris yet, but perhaps she should. It couldn't hurt to look the place over from a business sense while I am there."

He gave a quick nod to himself. "Yes, I can make this a good use of my time. I shall look for that wretched freedman and also look for local opportunities. I'm developing a plan for buying and selling Antonia's properties to consolidate land parcels so that more of them will be contiguous. ... and I'm not sure what else I'll do yet. I'm no farmer, but I'm working on it."

The *strategos* nodded his understanding. "I wish I could accompany you tomorrow, but I have some petitions I need to investigate. I wish you luck, Alexander. I hope you find your man."

****

"Master, Look."

Amarantus touched Alexander's arm to get his attention and pointed.

"Could that be the same man that we saw in Karanis?"

That morning Alexander and Amarantus had joined young Leah, her lady companion Hannah and the small troop of servants who were traveling with them. It had taken no more than two hours to reach the nearby Great Labyrinth travelling first by barge and then by donkey cart. The small party had spent the past hour wandering around the Great Labyrinth admiring the architecture and studying the carvings on the pyramid.

Now Alexander followed his servant's pointed finger to see the back of a man in the distance. He squinted in the bright sunlight and gauged that the man was medium height and medium build, maybe a few gray streaks in his dark hair. Alexander couldn't see the man's face, but since he had never met Hierax he wasn't sure what he looked like anyway. But what Alexander did have was a general description of the land agent and, perhaps more importantly, a description of his clothes. Apparently, Hierax had a couple of fancy tunics that he wore everywhere and Alexander had a good description of each of them. That man up ahead was wearing a blue tunic that seemed to fit the description well enough.

"Ranti, you may be right," he nodded. "I think he is headed for the necropolis over there. I'm not sure if a necropolis would make a suitable hiding place for a man, but I guess I will find out."

Alexander thought for a moment, then nodded to himself. "I'm going after him. I won't know if he's the right man until I talk to him, but I need to try. ... You, Ranti," he pointed, "I want you to stay here with the ladies. I believe they are expecting my protection so I can't leave them alone for very long. If they notice I am gone, please explain to them that I'll return very shortly."

With that, Alexander stepped away following in the direction of the unknown man in the blue tunic. As he got closer, Alexander realized that the necropolis was primarily underground. Fortunately, at the entrance he was able to rent the use of a small clay oil lamp. The merchant asked if he would like to wait for a guide to take him through the tombs.

Alexander considered it, but decided to go on alone. For one thing, he had already lost sight of the unknown man whom he was following. It was likely that the man had entered the necropolis, but Alexander had not actually seen him do it. Alexander felt he should keep moving or he would lose track completely of the elusive land agent – assuming the man in the blue tunic even was Hierax.

The oil lamp fit easily into the palm of his hand and provided only a small amount of illumination and a lot of background shadows. It would have to suffice. Alexander descended the mud brick steps into the cellars where the tombs were kept. He reached the bottom to a complete blanket of silence. Somehow he had thought he would hear the other man's echoing footsteps ... or *anyone's* footsteps for that matter. But, no, this underground burial site was utterly quiet.

Alexander did not know the floor plan of a typical Egyptian

cemetery, and certainly not the layout of this underground one. In front of him stretched out a long corridor. Looking ahead, Alexander could see that there were a few torches in sconces on the wall, but they were spaced very far apart. The torches provided some faint illumination in the gloom, but Alexander had to admit that being in this dark cellar filled with tombs of the dead was … well, *disconcerting*.

Alexander hesitated then decided that there was nothing for it but to move forward. With his small oil lamp held high, he stepped forward slowly. The floor was paved and seemed to be level. After twenty or thirty feet, Alexander realized there was another hallway that split off perpendicular to the one he was on. Peering down it, he could not see even a glimmer of light. *Hmmm*, the man he was following was unlikely to have turned in there.

He continued to pace down the central corridor. Twice more Alexander passed connecting aisles. Like the first one, neither of these had any light shredding the darkness. He kept going deeper into the burial chambers. Up ahead, Alexander saw another passageway that led off the main corridor that he was on. This time, there was a faint glow of light shining out the entrance.

As Alexander reached the doorway, that faint light disappeared. *Hunh*, he had seen no one leave, so someone must still be in there. He wasn't happy about looking for a man who seemed to be wandering around in the dark, but if Hierax was down there … well Alexander wasn't going to hold back out of fear. But Lord, it was dark in there.

Holding his small oil lamp down so he could watch his step, Alexander moved into the side aisle and started to slowly edge his way toward the back.

The floor here was mud brick and not as level as the corridor from which he had just turned in. Alexander had paced maybe ten feet holding the oil lamp low so he would not trip over the uneven pavement. Small oil lamps were known for casting strange flickering shadows. In unfamiliar surroundings, they could feel gloomy. In this underground cemetery, however, the shadows were downright eerie and Alexander had to pause to rein in his imagination which was running rampant. *This* was *just* an underground room, like a cellar. There was *no one* here; *nothing* to be concerned about.

That was when he heard the sound.

Alexander startled and muttered, "*Merda.*"

He had been holding the lamp low so he could watch his footing. Now he raised the lamp to look around, but he had lifted it too close to his face. The closeness of the flame in the inky darkness of the corridor caused Alexander to jerk his head back and turn his face away. He blinked and squinted trying to adjust his eyes to the light.

What was that? Another sound. From where? The passageway was creating a slight echo effect so he could not be sure of the direction. If that was an honest man who had made that sound, Alexander felt sure he would have called out. None of this sneaking up on strangers. Holding the oil lamp at arm's length, Alexander thought he heard a footstep and spun to his right.

In the light he could see a man's face no more than a foot away from his own.

"*Merda!*" Alexander swore again as he stepped back. How did that man get so close to him without him even realizing the man was there?

Alexander took another step back and whirled to his left. Another man's face loomed before him. Another? How did they *both* get so close without him hearing them?

Was he surrounded? His breaths started coming fast. Two steps backward and Alexander twirled again to his right. Another face, but this time it was a woman's. He hesitated; was this woman one of the would-be attackers, or was she a victim, too? Wait. What was wrong with her? She wasn't moving at all – just staring at him with wide open eyes. Oh Lord, could it be that the Egyptians made undead people to wander the halls of the necropolis? Alexander felt chilled and felt bumps rise along his skin.

Suddenly ... another sound. This time Alexander heard definite movement, soft footfalls, the swish of fabric. He twisted to see another face before him. Lord! It was the same unmoving woman's face he had just seen staring at him, except ... this one was moving. How could there be two of them?

Alexander sucked in a loud breath and took another two steps back. He shifted the oil lamp to his left hand and began to fumble to release his *xulons* from their sheath at his side. He wasn't sure how two men and two women had so silently sneaked up or what they wanted with him. But Alexander knew he wasn't going down without a fight.

A voice broke the silence; a woman's voice.

"*Umm*, you do realize they are just portraits, don't you?"

"*Huh? What?*" he grunted out loud. Alexander was still breathing hard.

The woman's voice responded. "Wait. Please, calm down. My name is Indike. I'm stepping forward so you can see me. Don't strike me, please."

A young woman moved in from the shadows. Holding his oil lamp up, Alexander studied her face, then turned and looked to his side. It was the same face, only this one was not moving. But wait ... it was ... *just a face*. There was no body below it. He whipped the oil lamp back around and studied the woman who had stepped toward him. *She* had a face *and* a body and she could move. He felt pretty sure that she wasn't one of the dead. The woman stopped a few feet away from him and smiled.

"This is your first time down in the tombs, isn't it?"

Alexander decided that she was definitely not dead. She sounded very much alive – and *amused*. Was she laughing at him?

The woman – Indike she had called herself -- took another small step forward. "You seem a bit taken aback by the portraits. That's how I guessed you had not been here before."

"The portraits?" Alexander echoed back dumbly.

Portaits? Portraits. Alexander moved his oil lamp around so he could study the faces that lined the passage around him. There. There were the two men who had just accosted him ... except they were just faces, no bodies. Portraits. *Hunh*. They indeed were just portraits, paintings of men's and women's faces. No men were attacking him. ... *How very embarrassing*.

Alexander heard an impatient snort and turned back to speak to the woman.

"Well, you got me on this one," he admitted. "These faces were ... most unexpected. ... Many of them are very realistic. I have never seen anything like these before."

"Not ever?" The woman seemed skeptical.

"Well, no. I recently came from Rome and there is nothing like these portraits there. Of course, there are statues and busts, and occasionally there are some people painted into frescoes that can be pretty accurate – but, no, there is nothing like this. Are there many of these? These portraits?"

The woman smiled, "Not that many yet. This style has only become popular for maybe the last ten years, maybe a little longer. I think the majority of the portraits are here in Haueris, but there are also some scattered all over the Arsinoite nome. I suppose there may be portraits all over Egypt, but I don't travel much so I wouldn't know."

Alexander moved over to the portrait of the unmoving woman he had noted earlier. He pointed and raised his shoulders in question.

Indike stepped over to the portrait hanging on the wall and nodded proudly. "Yes. This one is mine. What do you think? Is it accurate?"

Alexander was confused. "Well, I suppose it is. In fact, *it definitely is*. It is very well done. ... But, but why? Why would you have a portrait made and then stick it in this dark tunnel?"

Indike blinked back in disbelief. "Well, it is my *ka* of course. Or it will be after I die."

Alexander didn't think that had clarified things too much for him. "Your, *uhhh kaaah*? That's an Egyptian thing, right?"

Even in the dim lamp light, Alexander could see the angry look that Indike gave him as her voice raised. "*An Egyptian thing? An Egyptian thing?* Who are *you* to mock our customs?"

Still holding the oil lamp in his left hand, Alexander held out his right palm in what he hoped was a placating manner.

"Apparently, I am an idiot, or at least someone who did not consider his words," he responded. "I apologize. I truly do. You see, not only am I recently from Rome, but I am also a Jew and we never have images made of ourselves. So I do not know the local customs ... however, I *would like* to know. Indike, will you tell me about your portrait?"

Alexander held his breath and hoped that was a good save. The best way to deflect someone's anger was often to ask the person to talk about themselves. At least that had worked for him in the past for men. Women were harder to figure.

Indike narrowed her eyes and gave Alexander a suspicious look, but then decided he was probably being sincere. Plus, she really, really liked talking about her portrait.

"*Hmm*, well I cannot explain *everything* to you as I would to a child, but simply put, after a person dies their body in prepared for the afterlife. However, the gods will not know who it is unless there is some image to represent the deceased. That is our *ka*. The *ka* has always been present at the tomb, but this style of representing the *ka* is somewhat new. It was only when Greek painters moved to Egypt, that this style was developed."

She looked up at Alexander and he nodded that he was following, so she turned back and gestured to her portrait.

"As you can see, this is not a fresco; it is not painted on the wall. The painting is on a wooden panel so it can be moved to where it is needed."

Alexander held up the lamp and looked at the portraits around him and turned back to Indike. "But you are still young. You don't look like you are about to die. In fact, most of these people look like they are in their twenties. Don't tell me they are all about to die ... or are they already dead?"

Indike let out a little laugh. "No, I am *not* about to die, pray to Isis. And probably none of these others are dying either. In Egypt, we spend many of our years preparing for our afterlife. In this case, it means having our portrait – our future *ka* – made when we are still young because that is how we hope to look in the afterlife. More importantly, though, we know that death can sometimes come suddenly. We wish to have our *ka* ready in case that happens."

Alexander nodded slowly. "Yes, I think understand that ... but tell me, why were you wandering around the corridors in the dark?"

Again Indike laughed. "I was not."

She held out her left hand and showed an unlit oil lamp. "The oil in the lamp ran out. I came to see my portrait and then I walked farther to see another portrait, one of my mother. I must have stayed too long, because my oil lamp went dry and the light went out. Since I have only been here once before, I was very worried about finding my way out until I saw your light and headed towards it."

Alexander nodded back to the wall. "Then you plan to keep your portrait here until you die?"

"Perhaps. Perhaps not," Indike shrugged. "If someone has their own house, they often hang their portrait on the wall. It is considered a mark of status." She shook her head. "I am not married yet so I have no home of my own. It is better to keep it here and hope that one day soon I will have my own house where I can hang it on the wall -- until it is needed for my afterlife."

Indike gave Alexander a quizzical look. "If you are not here about a portrait, then *why* are you here?"

Alexander could have smacked his own forehead. Shortly after he had entered the tombs, he seemed to have completely forgotten why he was even here. They were just that *eerie*. Perhaps it was not a lost cause.

"Actually, I was following a man. – I just need to talk to him," he added as Indike gave him a suspicious look. "Perhaps you saw him? He was wearing a good blue tunic with embroidery."

Indike held out a hands palm up. "I'm sure there are several men who dress like that. Having one's portrait made is still costly, mostly only the rich can afford it. Does this man you are following have a name?"

"He does. His name is Hierax, he is a freedman of the Lady

Antonia Minor in Rome and he has been working as her land agent."

Indike bit her lower lip and slowly shook her head. "I know Hierax, or at least know of him. My parents lease land from Antonia and I know they pay him the rent." She thought a moment. "I do know what Hierax looks like and I have never seen him in this area at all – not in or out of the tombs. My portrait was painted outside the Great Labyrinth where there was daylight. Before I came for my portrait, I was here for my mother's and my brother's, so I have been several times.

"I have never seen Hierax in this area," Indike repeated. "But that, of course, doesn't mean that he has never been here. I can only speak to what *I* have seen – or I guess I should say *not* seen."

"So, definitely not today? " Alexander pressed. "You did not see him come into the necropolis shortly before I did?"

Indike let out an exasperated gasp. "What is your name?"

"Oh, apologies, I should have said. It is Alexander – Gaius Julius Alexander. Now that I have returned to Egypt, the Lady Antonia has asked me to take over management of all her estates everywhere."

Indike nodded slowly, "Well, Alexander, when I just told you that I have *never* seen Hierax in this area, the word *never* did include today. Please believe that I do know what the word *never* means."

She smiled to take away the sting of her remark and Alexander couldn't help but smile back. Indike was obviously clever and in the lamp light he could tell that she was an attractive young woman, as well. *Hmmm,* if her parents leased land from the Lady Antonia, then it was likely he would be seeing her again.

Once again Indike broke into his musings, "Alexander? ...

Look at your lamp. I have a feeling that you do not have a lot of oil left. May I suggest that we both depart at once before it runs out?"

She was right. Of course, she was right. The oil lamp wasn't empty yet, but there was unlikely to be much more time for exploring. Alexander nodded his acknowledgement.

"Yes, a good notion." He gestured downwards. "The bricks in the floor are uneven here. May I suggest that you hold onto my left arm and I will hold out the lamp in front of us. Then, hopefully, we will make good time and be out of here before the oil runs dry."

With Indike holding onto his arm and a sputtering oil lamp held before them, they somehow managed to awkwardly find their way out of the passageway without getting their legs entangled as they edged forward step by step. Once they got into the main corridor the light of the occasional torch did help. Still arm in arm, they climbed the last few steps and stumbled outside, both laughing as the oil lamp went out just as they passed back into the daylight.

Indike tugged on Alexander's arm and pointed with her chin. "Are *they* with you?"

Looking up, Alexander realized that not too far away was the party that he had recently left behind for this foray into the necropolis. The girl Leah had her arms crossed before her and was giving him a strange look. So was Hannah her lady attendant. Well, Alexander had always been clear that he was here to look for the land agent. If they were upset that he had left them for just a few minutes to seek Hierax, what was he to do about that? It was not like they had been abandoned. They had their own men servants and he had left Amarantus with them.

Speaking of whom, Alexander could see that his servant was eager to tell him something.

"What is it, Ranti?"

"Master, the man we were watching came back out. I don't know if you saw him yourself, but I do not think he was Antonia's land agent."

Ranti shook his head to reinforce his opinion. "From the back, he may have looked similar, but *we saw* him from the front." He gestured at Leah, her companion Hannah, and then back at himself.

"The man we just saw had a scar, a long one, down his right cheek. So far, no one has described Hierax as having such a scar, so *we think*," again he gestured at Leah, Hannah, and back at himself, "that he is not the man that you are seeking."

Indike spoke up. "It is true, Alexander. As I told you, I know what Hierax looks like and he does not have such a scar."

Alexander pressed his lip together and with difficulty refrained from swearing. If Ranti was correct, and Indike as well, then Hierax was probably not in this area – probably never was in this area. Once again, he had wasted his time looking for the wretched freedman.

"Humph."

About the same time that he heard the sound, he felt an elbow nudging him in the side. Startled from his thoughts, Alexander looked up to see Leah was looking at him, then turning her head to look pointedly at Indike, and then back at him again. He turned and realized that it was Indike who had elbowed him and she was looking pointedly at Leah and back at him.

He placed his palm on his forehead. "My manners. I apologize." He gestured to his side. "This is Indike from Crocodilopolis. Her parents lease lands from the Lady Antonia so their contract will be part of my new responsibilities."

He gestured in front of him. "And this young lady is Leah.

She is visiting from Judea where her father is ... did you say he was a merchant?"

Leah seemed to hesitate, then nodded. "Yes, Abba – my father – is a merchant. Jacob, the merchant. We live in Jerusalem." She turned to her side. "This is my traveling companion, Hannah."

Alexander nodded. "Oh and, Indike, this is my man Amarantus. He is my secretary among other things, so there is a good chance he will be acting in the Arsinoite nome. You can tell your family to assume that he speaks with my full authority."

The ensuing small talk after the introductions were made seemed awkward, but Alexander wasn't paying much attention. He was thinking that this was another lead on the land agent that had gone nowhere. He had come all the way to this Great Labyrinth for nothing.

Suddenly, he blurted out, "This trip was a bust. I can't believe I have wasted another day."

Indike, Leah, and Hannah stopped chatting and turned to stare at him. Then they turned and looked at each other. Amarantus pursed his lips and raised his eyes to the sky.

Alexander did notice that all conversation had suddenly stopped, but it took a few moments more -- and a few meaningful looks from Ranti -- before it finally did occur to him that he had been less than gracious to the ladies. Actually, he had been flat out rude. He could do no more that day about the land agent so he needed to push those thoughts out of his mind. –And for now, he would apologize and try to enjoy the rest of his day with the lovely Indike and the feisty young Leah.

And indeed he did. Alexander had a surprisingly enjoyable time. Leah's attendants had brought a picnic lunch and he and Amarantus had found a shady spot under a small grove of date palms. Both he and Leah had insisted that Indike join them and she turned out to have a wealth of knowledge about the Great Labyrinth and the whole area in general.

Although they did not go inside the Great Labyrinth temple building itself, Indike guided them on a tour around it telling them about the architecture, the statues, and the carvings on the pyramid. She was very amusing, occasionally pointing at an engraving of a god and then launching into a tale of one of the god's adventures often with him or her acting as a trickster. They leisurely wandered, rested, stopped at a booth for honey cakes. Soon they were all chatting as if they had quickly become old friends, despite their many outward differences.

Long before dusk, they all returned to Crocodilopolis. Indike had picked up her family's man servant in Haueris and they rode on the same barge together. Before they had arrived back in the nome's capitol, Alexander had a thought. He whispered it to Amarantus who took off in a hurry as soon as he could disembark. Alexander begged the ladies to wait just a few minutes longer before returning to their houses. They cast a curious look at him and then in the direction in which Amarantus had gone and then at each other, shrugged and kept chatting.

Fortunately, it did not take long for Amarantus to return carrying a small basket. Alexander gave a formal bow and spoke, "Ladies, I know I was inexcusably rude at least once today. Yet you still honored me with your company and a most enjoyable day. I wish to give you each a small token to show my gratitude to you for sharing your precious time with me today."

Perhaps those words were too formal? Too impersonal? Alexander didn't know so he moved quickly. Amarantus opened the basket revealing three parcels wrapped in wool, each about the length of a man's palm. Alexander took them out one by one and presented them to Indike, Leah, and Hannah. They were three of the glass blown pieces he had purchased in Karanis, not the bigger ones, but the smaller cosmetic vials that he had first noted. Each one was different but of finely shaped colored glass and the obvious work of a true artisan.

Alexander was pretty sure that the ladies each liked their gift, but the response was different from each of them. Hannah was demure. She dipped her head and murmured a shy thank you. Indike accepted with a gracious nod of her head. He had a feeling that a lovely young woman like Indike was accustomed to receiving a lot of little gifts. But then Indike captured his eyes, tilted her head, lowered her lashes, and gave him a little smile. Alexander found it … charming.

Little Leah, though, had yet a different reaction to her gift. She cupped both hands around the little glass vial and then lifted it before her as if it were some precious offering.

"*Ah*, I see yours is the purple design," Alexander said to her. "That was one of my particular favorites. I ordered several matching pieces for my home in Alexandria."

Leah's eyes shone as she looked up at Alexander. Those weren't tears were they? No, of course not; why would they be?

"Oh, Alexander of Alexandria, this is the most special gift I have received in a long time. I shall keep it with me always."

Alexander was glad Leah liked it, but her response seemed perhaps just a little too effusive. She obviously came from a wealthy family. No doubt, she had many glass cosmetic vials at home. He could think of no reason why Leah should consider the one he gave her to be more special than any other. Still, Alexander smiled at her and said that he was pleased she liked it.

Later that evening back in the Archon's house in Crocodilopolis, Alexander stopped to ponder why he had such a feeling of inner calm, of ease. Could it be that it had been weeks since he had a chance to spend some leisure time with some interesting company? No, that couldn't be so. Alexander had visited with Dion and Sabinus at the beer house twice now.

...But today felt different. Was it because he had spent the day in the company of such lovely and intelligent ladies? It occurred to Alexander that maybe ... maybe today felt different because he had been ... *lonely? Hunh.*

206 *Kass Evans | Toga in the Wind*

14. Melee

"I find that I am in agreement with the villagers. That *nothus* is a thief."

Sabinus grinned back across their small table in the beer house. "A thief, *eh*? How do you figure that, Alexander?"

"I know he is a thief, because he has stolen the last of my patience."

Sabinus snorted. Dion made a thin smile. Back in Crocodilopolis and back in the beer house, Alexander was expressing his growing frustration to his new acquaintances.

He blew out a breath and ran both hands through his hair. "I realize now that searching for Hierax at the Great Labyrinth was a long shot idea. It's just that I can't think of where to look next. Since I've never met the man, I don't know his habits or what to expect from him."

The *strategos* Dion shrugged, "I suppose you could always check with his friends. Maybe they know where he is."

Alexander stared; then he dropped his head with a groan. "*Of course.* Of course, that's the answer. Everyone has told me over and over right from the beginning that Hierax '*runs with the bastards.*' Those are the priests of Kronos, right? And they're all in Tebtunis, aren't they?"

The *strategos* nodded in agreement. "Yes. One or two of them may travel occasionally, but all of the priests of Kronos in

Egypt are in the village of Tebtunis. And they are all associated with the temple of the crocodile god Soknebtunis. ... Soknebtunis and Kronos are two aspects of the same crocodile god, of course. In Egypt, gods sharing a temple is common enough."

Alexander looked from Dion to Sabinus. "So how do you think I should do this? Should I just go to the Soknebtunis temple and ask if there are any Kronos priests around?"

Sabinus gave a careless wave of his hand. "You could do that. Or you could just ask Kronion – that's my former woman's son. "

Alexander turned his attention to Sabinus. "Kronion? *Umm*, didn't you say that you had a priesthood created for him?"

"Oh, yeah," Sabinus replied nodding his head. "He's a priest of Kronos at the crocodile temple in Tebtunis. More to the point for you though, Kronion seems to know Hierax quite well. Probably he could tell you where your missing land agent is. You just tell Kronion that it was *I* who sent you. He'll assist you if he can."

Alexander rubbed slowly at his chin. "Sabinus, that is ... helpful, very helpful. Indeed, that is exactly what I will do. *Hunh*. It looks like I'll be travelling to Tebtunis after all."

Dion tilted his head thoughtfully and sucked at his lower lip. "I think I will go with you, Alexander. Tebtunis is within my area of responsibility in the nome and I do try to travel to each village as much as I can."

Alexander gave Dion a grateful nod. "Good. We leave tomorrow."

****

"Master, I found the crocodile temple and asked for Kronion as you told me." Amarantus had just returned to the house in Tebtunis where Dion and Alexander were staying.

"The Kronos priests said that Kronion was not there, but that he is expected to be back by this afternoon. ... *Oh, and, uh,* Master, it appears they are having a festival."

Alexander snorted. *"Another festival?"* He turned to Dion. "Exactly, how many festivals a year does each village have?"

The *strategos* shook his head and shrugged. "Not that many – usually no more than thirty or so a year. Of course, some of the festivals last for multiple days and many of the villages also celebrate the Roman holidays as well – like Augustus's birthday. Overall, though, it is not that much."

Dion observed Alexander's skeptical look and decided to elaborate.

"This is not a bad thing, Alexander. Those festivals are good for the landlord and the workers. A few days a month, the people get to spend some time with music, dance, storytelling and then they come back refreshed and ready to work."

"Hmm," was Alexander's only reply.

Amarantus edged up to Alexander's side and whispered, "Master, if you can spare me later, I would like to go to the festival. They said someone will play a double flute and they have hired castanet dancers. I have never seen that before."

Dion smiled at Ranti's enthusiasm and turned back to Alexander. "Unfortunately, I will not be able to accompany you on your visit to young Kronion, Alexander. Nome business again; a land dispute has come up that I need to settle. However, if you are still here in two days I will travel back with you."

"Agreed," Alexander replied. "I can only hope that by then I have gotten a lead on Hierax. I am very tempted to go to his house and force my way past his annoying steward so I can search it."

"His steward?" Dion replied. "Oh yes. I guess I have heard that Hierax had acquired a steward for that little house of his. It doesn't surprise me one bit since he is always putting on airs. That man would do anything to make himself look more important, more elite."

"Elite, *huh*? *I* will show him elite," Alexander said as he pointed both thumbs at the two *clavi*, the narrow purple stripes on his white tunic. Alexander nodded firmly to himself. "I have decided. That is what I will do. First, I will make every effort here in Tebtunis to find his whereabouts. After all, he is a Roman citizen so I will give him that much courtesy. But if I can't locate him, then I *will* start searching his property and confiscating whatever I need."

Dion shook his head. "*I cannot* give you permission for that, Alexander. I am just the *strategos*. If you wish permission to enter and search the house of a Roman citizen, you will need a higher authority than mine. Believe me, *Marcus Antonius* Hierax is very aware of his rank and status of being the Lady Antonia's freedman. He will use that to thwart you if he can."

Alexander was not deterred. "*If* he can. I doubt very much that his influence could exceed mine, especially with the Lady Antonia backing *me*. ... That *asinus*. Let him try."

A short time later, Amarantus was guiding Alexander toward the largest temple in Tebtunis. The crocodile god Soknebtunis was the village's main deity and so his temple was situated in the most prominent location. Through the center of the village was a long causeway which was lined with statues of lions at rest. The temple of Soknebtunis and Kronos lay at the end of the causeway and was fronted by a large walled courtyard.

"Master, there was a procession and crocodile offerings this morning. I guess it was like what we saw in Karanis. Then everyone was supposed to rest during the hottest part of the day. Now the priests will be gathering in the temple courtyard for the next part of the festival. The temple servant told me that all of the priests of Kronos will be there. Since they have their heads shaved so oddly, we should be able find them easily and ask which one is Kronion."

Alexander had originally hoped that he would be able to go to the temple, talk to Kronion, learn the location of Hierax and get away before any further festival activities started up. He was a Jew. A festival for crocodile worship was not a thing he had any desire to attend.

That expectation was dashed as Alexander walked the causeway toward the temple and noticed the way was becoming increasingly crowded. People had lined the road as if expecting a processional, but instead of a feeling of happy anticipation there seemed be a sense of *tension* in the air. Alexander did not know if that was normal for worshippers at this festival, so he ignored the tension and kept walking toward the temple. The path was obvious and the temple was unmistakable.

As he and Amarantus neared the temple, Alexander pushed forward through the crowd hoping to see one of those Kronos priests. Before him was the courtyard spread out before the temple doors. *Hmm.* No priests were there – at least not yet. The crowds seemed to have left the space in the center of the courtyard open so something must be expected to happen there. Alexander didn't care; he just wanted to find Kronion and get out. He was already feeling too closed in by the crowds.

Around him there started a low murmuring and the crowds began to stir and shift. Almost as one, all of the people seemed to turn and look in the same direction, so Alexander turned and looked in that direction, too. Something was happening. There were loud voices chanting. In fact, he could hear the voices, well before he ever saw who was making the noise.

"Kronos! Kronos! Kronos!"

A line of white robed men appeared from one corner of the courtyard, somewhere from the shadows. They were all chanting the name of *'Kronos'* in unison. To Alexander's ear, it did not seem that the god's name was being invoked with any particular reverence. Indeed, he had heard similar sounding chants at the chariot races back in the Circus Maximus in Rome.

Alexander noted that the chanting men who approached from the far end of the courtyard each had shaved a circle on the top of his head leaving a fringe of dark hair hanging down around his ears.

The shaved pates made it pretty clear that these must be the priests of Kronos. The *strategos* had said that they were forbidden from shaving their heads completely since they did not have a legitimate priestly lineage. To Alexander, they looked ridiculous, but they seemed to wear their partially shaved heads with pride.

Then Alexander realized that each man, each of these priests of Kronos, carried a *xulon*; some men carried two. Unlike the two short sticks Alexander wore in a sheath at his side, these priests carried the full-sized *xulon*, each a good three to four feet long.

Alexander held his chin and frowned. *What was happening? Why were the Kronos priests armed? Were they expecting to have a stick fight?* Perhaps there was about to be some sort of ritual using the *xulons*?

Aaah, he thought. Perhaps, there was going to be a competition. Now, *that* would be worth seeing. The temples in Egypt had long traditions of training and fighting with the *xulon*. Whatever these priests were about to do with their sticks, it should be interesting. Alexander began to push forward into the crowd hoping to get a good view of whatever spectacle was coming.

Other than the constant chanting of the name *Kronos*, nothing seemed to happen at first. The crowd around Alexander continued to jostle each other and seemed to be growing increasingly restless. Then almost as one, everyone turned to look in another direction. A new chant came up from the opposite side of the courtyard.

"The great, great god commands you! The great, great god commands you! The great, great god commands you!"

This new group appeared to be the more traditional priests. They were also dressed in white tunics, but their heads were completely shaved. Like the Kronos priests, each man carried one or two *xulons*, as well.

Alexander looked from one group of priests to the other. *What was going on?* Was this the first part of a *xulon* ritual? The people in the crowd around him seemed to have a look of anticipation. Of course, as a Jew he didn't know what was normal for Egyptian rituals ... *but* something didn't feel quite right to him. The crowd had started splitting itself in two directions. Some went to the side of the priests chanting '*Kronos*.' Others moved in the direction of the traditional temple priests. *Huh.* Perhaps, there would be a competition and these would be the sides of the two challengers?

Alexander had not noticed how far he had edged into the temple crowd, until he realized that he was being swept into the direction of the traditional priests. As the crowd converged around him, he was being shouldered and shoved forward. Since Alexander didn't speak Egyptian, he had not recognized at first the angry mutterings that were coming from the people on every side. The mutterings weren't directed *at him*; no, not at all. The anger was being aimed in the opposite direction – at the priests of Kronos. And the followers of the priests of Kronos appeared to be giving it right back.

At almost six feet tall, Alexander stood half a head above most of the crowd. Egyptian men were typically no taller than 5 foot, 6 or 7 inches. Despite his slight height advantage, Alexander stood up on the balls of his feet trying to get a better view. From what he could see, the crowd had definitely split into two opposing sides. On the far side were the Kronos priests surrounded by what must have been their followers. Facing them were the traditional priests of Soknebtunis.

The followers on both sides had started shouting insults, shaking fists, or brandishing *xulons*. --At least Alexander thought they were mutual insults. The priests of Kronos were shouting in Greek and those words he could understand, but the traditional priests and their followers were shouting in Egyptian. The angry tone was pretty clear, even when their words were not.

Looking around him, Alexander realized this was *no* ritual, *no* sporting competition. *This was a mob* – and it looked like soon there would be a riot. He had thought that he might get to see a competition with the *xulons*. Now he was pretty sure otherwise and Alexander knew that *he should not be here*.

He tried to move back, but the crowd was too dense behind him. Indeed, Alexander realized that he was only two men deep from the very front. He had a good view of the courtyard, but that was *not* what he needed at the moment. What he needed was to find a way clear before any trouble started. Alexander was a Roman and a Jew. Whatever was about happen with the crocodile priests, it was *not his* fight. Alexander reached down and patted the *xulons* in the sheath at his side. It was good that they were there, but he hoped he could slip away with no need to use them.

There was a sudden increase in the crowd noise directing Alexander's attention forward. One of the priests of Kronos with the distinctive shaved circle on his head had stepped forward with a *xulon* in each hand. While the other Kronos priests wore tunics, this one wore a kilt – white linen pleated and knotted in the front.

Over his shoulders and chest were wrapped padded bandages to protect his body.

Hmm, Alexander thought that this might be the Kronos high priest; or, perhaps he was their champion. Whichever one he was, this priest was issuing some sort of angry challenge. The Soknebtunis priests had not responded yet, but then slowly their line parted creating a path down the middle.

"*Wooooh*," the crowd moaned, some in awe, some in fear.

Alexander soon realized why. Out through the front line of the traditional priests stepped the great, great god Soknebtunis himself. He looked just as Alexander had seen him depicted on various carvings on temples. The god was tall with the body of a man and the head of a crocodile. He was wearing the royal blue and white striped headdress of the pharaohs. Like his Kronos opponent, the crocodile god wore a sheer kilt of the finest white linen, shoulder and chest padding. He also carried a *xulon* in each hand.

The sight of the living god appearing amongst them was too much for many in the crowd. Some began to swoon, others to simply sway and moan. Most eyes stayed on the center of the square where the crocodile god stepped forward and faced the priest of Kronos. Alexander could not see the crocodile's mouth moving, but the sound of his voice rang forth. Soknebtunis spoke in Egyptian so Alexander could not understand the words, but the god's intent seemed clear. He pointed at the Kronos priest then flicked one hand dismissively. Soknebtunis appeared to be ordering the Kronos priests away. A few more words, another dismissive gesture and the crocodile god turned slowly, disdainfully and started to walk away.

"*Whuuuuuh*," a collectively gasp suddenly sprang from the crowd.

The Kronos priest was stepping after Soknebtunis. He was

– *oh no, he really was* – he was going to strike at the god from behind. At the last moment, Soknebtunis whirled around and swept the Kronos priest's attacking *xulon* aside. There was only the barest hesitation, then the Kronos priest raised both his *xulons* and launched a renewed attack. The crocodile god Soknebtunis raised *his xulons* and answered in kind.

Alexander would have really liked to watch a man and a god fighting with sticks. Clearly, each was a master of the *xulon*. The crowd around him, however, had gone wild. When the Kronos priest had tried to strike the god Soknebtunis from behind, it ignited a battle among their followers.

In a flash, it seemed that everyone in the crowd, man or woman, had produced some sort of weapon. Not everyone had been armed with a *xulon*; in fact, most were not. Few peasants would have been able to afford the cost of a hardwood *xulon* and the training to use it. But a variety of other weapons appeared, especially staves and clubs, and what may have been farming implements.

It seemed that the followers of the priests of Kronos had come better prepared for a fight, and, they were now energetically laying into the followers of the traditional priests of Soknebtunis. At least it probably started that way. With all the yelling, shoving, and waving of weapons, Alexander wasn't sure how anyone could tell which side was which anymore. It looked to him as if everyone just seemed to start beating on whoever was nearby. Did they even know whether they were hitting friend or foe?

Unfortunately, Alexander was about to become an unwilling participant. Earlier, he had pushed his way near the front so he could see what was happening. That was a mistake. Now he had to extract himself from the middle of a giant brawl. He did *not want to fight*, but he would need to be ready to defend himself. Alexander opened the sheath at his hip and withdrew his two *xulons*. He had a brief flash of amusement about how he could tell the *xulon* master how his shorter sticks had saved him in this near shoulder-to-shoulder brawl.

... if they saved him. That moment of mental distraction had caused him to lose awareness of his immediate surroundings. Now, Alexander's eyes widened and he stumbled back as one - no two - separate clubs were descending toward his head. Defending against a club was different from a *xulon* or a staff. A club was usually heavier with more force behind the swing; it required greater strength to stop one. Still, Alexander hoped the standard positions he knew would work and he set his feet and then crossed he arms into an upward X. It should allow him to sweep the incoming clubs to the side rather than having to stop them outright – and it did at first. His left *xulon* knocked one incoming club off to the side.

A strong shoulder shove pushed Alexander out of the way of the right club that had been descending toward him. Alexander half stepped, half stumbled to the side, then his brows furrowed as he realized *who* had just shoved him. It was not someone who had come to fight beside him. No, apparently he had been blocking the way of a group of ... angry women. Several Egyptian women forced their way by him while screaming and waving clubs. One woman pointed her club in the direction of a Kronos priest and then with a string of Egyptian words the group of women rushed at him.

Alexander did not have a chance to see what became of them since he had to concentrate on defending from the fighters all around him. He berated himself for being so foolish as to get in the middle of all this. Priests of Kronos, or, priests of Soknebtunis? He did not know what their differences were and he did not care. All he wanted was to find Kronion and make Kronion tell where the wretched land agent was hiding.

But first, he had to get out of this mess. Alexander held his left *xulon* vertically before him, hopefully ready to block any attack from the front or either side. Then he flexed his elbow and held his right stick over his shoulder ready to swing down like a club. Slowly, he inched back trying to get away from the fight.

D-la—d-la—d-la – d-la – d-la – d-la – d-la.

Suddenly, Alexander heard a strange ululating call. This was immediately followed by *clack, clack, clack, clack.*

Huh? What? Alexander jerked his head around looking for the source of these strange new sounds. *Oh.* Over there. On top of the wall. *Hunh.* Two castanet dancers had climbed up onto the temple's courtyard wall and they were now clacking their instruments and swaying sinuously. Periodically, they trilled or let out another ululating call. Before long someone started slapping his thigh in time with the castanets. Then others started in as well picking up the beat.

The fight continued below them, but Alexander could see that a good number of the combatants were now nodding their heads to the rhythm of the castanet dancers' music. The scene was … astonishing. Alexander's mouth fell open and he just stared at the bizarre sight … *when he should not have.*

Suddenly, Alexander's knees buckled and he fell to the ground. It took but a moment to realize that someone had struck down on the end of the *xulon* that he had thrown over his shoulder. Nothing about his position had prepared him to be hit from behind. Forced to his knees, he felt a blow that skimmed across his right shoulder almost reaching his neck. *He was in danger.* Alexander threw his body to the left and then rolled onto his back so he could get his *xulons* up to protect himself.

The *xulons* would not be enough. He knew he needed to get to his feet before he got stomped into the ground, but Alexander could only stare wide-eyed as he saw a spear being thrust towards his chest. His mind was *too slow.* He needed to cross his *xulons*; he needed to prepare to block, but he was moving *too slowly.*

Alexander could not hold back a choking gasp as a *xulon* came out of nowhere and jabbed his assailant so hard in the chest that he might have heard ribs crack. Both spear and assailant disappeared back into the mob. Alexander blinked and looked up to see his rescuer.

"I still say your stick is too short."

"Hunh. It's ... you," Alexander replied still lying flat out.

And it was. It was the man who had fought beside his *xulon* master back in Alexandria. The man who was Nubian, or, maybe part Nubian, who didn't speak much Greek -- except he had just spoken to Alexander in fluent Greek.

The man stuck out his hand and pulled Alexander to his feet. "You will rise now," he said. Then he seemed to smile, shook his head and added, "And next time, fight better."

Alexander was back on his feet, but still felt a little breathless. He wanted to thank the Nubian *xulon* fighter for his help, but before he could, the man was gone. Somehow they had moved onto the outskirts of the fighting. Alexander sucked in a huge grateful breath and continued to fall back away for the mob.

"Master, we did not have festivals like this in Rome." Amarantus had somehow appeared at Alexander's side gripping his own *xulon* and casually jabbing anyone in the belly that came too close.

Alexander laughed, relieved that his servant had been able to find him in the mob. "No Ranti, we did not. Those castanet dancers, in particular, certainly do add a bit of spice to a strange occasion." He gestured toward the two women who were still on the courtyard wall swaying and clacking away. "Look, they seem to be having a calming effect on the crowd."

Amarantus glanced up at the castanet dancers, but then used his *xulon* to point to a spot below the women in the middle of the courtyard.

"Perhaps the dancers are having an effect, master, but I think *that* is what is really controlling the fight. See there. The crocodile god is beating that Kronos priest really badly."

Alexander looked over to where the fight first began when the champion of the priests of Kronos had challenged the traditional priests. Then, their champion had tried to attack Soknebtunis from behind. … That had been a mistake.

As they watched, the crocodile god beat the Kronos champion to the ground and held the tip of a *xulon* to fallen man's throat. That changed the fight completely. All around, the mob stopped and let out varying noises – everything from moans of defeat to cries of victory. Suddenly, the followers of the priests of Kronos all broke and ran.

Amarantus let out a happy hoot and began poking their former assailants in their rears as they ran by. Alexander was trying to stay back to avoid the rush, but then a man staggered up and collapsed before him. Looking down he saw the curious shaved pate of a priest of Kronos. *Hunh.* Maybe tonight would not be a complete waste.

Alexander grabbed a handful of the man's tunic and dragged him backwards until he found a quiet spot in the shadows. After glancing around to make sure they were alone, Alexander squatted next to the priest, grabbed his shoulder and shook it.

"*Hey*, wake up."

With a groan, the Kronos priest opened one eye then closed it. Alexander gave his shoulder another vigorous shake.

"Are you Kronion?"

"Huh?"

"*Hey*, answer me. Are you Kronion?"

"No."

"Well, have you seen Kronion?"

"No."

Alexander squeezed the priest's shoulder harder and gave it another vigorous shake.

"Where is Kronion?"

The Kronos priest shook his head. *"I-* I don't know. He was supposed to be here, but he didn't show up."

"Well, I'm looking for him. Do you know where he might be?"

The Kronos priest shook his head again. "I don't know. Maybe he is with Hierax. He is with him often enough."

"That's good. That's good," Alexander tried to say encouragingly. "Kronion and the land agent may be together, but they are not at the land agent's house. Where else might they be?"

The priest groaned again. "How should I know? ... Maybe they are at the secret warehouse."

Alexander tried not to roll his eyes. "And where is this secret warehouse?"

The priest tried to sit up, but Alexander pushed him back down. *"Where. Is. It?"*

"If- If I tell you, will you let me go?"

Alexander looked down at the priest and saw a young man's face looking back at him, a boy really. He couldn't have been much more that sixteen or seventeen -- old enough to get himself *into* trouble, but not old enough to know how to get himself *out* of trouble.

"Yes," Alexander assured him. "I am really looking for the man Hierax. If that is his secret warehouse you mentioned, I need to go there. If you tell me where it is, I will help you get away unhurt."

The boy priest's eyes got big and then he nodded yes. "I should go home now. My father will want to know where I am."

"I think that is a good idea," Alexander said. "Last I saw, the priest of Kronos was taking quite a beating from Soknebtunis. I don't think you want to go back and share any of that. ... Tell me about this secret warehouse."

The young priest barely hesitated. "It *is* the warehouse of Hierax — just his. No one else uses it. He and Kronion are friends, so sometimes Kronion goes there to help him with – well, I don't know with what. Once, Kronion brought some of us there with him. Hierax wasn't there when we went. Mostly we just played dice, ate and drank beer. Kronion paid for the beer for everyone."

Again, Alexander resisted the urge to roll his eyes. "*Uh, huh.* Kronion sounds very generous. Now tell me. This warehouse. Where. Is. It?"

"It's not hard to find. Just take the road – the only road that runs southeast of Tebtunis. Stay on it for about two-three miles. Actually, it is not really a road. It's more of path of sorts. You would do well to take donkeys since that area isn't cultivated yet."

Alexander questioned him further, but the young priest didn't seem to have much more to add. So Alexander grabbed the young man under his arms and lifted him up. The kid was unsteady, but Alexander held onto him until he seemed to gain his feet. The boy brushed off his tunic and looked up at Alexander with big eyes. "May I go home now?"

"Yes," Alexander replied. "Do you know your way from here?"

The boy priest nodded his head vigorously. "Yes, yes. If I follow this wall, there will be a place where I can climb over and get into the village."

Alexander looked the boy in the eye. "Go straight home to your father. Do not stop at the beer house. Do not stop at the temple. Do not visit any your friends. Just go home."

He turned the boy around and gave him a gentle push in the right direction. The young priest of Kronos didn't hesitate, but took off running.

Alexander walked over to where he could see Amarantus was waiting for him. "Ranti, it appears that Hierax keeps some sort of warehouse southeast of here. It's not listed as one of the Lady Antonia's properties, but I have a feeling it's important. We'll hire a couple of donkeys and head out tomorrow. ... But first, I suppose I had better report this fight to the *epistrategos*."

Titus Serenius, the *epistrategos*, had asked Alexander to report any trouble he saw with the priests in Tebtunis. Serenius had even had his brother Philo write to him to remind him to do so. The melee fight they just witnessed certainly qualified as priestly trouble. So after returning to the home where they were staying with Dion, Alexander took out a small scrap of papyrus and wrote a quick message.

G. Jul. Alexander to Ti. Serenius, epistrategos of the Arsinoite nome. Many greetings and good health. Be advised that there was a mob fight in Tebtunis this very evening. It appeared that the priests of Kronos chose to challenge the traditional priests of Soknebtunis. I was present and saw a priest of Kronos strike the first blow using a xulon. All priests and many others present were armed with xulons and other weapons and there was a large fight between the two priestly factions and their supporters. I left soon after the fight began and am unaware of resulting injuries or property damage. As you requested, I report these actions to you. Farewell.

Hmm, now where to send it? Alexander wasn't sure if the *epistrategos* was in Alexandria or Crocodilopolis. Titus Serenius had indicated that he would come if the priests caused additional trouble. Finding someone to carry a message all the way to Alexandria would be difficult. The nome capital Crocodilopolis, on the other hand, was no more than 30 miles away by canal – much less by land. Getting a message there should not be too difficult.

Alexander decided he would send the letter to the imperial scribe for the nome who worked out of Crocodilopolis. Then if the *epistrategos* was not in the city, the scribe could arrange to have it sent on. An imperial scribe would certainly have established routes for exchanging mail with the government in Alexandria.

Alexander consulted with Dion on how to direct his letter. A *strategos* should know how to get a letter to his superior, the *epistrategos*. Dion not only knew, but went one better, and took Alexander to a camel driver who was about to leave for Crocodilopolis. Apparently, it was much cooler for camels to travel by night. Plus going overland would cut the distance in half of that of a barge on the canals.

After providing the camel driver with the letter and money, Alexander headed back to the house. He let out a long breath and felt relieved. That was his civic duty and now it was done. It was time to plan this trip to the secret warehouse and maybe -- just maybe –he would finally catch up with Hierax there.

15. An Evil Goat

Back at the house where he was staying in Tebtunis, Alexander found a private letter was waiting for him. Initially, he assumed it would be from his brother Philo, but the handwriting on the outside of the folded papyrus was not familiar.

> *Indike of Crocodilopolis to G. Jul. Alexander, greetings. I have sent this letter with the camel driver who is going to Tebtunis. Know that I have spoken with my parents regarding the land agent Hierax. Hierax came to collect the rent thirty-three days ago. He was paid in coin and wheat and there is a receipt. My father has consulted with others from the local villages who also lease land from the lady Antonia. No one has seen the land agent since that day. Farewell.*

Hunh. Alexander sat back and rubbed at his chin. It was good of his new acquaintance Indike to write to him with help for this mystery of the disappearing land agent. Young Leah had tried to help him, too, which was why he had even been at the Great Labyrinth in the first place. Alexander recalled how startled he had been at seeing the *ka* portraits in the necropolis. That, of course, had led to him meeting Indike and then spending a very pleasant afternoon with her and the little one, Leah. He smiled at the recollection.

Alexander pulled his thoughts back to the present and the contents of Indike's letter. *Hmmm,* so she writes that no one around

Crocodilopolis had seen the land agent in about thirty-three days. That would have been close to the time that crops and animals were reported missing from the villages of Philadelphia, Karanis and others. Indike's father had seen the land agent and had a dated receipt. The villagers up north of Lake Moeris said they had not actually seen the land agent, but thought he was the reason for at least some of their missing goods.

The time specified of thirty-three days ago was significant because that was about the earliest that Hierax may have heard that the Lady Antonia was sending Alexander to replace him. Alexander knew that Antonia had not written to her freedman beforehand. She had given Alexander a letter and left it up to him to decide how to break the news to the land agent. Still, there would have been enough people in Rome who knew of her decision that a letter could have been sent ahead to warn the land agent.

Would knowing of his dismissal in advance have caused Hierax to act so deceitfully? He *was* a Roman citizen whose patroness was Augustus's own niece. Would he have stooped so low as to have sneaked from property to property and taken rents and, apparently taxes, without leaving receipts and then hid that all away?

Alexander did not know, but he certainly needed to find out. Early the morning after the fight of the crocodile priests he and Amarantus were astride donkeys headed southeast of Tebtunis. They followed a simple dirt path that did not appear to be used regularly. After riding in silence for awhile, Amarantus broke into Alexander's thoughts.

"Master, was that really *a god* we saw? The crocodile man? He fought like a god – at least he beat the priest man."

"No, Ranti," Alexander shook his head and smiled. "I don't think that was a real crocodile god, although at first I was surprised and taken in myself. I am pretty sure that was just a man wearing a crocodile mask."

Amarantus looked disappointed. "Yes, I thought that, too. But it would have been good to have seen an actual god. We could have gone back to Crocodilopolis and told Indike, Leah, and Hannah all about how we fought beside a god with sticks. Master, I think that would have impressed them."

Alexander laughed. "Yes, Ranti, it probably would have – at least Indike. She's Egyptian and so she believes that their gods can take physical form. But remember, Leah is Jewish. She may be curious enough to want to see it for herself, but I imagine that she knows that a man in a crocodile mask is *not* our Lord God. Same for her companion Hannah."

Amarantus let go of his donkey's reins long enough to raise his hand palm up. "It is said that there is a lot of magic here in Egypt. Maybe we will be lucky and get to see a real god someday."

That was not an item on Alexander's list of things to be desired, but he merely smiled at his servant and they rode on.

There were no mile markers like there were on Roman roads, but after what felt like about two miles Alexander saw some buildings in the distance. He pointed them out. "Ranti, does that look like a secret warehouse to you?"

Amarantus lifted a hand to shade his eyes. "Master, I think it must be. There are no people in sight. In fact, look, there are no crops planted, no canal; no reason for anyone to be here. ... Wait. Master, are those cows? There," here pointed, "behind those two buildings."

Alexander looked to where his servant was pointing. "I think they are cows, Ranti. It looks like there are *four* of them. *Hmm.* That is the same number that are missing from Philadelphia."

He jabbed his forefinger toward the cows. "And *that* is not a typical cow pasture. Without a canal, there is no water source and no natural grass for feed. No one would deliberately raise cattle in that environment. I think that must be Hierax's secret warehouse. Let's go take a look."

The two young men rode their donkeys up next to a large rectangular structure that had several smaller buildings scattered around it. Alexander looked around, but he saw no sign that anyone was there. Nevertheless, he called out in Greek and then in the few words he knew of Coptic, the Egyptian language. There was no answer. That didn't feel right. Someone had to have been here recently. At the very least someone had to be coming to provide water and hay for the cows. Well, the place seemed to be abandoned now.

Alexander dismounted and walked up to the front of the largest building. It was made of mud brick and had a wooden door with a Roman-style iron lock. Amarantus took the reins of both donkeys and led them to a trough of water. *Huh*, a trough of water? Well, that proved that someone must have been here. Troughs of water did not last that long, this close to the desert.

"Ranti," he ordered, "walk around this building and see if there are any other doors or windows. While you do that, I'll check on these smaller structures."

As Amarantus walked away, Alexander turned toward the nearest building. It may have been a shed, although he supposed it could be used for various types of storage. Alexander nodded to himself. It was time to go exploring.

Just to be sure they were alone, he called out again. Once again, no one answered his hail, so Alexander concluded that there was no one around to hear him. So he wasn't paying enough attention to his surroundings at all ... not until he heard a soft footfall behind him and then felt the pain in his head as he slipped into darkness.

****

"*Ooooooo.*"

Alexander woke up feeling someone rubbing his face with a rough, wet rag. Slowly, he opened his eyes and immediately jerked his head back in alarm at the sight of a pair of big brown eyes staring deeply into his own. They were too big. His mind felt fuzzy, but he could tell those eyes were too big for a normal human.

"*Moooooo.*" In the dim light, he could see that someone was about to wipe his face with that rough, wet rag again.

Alexander tried to move out of the way, but could not. Vaguely, he realized that in fact he was quite immobile. He squirmed and felt around until he realized that his ankles had been tied together and his wrists were bound as well. Where was he? Inside somewhere, apparently, but where? The rough rag descended again.

"Stop it!" Alexander shouted. "Get away from me!"

The dark figure did move back a little and Alexander saw that he had been staring up into the soft, brown eyes of a ... red calf. As the tongue darted out, he realized what exactly had been wiping his face.

"*Ewww.*"

"*Moooooo,*" the calf seemed to low mournfully in reply.

"Indeed, little *uhh* cow," Alexander responded as he rubbed his cheek on the shoulder of his tunic. "I don't think either of us is happy to be here right now."

Fortunately, the red calf stopped trying to lick him and

moved away. As it did so, a shaft of light came through some palm fronds that made up the roof. It was enough light for Alexander to lift his head from the floor and inspect his surroundings. First, he checked his bindings. Both his hands and feet had been tied with a thick cord made from woven papyrus strips. *Huh*, this was probably better than if he had been tied with leather strips. Papyrus would stretch... eventually. He pulled hard with both arms, but his wrists remained tightly bound.

Alexander repeated his efforts with his legs straining to snap the papyrus cord. It held fast. Using the heels of his boots, Alexander was able to scoot backwards until he could sit up and lean against a wall ... but the wall of what?

"*Moooooo*," the little calf lowed again and moved farther away. This was followed by another sound. *What?* Was that a snort? Then *naaa*. Alexander's eyes were now becoming accustomed to the dim light filtering through the roof of the shed ... or was it a stable? No, no, it was too small to be a stable. One room, four walls. *Hmm*. It was a shed; not much of a shed, mostly reed stalks tied together and stuck vertically into the ground.

Alexander was currently resting his back up against the reed walls of a large shed. ... And his companions were a small red calf ... and, *uh*, behind her the snort had come from a ... wheat-colored mare. *Naaaa*. He looked past the calf and the horse and saw a truly evil looking billy goat. Alexander hadn't really thought of a goat looking evil before, but there was something about the huge deformed face of this goat that was just wrong.

It did not escape Alexander that he had received exactly three petitions for missing animals from the village of Karanis: one red calf, one wheat-colored mare, and one evil goat. He was nowhere near Karanis now, but what were the chances that these three animals could be anything other than the missing ones from Karanis?

Naaaa. Alexander cast a suspicious look at the evil goat and thanked the Lord that no one had claimed to be missing a big, cranky sow as well.

They were all shut into a shed that was about 12 feet square – too small for the current company. There was a door on the opposite wall, but there were no windows. What light and air there was came from gaps in the roof. Looking down, Alexander realized that he had been tossed onto a pile of hay – the *only* pile of hay in the shed. No wonder the animals all seemed to be regarding him so intently. He was blocking their dinner.

Now that he was sitting up, Alexander could look down to see that the knife that had been attached to his belt was gone. He thought about his *xulon* sticks, but remembered he had left them in their sheath still attached to the donkey's pannier.

Alexander was alone, restrained, and unarmed. Where was Amarantus? Well, at least he wasn't gagged. Alexander took in a deep breath and shouted for Amarantus over and over again, pausing each time to strain to hear a reply. Nothing.

Again he tugged on his bindings, but they didn't loosen. He looked towards the door on the opposite wall. Would it be locked or blocked off with something heavy? No doubt, Alexander would have better luck removing his bindings if he could just get out. Maybe Ranti would be out there looking for him. He thought of calling out for help again, but then held back. Clearly, *someone* had knocked him unconscious and put him in the shed, and that someone could still be nearby.

He *needed* his servant. Alexander didn't know if he could free himself alone. *Alone ... hmmm.* He wasn't exactly alone, was he? Alexander looked at the calf, the mare, and then his eyes settled on the goat. 'I wonder,' he thought. '*I wonder if you're really as hungry as you look. ... I wonder if it is true that you will eat anything.*'

Flopping over onto his side, Alexander grabbed a handful of

hay and then squirmed back into a sitting position resting against the wall of the shed.

Naaaa. All three animals were staring at the wad of hay he was holding, but it was the goat that interested Alexander. "Yes, yes, you are very hungry – I hope. Wait just a minute, goat. I'm preparing a nice treat for you."

It wasn't easy to do with his wrists bound, but slowly Alexander was able to wrap several strands of hay around his wrists covering the papyrus cord that bound them. He had to use his mouth and chin to bend the strands of hay and hold them in place. With a little saliva and stiff fingers, a nice golden loop of hay was wrapped around the papyrus cord. Then Alexander angled his body and held out his wrists toward the goat with some extra strands of hay sticking out to act as an enticement.

"Dinner, my ornery friend," Alexander coaxed. "Come and nibble on this." He shook his wrists to make the wheat wave back and forth.

The goat fixed its eyes on the wheat.

"Come on, goat," Alexander almost crooned. "Come and get a nice mouthful of wheat with a nice piece papyrus cord to chew on."

The goat took a tentative step forward. Alexander almost gasped in delight. Would the goat come to chew on the hay and also chew through the papyrus cord binding his hands? Eagerly, he waved his wrists with the hay back and forth to tempt the goat. Too late, he realized that the goat saw this not as a temptation, but as a *taunt*.

Suddenly, the goat took its eyes off the hay and fixed Alexander with an angry look on its big deformed face. Alexander could tell instantly why so many people thought that the goat could curse when it gave the evil eye. It *was* scary looking - really, really scary looking.

The goat lowered its head and made a run straight for Alexander. *Merda*, he shouted and managed to throw himself to the side at the last moment. The evil goat continued to run straight at where Alexander had been sitting. *Bam!* The goat rammed into the wall, shook its head from side to side and backed away slowly.

Alexander looked at the spot where his head had been. The goat had rammed hard into the vertical reed poles -- hard enough to crack one. *Hmmm.* Maybe the notion of getting the goat to eat through his bindings had not been very realistic, but perhaps he could get it to bust up the wall. Alexander scooted and squirmed until he had his back up against the place where the goat had last hit. Slowly he began to wave the hay around and yell taunts, "Stupid goat! I have this hay and I'm not going to give it to you."

He held his wrists up and waved the hay around. "You're not going to get any of this hay! In fact, I'm going to eat it myself just to keep it from you. Stupid, evil goat. No one likes you." Lord, he was glad that there was no one there to hear him trying to insult a goat.

Once again the goat gave him an evil look put its head down and rushed straight at him. Once again, Alexander threw himself to the side at the last moment although a goat's hoof clipped his thigh as he fell. "*Bam!*" The goat shook its head as it backed up. One of the reed poles was definitely split.

Alexander looked from the cracked pole to the hay in his hand then back at the goat. He didn't think the goat was going to fall for that one again. With one pole split, and it looked like at least one or two more cracked, Alexander wondered if he could kick a hole through the wall.

He scooted over until he could lie on his back before the wall. His ankles were still tied together, but Alexander was able flex his knees, bring them almost to his chest and strike out with both his boots at the wall. The reed poles cracked further, but there was no opening yet. He prepared himself to strike out again with both feet.

Naaaa. ... Oh *merda*. That evil goat was getting ready to make another charge at it. Just in time Alexander was able to roll aside as the goat charged by him, head down forehead facing the wall. *Bam!*

Crack! Crack!

Two more of the reed poles were definitely split and Alexander could see sunshine rays coming through. Lying on his side, he looked back over his shoulder at the goat. For the moment, at least, it seemed to have lost interest. That might change once he started trying to enlarge a hole. No time to waste, then.

Alexander rolled back until he was lying in front of the wall with his knees pulled back to his chest and struck out as hard as he could. There was a satisfying crash as a hole appeared in the wall. Now, he only had to enlarge it so he could get out.

Naaaa. ... *Oh, double merda.* That evil goat was coming again. Once more, Alexander rolled to the side and forced himself up onto his knees. His body was really starting to ache from trying to move with his wrists and ankles tied. Still, he forced himself to lean way back as the large, shaggy head rushed by him.

Bam! Crash!

The goat's head now stuck out of the shed in the new hole it had created. Unfortunately, the rest of the goat's body was still in the shed. Alexander squirmed back as the goat stomped and shoved looking to force its head free. The reed walls began to crack and split as the goat shoved its broad shoulders into the wall. Then with a loud crack the goat's shoulders were through. It squirmed and kicked until it was able to push its body the rest of the way through the broken wall and on to freedom.

Alexander waited a moment to make sure the evil goat wasn't coming back. On his knees with his wrists and ankles still tied, he edged closer to the hole in the wall. It wasn't human sized, but he could make it work. Reaching out with his tied hands he clutched at one side of the opening, forced his legs up into a crouch and then dived through the opening the goat had made.

Ooof. Alexander's forearm and shoulder hit the ground hard. Somehow he had pictured himself diving through the hole into a perfect somersault. His actual dive had been considerably less elegant, and much more painful.

With a groan, Alexander rolled onto his back and stared up into … the face of a horse … and over that was the face of … *Sabinus?*

For a moment both men just stared at each other. Sabinus rubbed his chin. "Well, young Alexander, it is not often that I am at a complete loss for words, but you definitely got me with this one. … I hope I can assume that you do not normally tie yourself up and accost domestic animals?"

Alexander blew out a breath. "No, indeed. I came here looking for Hierax. But before I could look, someone hit me over the head from behind. When I came to, I was tied up in that shed with what appears to be some stolen animals."

He looked up at Sabinus. "You could *untie* me, you know. It would be greatly appreciated."

"*Huh,*" Sabinus swung down from his horse and drew a knife from the sheath attached to his belt. It didn't take too long for him to saw through the papyrus bindings.

Alexander sat up and rubbed at his chafed wrists and ankles. "*Ooh,* that's better. Imagine being tied up helpless at close quarters with that evil goat."

"Evil goat?" Sabinus looked puzzled. "Oh, you mean that

one?" he pointed. "The goat that came out just before you?"

At Alexander's nod, Sabinus laughed. "I suppose it does look a little evil. That, my friend, is a *Damascus goat*. It's an actual breed of goats."

Alexander was incredulous. "You mean there are *more* of them?"

Sabinus nodded. "Yes, there are. Actually, there aren't too many in Egypt, but there are whole herds of them up in Syria."

Alexander shuddered. He hoped there weren't any more of them in the Lady Antonia's pasturelands.

"*Masteerrr!*" A voice called from somewhere behind one of the buildings.

"Ranti!" Alexander yelled. Sabinus followed him until he found his servant tied up and left face down in the sand. Using the knife Sabinus handed him, Alexander cut Amarantus free. His servant's story was the same as his own. Thinking that the area was abandoned, he wandered around not paying much attention to his surroundings. Like Alexander he had been hit on the back of his head and woke up groggy and bound hand and foot.

After freeing Amarantus, the men took a good look around the area, but this time there was definitely no one else there. They even kicked open the door of the brick storehouse to see what was inside. Alexander and Sabinus each gave a long whistle as they entered and saw the interior stocked full with wheat, barley, various jars, and more.

Amarantus followed them in and curled his lip. "Master, I think you will need an inventory of all that is here, and that will take a long time."

"You are right, Ranti," he replied. "But I wonder how all of this stuff got here without anyone noticing? And who was the man who hit us?"

Alexander turned to Sabinus.

"Are you sure you didn't see who attacked us? You must have arrived soon after we got our heads cracked. Aside from these buildings, this is wide open space. There is no other place to hide. Didn't you see *someone*?"

Sabinus chewed his lower lip. "No, I didn't see anyone else, at least no nearby. There might have been a donkey and rider in the distance -- not on the trail from Tebtunis, but the other way." He shrugged. "Although, I wasn't looking too closely at them since, of course, I didn't know that you were in the area, let alone tied up."

Alexander leaned forward. "Could you have possibly seen Hierax on that donkey? Could it have been that freedman who attacked us?"

Sabinus tilted his head and thought for a moment before slowly shaking it side to side. "I don't know. Could be. I'm not sure if I would have been to recognize Hierax from a distance. *I would like to talk to Hierax, too.*" He looked around. "Clearly, someone was here if you got conked on the head. And someone must have been taking care of the animals and probably guarding the buildings, too."

Sabinus paused and looked at Alexander's dusty tunic up and down.

"I wouldn't be surprised if that thing you're wearing scared 'em off. Whoever hit you probably realized what those two purple stripes meant and decided that he wanted no more part in attacking a Roman noble. Old Hierax probably wasn't paying his people enough for that – if it even was one of his people."

Alexander shook his head in disappointment. Then he fixed his rescuer with a suspicious look.

"What are *you doing here*, Sabinus?"

The other man shrugged. "Oh, I was just in the area and heard the banging in that shed. I decided to take a quick look and see what it was."

Alexander cast a wide look around him and saw only the quiet expanse of uncultivated lands, the brick storage building, the small shed in which he had been tied – and not much else.

"Come on, Sabinus. There is nothing out here for miles except that storage house. No one *just happens* to be in this area ... and on *a horse*, no less. You are here for Hierax, aren't you?"

Sabinus waved a negligent hand. "Actually no, I am not, at least not particularly. If you must know, my former woman can't find her son. She pestered me to come looking for him."

Alexander's look was skeptical. "You mean Kronion, right?"

Sabinus nodded.

"...And you happened to come looking for her son on property owned by Hierax that appears to be full of stolen goods?"

Sabinus shrugged and nodded. "Yeah, young Kronion was friends with Hierax. I can't imagine *why* he was because there was a pretty big age difference between them, but *ehh* not my affair."

"Not so fast," Alexander replied. "If you are *here* now, then you must have known about this place. Why did you not tell me that Hierax had this secret warehouse?"

Once again, Sabinus simply gave an indifferent shrug and waved a negligent hand. Alexander thought the man was a master at dissembling. But now Alexander was feeling both angry and confused. He gestured at the warehouse.

"I think this is the Lady Antonia's property, and no doubt, quite a lot of it is stolen from others as well – like that evil goat over there. Sabinus, were you *even* going to tell me about it? Were you planning on letting Hierax keep all of this?"

Sabinus shook his head and gave a mirthless smile. "No, Alexander, I never planned to let *Hierax keep* the Lady Antonia's property."

He looked around. "It is apparent that young Kronion is not here. If you have seen all you need to see, I suggest we ride back to Tebtunis together. Riding with me should keep you and your man out of trouble for awhile."

Alexander wanted to glare at Sabinus, but his head hurt and honestly he really did want leave this miserable place and return to Tebtunis. But first he needed to settle things. He tapped his lower lip.

"Yes, let us return. There is nothing much I can do here right now except secure the place as well as I can. When we get back to Tebtunis, I will speak to our *strategos* Dion and arrange to retrieve these items and get them moved into one of Antonia's real storehouses."

He thought for a moment and nodded sharply to himself. "I am going to assume that *everything* here actually belongs to Antonia or one of her tenants. If Hierax has a problem with that, then he can just come and tell me."

Sabinus shrugged indifferently. "It makes no difference to me. But don't be too long. *I* have no more business around here."

Fortunately, there was a well with a bucket on the property, so Alexander had Amarantus get water for all the animals including those in the shed. He found some rope made of twisted papyrus and used that to repair the hole in the shed where the goat had busted its way through. After coaxing the evil goat back in the shed using water and fresh piles of hay, he finally turned to go.

Sabinus waited by his horse and Ranti walked up leading their two donkeys by their reins. Alexander took one last look around and nodded to himself. He hadn't found the missing land agent, or any of Antonia's records or rents collected *in coin*. They had found no money in the warehouse. Still, Alexander was pretty sure he had found much of Antonia's rents that Hierax had collected in goods. He had even solved the mystery of the missing animals from Karanis and Philadelphia. At least he had solved *where* they were. *Why* Hierax had stolen these animals and brought them clear across the nome to hide them here -- well, he couldn't imagine any reason for that.

Alexander and Amarantus mounted up on their donkeys and set off back to Tebtunis with Alexander riding next to Sabinus on his tall horse.

Sabinus looked down at Alexander and said, "You are welcome, by the way. If I had not come along and rescued you, you might not have made it."

Alexander sucked in a breath and took time to think before answering. Riding next to Sabinus's horse on the shorter donkey with his feet almost trailing the ground made Alexander feel ... well, ridiculous. Not a shred of *gravitas* here. Indeed, if the people he knew in Rome saw him trotting along on the little donkey in his *eques* tunic, he would be a laughing stock.

Still, Alexander was not in Rome now and Sabinus did rescue him. Did he *trust* Sabinus? Nope, not for a moment. He *liked* him. Sabinus was excellent company despite his occasional tendency towards sarcasm -- or maybe because of it. He was almost always amusing.

Alexander couldn't quite say why or what it was, but there was just something about Sabinus that felt a little ... *off*. For today at least, Sabinus had certainly come through for him. He appeared to be on Alexander's side – or on *Antonia's* side at least. And for now, that would have to be enough.

Bouncing up and down on his little donkey, Alexander

looked up at Sabinus on his big horse and put on his best grin.

"You *did* rescue us. We were both knocked out and bound. It was lucky that you came, Sabinus. ... and doubly lucky, that you *already knew* where Hierax was hiding Antonia's stolen property."

Sabinus shot him a quizzical look, but Alexander had already turned his face forward looking toward the village of Tebtunis somewhere in the distance.

16. Another Corpse

"I will look into it personally later today, Alexander, but first I have to go view a dead body."

After leaving the secret warehouse, Alexander had returned to Tebtunis to locate Dionysodoros. He wanted to hire the *strategos* to inventory and retrieve Antonia's goods that had been hidden there. Alexander knew he needed to find local men whom he could trust and delegate some of the responsibility for Antonia's properties in the nome. He felt confident that Dion was just such a man.

But for now, it appeared Dion's duties as *strategos* would have to come first.

"A dead body?" Alexander asked. "A local person?"

"Actually, no," Dion replied. "Or at least, I don't think so. So far, I have only been told that a man's body was pulled from the canal just east of Tebtunis. I was also told that the man was not an Egyptian."

"Not an Egyptian?" Sabinus had been standing nearby and had overheard their conversation. He rubbed his chin. "Not an Egyptian, you say. What then? A Greek, a Roman?"

Dion held up his palms indicating that he did not know.

"*Hmmm*," Sabinus responded. "I think I will ride along with you Dion."

Alexander was about to turn away when it suddenly

occurred to him that the man for whom he had been searching could certainly be described as *not an Egyptian. Huh.* He turned to Dion. "I think I will ride along with you as well."

The *strategos* seemed puzzled that these two Romans wanted to go view a dead body with him. He shrugged off the thought. They were good company and if they wanted to come, then why not?

"Very well," Dion said. "But first, Alexander, I am going to send a couple of my own servants to guard that storage building you found. If you two have not eaten yet, I suggest you stop at the beer house before we head out. From what I have been told, the body was found only a couple miles outside of Tebtunis, but where we are going there is nothing but farm fields. We will be riding donkeys and following the canal east."

Alexander and Sabinus did stop at the local beer house for drink with some bread, cheese, and olives. They ate quickly and rejoined Dion by the stables. Amarantus was already there and had arranged to keep the two donkeys they had rented for their trip to the secret storehouse.

There was a local man with the *strategos* who silently mounted a donkey and took the lead. Alexander guessed that this must be the one who had reported the discovery of the body.

As they rode out of Tebtunis, Alexander could not help but note that once again Sabinus was on horseback, while all of the other men trotted along on donkeys with their feet practically touching the ground. His donkey mount made Alexander feel slightly ridiculous. An *eques* and a future Alabarch should not be seen with such a loss of *dignitas. Hmm,* Alexander vowed to speak to his father about how to travel in Egypt without this loss of dignity, a challenge that never arose when he had lived in Rome.

Sabinus, for his part, seemed not to notice the difference in their mounts. As they trotted towards the canal, he turned to Dion then pointed with his chin at the local man who had ridden out with them. "Is that the man that found the body?"

Dion nodded. "Yes, he is one of them. They sent him to find me because he was the fastest on foot. I've loaned him a donkey for now, and I expect I'll be using that same donkey to bring the body back."

"So what does he say about the body?" Sabinus asked. "Is he sure he doesn't know who it is?"

"Not a big talker, that one," Dion shook his head. "He only speaks Egyptian, but that is no concern. I speak Egyptian, too. Some of these field workers live outside of Tebtunis and rarely come into the village. They may be hard working, but they are not a very social lot. They just don't have much to say."

He held up a hand to stop Sabinus from trying to press the local man for more detail. "It is only a couple miles, less than an hour away. We will find what there is to know soon enough."

Alexander listened to them talk, his mind considering the possibilities. As they trotted along the path beside the canal, Alexander became more and more certain of his conclusions. Finally, he turned to Dion and Sabinus and cleared his throat to get their attention.

"I know who the body is," Alexander said. "...Who it *must* be. Since it is not an Egyptian, there really is only one likely possibility."

Both the *strategos* and Sabinus twisted on their mounts so they could face him with curious looks.

Before they could question him, Alexander held up one finger. "Point. The body was found just north of the secret warehouse belonging to Hierax." Second finger. "Point. Hierax cannot be found. He is not north of Lake Moeris, not south, or east of the lake, not in Crocodilopolis, not at the Great Labyrinth, not in

Tebtunis, and not at his secret warehouse. It is a matter of simple deduction. Since Hierax is not anywhere else and no one admits to having seen him, then the solution *must* be that this dead body is my missing land agent."

It was a clear case of logical deduction. Alexander looked at his companions expectantly.

Both Dion and Sabinus furrowed their eyebrows as they considered his words. Alexander pushed on "It *is* him. It has to be. I've searched everywhere and Hierax is nowhere to be found. It is an obvious conclusion. If no one has reported seeing him *alive* in weeks, then he *must be dead*. And so far, I have only heard of one dead body that hasn't been identified; this one. Therefore, it must be Hierax."

"I suppose that is logical," Dion replied hesitantly. "Well, we will find out for sure soon enough. Look ahead. That must be them up there."

While Egypt was not a land with any forests, there were some trees. Softwood trees like acanthus or palm grew where there was irrigation and that included near the canals. Up ahead, Alexander saw a small copse next to the canal with some shade provided by a handful of date palms. He couldn't control his eagerness and urged his donkey ahead. There was a body on the ground covered by a course linen cloth with another local man squatting down next to it. The latter didn't move or speak, but watched as the mounted men approached.

Alexander got there slightly ahead of the others, dismounted and placed himself next to the body on the ground. He waited for the *strategos* Dion and Sabinus to arrive and dismount.

"I think my search has finally ended," Alexander said. "This must certainly be Antonia's former land agent, the freedman named Hierax."

With that, Alexander grabbed the course linen cloth and pulled it back off the body. Then he made a flourish and waved to the head of the dead man ... the head with ... *a circle shaved onto the top* ... the head of what could only be *a priest of Kronos*.

"*Oh, by the gods no,*" Dion groaned and stalked over to stare at the body's face. "Not an Egyptian, not a Roman, but a *Greek*. ... This *is Kronion* isn't it, Sabinus?"

Sabinus walked over and stared at the body. His usually expressive face had turned to stone – no sneer, no laughter, no expression at all. He looked up at Dion and gave a curt nod to confirm the identity of the corpse.

"I am sorry, Sabinus," Dion said. "I know you, *uh,* cared for the boy."

Sabinus still said nothing but stepped back a few paces. The *strategos* looked to the still astonished face of Alexander.

"Well, it is not your land agent after all, Alexander. Let's take a look and see how young Kronion died. Can you help me with this?"

It would not be a pleasant task, but Alexander did kneel down next to the body to do what he could. He was glad that he had never known this Kronion in life or the morbid and decaying remains in front of him would have been too hard to take.

Dion looked up at Amarantus. "I know you often act as Alexander's secretary. Would you be able to take notes on what we find here?"

Amarantus looked at Alexander who nodded his agreement. "I have a wax tablet in my bag," Ranti said. "I will take notes on wax now and transfer them to papyrus later if you need that."

The *strategos* shook his head sadly at the body and began. "I would say the boy has been dead for at least a week. It's impossible to be certain. Usually, in this heat, a body deteriorates quite fast, but, look at the hands. See how the skin is wrinkled on the fingers. There is the other swelling and bloating, too. I think that it was submerged under water for a while – days perhaps. It is true, the body is in rough shape, but it is in a different way than it would be if it had been lying in the sun."

The *strategos* started at the head and continued to examine down the body. "I will want my physician to look at him, but I think this will be what caused his death."

He pointed at the legs of the corpse. "Look at these marks. It looks like teeth have torn into his legs – maybe that's what dragged him under water. Certainly, there would have been considerable loss of blood."

Alexander looked up. "Do you mean like a crocodile? Do you think he was attacked by a crocodile?"

The *strategos* tilted his head, "So it would appear."

The local man who had been squatting near to the corpse shifted and began speaking softly in Egyptian to the *strategos*. The *strategos* answered and the man appeared to repeat himself, this time pointing at the corpse's wound. Being fluent in both Latin and Greek, Alexander was accustomed to understanding what was being said. With his Egyptian limited to a few words that he remembered from his childhood, he was now lost.

"What is it?" he asked impatiently. "What is he saying?"

The *strategos* rubbed at his chin. "He says it is *not* a real crocodile bite. He says these wounds were meant to *look* like a crocodile bite."

Alexander was confused. "But why not a real crocodile? Doesn't this look like a real crocodile bite to you?"

"Actually, no it doesn't – at least now that this fellow has pointed it out to me," Dion replied. "Look again at these bite marks." He pointed to one leg and then the other.

"See how every tooth would have to have been the same size and evenly spaced? That is not what a real crocodile bite looks like. The crocodile's teeth do not have such even gaps between them; they are different sizes and they curve inwards. Plus with a real crocodile, the wound would show a lot more tearing as the crocodile works its jaws to secure its victim."

Dion gestured again to the bite marks on the young man's legs. "Truly, I think these marks were made by a metal trap -- something made to look like a crocodile bite. But for someone who has seen a real crocodile attack, these marks don't quite fit."

They heard the swish of sand and looked up to realize that Sabinus had been standing not far behind them quietly watching and listening. He gave Dion a quick nod that seemed to confirm that he agreed with his findings. Then he turned and walked away.

After Sabinus had gone some distance, Dion murmured to Alexander, "He never legally acknowledged the boy, but everyone pretty much knew that Kronion was *his son*. I suspect that Sabinus is taking this death pretty hard. He is going to want to find whoever caused this."

"Are you sure this could not have been an accident?" Alexander asked keeping his voice low.

The *strategos* shook his head. "No. I don't think so." He paused to collect his thoughts then continued.

"The boy was a priest of Kronos. He had no reason to be away from the temple, or to leave Tebtunis at all. We do know ... *now*," he glanced toward Sabinus. "We do *know now*, that young Kronion was aware of the secret warehouse of Hierax and that he had spent some time there. He even took his friends to see it."

Dion raised his arm and pointed toward the north. "In fact, that secret warehouse is that way, probably at most a mile from here. ... Of course, there is no proof for it, but my instinct tells me that there may have been some type of falling out between the two of them, Hierax and Kronion. We may never know what happened, unless we can catch Hierax and he tells us."

Alexander tapped his chin twice. "But why a crocodile? Why would anyone have a metal trap that would resemble a crocodile bite? I presume that such a thing is not used for fishing, farming, or dredging canals, is it?"

Dion shook his head. "No. I can't remember ever seeing any kind of tool that would make a mark like that. I can think of no reasonable explanation for why such as thing would even exist – other than trickery... and malice. I suppose this trap may have been made to keep people away from Hierax's secret warehouse."

Alexander chewed at his lower lip. "That still doesn't quite satisfy the question of *why*. Why would anyone attack someone with a trap or tool that would like a crocodile bite?"

The *strategos* considered for a moment. "Perhaps someone thought there was some meaning to having a priest of the crocodile god appear to be attacked by a crocodile. Remember, that these crocodile priests of Kronos are very controversial in Tebtunis. Maybe there was some message intended there."

"Or, maybe there was no particular meaning. It was simply a ruse," Alexander added. "... a ruse to get away with a crime. *You* realized it wasn't a real crocodile bite, but most people would have thought that it was. *I* would have guessed that was a real crocodile bite and assumed the whole thing was just a terrible accident."

Dion slowly nodded. "Probably both of our ideas are correct. I don't know. At this point, maybe we shouldn't try to over-think it."

Alexander had nothing more to add. He was, *well*, he was still flummoxed over the true identity of the body. It had felt so certain when they left Tebtunis that the corpse would be the land agent. The logic had seemed so sure; all of his rationale was completely cogent. Yet, his conclusion had been very wrong. The body was *not* Hierax. Where that wretched freedman could be now, Lord, he did not know.

The two local men tied the body of Kronion onto the extra donkey then Dion, Sabinus, Alexander, and Amarantus rode back to Tebtunis mostly in silence. Alexander wanted to talk, at least to vent his frustration that once again the land agent had eluded him. It was out of deference to Sabinus that the men stayed silent. Every now and then, Alexander glanced at him, but the face of Sabinus remained stiff and expressionless as if it had been carved in stone.

Hmm, Alexander couldn't imagine what Sabinus was thinking and didn't know him well enough to ask. ... but if Alexander had to guess, he would guess that Sabinus was thinking much the same thing as both the *strategos* and himself. Kronion's death was very likely caused by Hierax, the freedman and land agent of Antonia Minor.

Dion had not translated aloud everything the local men had said. Of this Alexander felt sure because he had understood just enough of the Egyptian to hear that the local men had repeatedly said the name of Hierax. He understood why Dion did not repeat their words aloud. It was a risky matter for a local Egyptian farm laborer to be making accusations against a Roman citizen which of course Hierax was.

Still, if Alexander had understood at least a little of what the Egyptian laborer had said, then no doubt Sabinus had understood it as well. Alexander thought it likely that the big Roman would like to have a *little talk* with Hierax. In fact, if Hierax had indeed caused the death of young Kronion as they all suspected, Sabinus would probably want to have *more* than just a few words with the man who had killed his son.

"Yeah, well, Sabinus can have him after me," Alexander thought. He had been searching longer and it was both he and the Lady Antonia who had been harmed by the man's duplicity and outright theft. Alexander had every intention of finding and settling things with Antonia's freedman before anyone else could get a chance at him. Yeah, Hierax was a Roman citizen, but he was just a freedman. Alexander was nobility, an *eques*. Plus, Antonia had given him permission to deal with the man as he saw fit.

Hmm, as he saw fit. Alexander liked the idea of that. He could imagine a lot of things that he would see fit. Next to him, Sabinus was silent, sitting stoically on his horse. Alexander had a feeling that he had better make sure he got to Hierax before Sabinus did.

They entered the village of Tebtunis and stopped by the temple of the great, great god Sobek and his counterpart Kronos to deliver the body of Kronion to be prepared for burial. Alexander noticed that the priests of Kronos that attended the body didn't actually seem that surprised at the young priest's fate. He wondered just how much these priests may have known, or suspected, about what had happened.

Sabinus stood off to the side talking quietly to a couple of the priests of Kronos who were so easily identified by the curious shaved circles on their heads. Alexander saw that they were almost all young, boys and young men. He recalled that Sabinus said he had purchased a number of priesthoods for Kronos, possibly to include the friends of Kronion. It seemed likely that these young priests of Kronos would know something about Hierax, but when he tried approaching them they quickly dispersed. He looked at Sabinus for answers, but the man still wore the same stony expression he had since they had identified the body of Kronion.

The *strategos* touched Alexander's arm to get his attention, and then shook his head no. "Now is not a good time," he whispered. "I know you want information, Alexander, but I suggest you stay away from Sabinus and those Kronos priests for now. I'm not sure what is going on with them, but I wouldn't trust your safety – or *my* safety -- around them at the moment. As you saw at the melee fight last night, they can be *unpredictable*."

Alexander nodded reluctantly. "I suppose you are right. Of course, there was no actual evidence that Hierax had anything to do with the death of Kronion. It is nothing more than a suspicion. I can't really see Sabinus or those Kronos priests bringing an official complaint against Hierax without some sort of evidence."

"An *official* complaint?" the *strategos* replied. "No, no I don't see them doing that either. No, definitely not anything *official*."

It wasn't the words themselves, but something in the tone that caused Alexander to look sharply at the *strategos*. Dion returned a small smile and a shrug. "I suppose with time we may learn if anything *unofficial* happens."

Before Alexander could ask him to explain further, Dion turned and walked away.

17. In the Wind

Alexander, Amarantus, and Dionysodoros spent the following morning at the secret storehouse south of Tebtunis. Together they had worked up a plan to inventory the stock and move everything to one of the Lady Antonia's own storehouses. Leaving them to it, Alexander had returned to the village and dropped off his rented donkey at the local stable. While he was walking down the causeway to the house where he was staying, he heard them.

Clop clop clop clop clop.

Alexander quickly stepped to the side at the sound of rapidly falling horses' hooves pounding up the causeway through central Tebtunis. Instead of passing by, they stopped not far behind him. This time it was not Sabinus on his big horse. In fact, Alexander couldn't tell who it was. There were half a dozen men on horseback encircling a seventh who may have been the one in charge.

Every man of them had a long linen scarf wrapped around his head covering hair, forehead, nose and mouth. Only the eyes could be seen through the dust that coated each rider and horse from head to foot. Clearly, the men had ridden far through the sands of the desert that day.

Alexander could think of only one likely explanation for a small band of men traveling on horseback to the village. These had to be *legionaries*. Local villagers may travel by donkey or camel, and certainly by barge on the canal. Horses, however, were not suited for general travel in Egypt. A group of men on horseback most likely meant the *Roman cavalry*.

Knowing that, Alexander took a closer look at the men's clothes and the horses' accoutrements. Metal helmets and breastplates may have been tucked away for the desert travel, but round shields and long swords were hung from every saddle – the weapons of cavalrymen. There was no question that these were Roman legionaries.

Or, at least, six of them were. The man in the middle turned his horse in a full circle as he cast an appraising look around the village of Tebtunis. He then turned his horse back and looked down at Alexander as he slowly unwound the long linen scarf that had been wrapped around his head.

"*Ahh, it's you,*" Alexander breathed as he recognized the man before him as Titus Serenius the *epistrategos* of the Arsinoite Nome and the seven smaller nomes that made up the Heptanomia.

Serenius returned a quick nod and said, "Did I ever mention that I *detest* desert travel?" He blew out a breath. "It's hard to avoid it, though; at least in *this* nome. *Hunh.* Unfortunately, I had a feeling that I should be ready for trouble with these crocodile priests. That's why I was already in Crocodilopolis with the legionaries when your letter arrived."

Before Alexander could respond, the *epistrategos* held up a cautionary finger. "We will *not* be discussing this in the street; and certainly not until I wash off this travel dirt."

He pointed at Alexander. "Can you find the home of the local councilman? I am staying in the house next to it, the one with the large courtyard. Come for the mid-day meal. I want an update from you before I decide what to do about these problem priests."

Alexander gladly made his acceptance. Actually, the timing was good because he had not made plans for the mid-day meal. Amarantus had been left behind at the warehouse working with one of Dion's scribes to sort things out so Alexander was on his own. It would be good to have a meal with someone who was of his own social class. As an *eques*, Alexander far outranked Dion, Sabinus -- pretty much everyone he had met so far.

Serenius was also of equestrian rank and in every way a good man to know. He was older that Alexander by at least ten years and well established in a very politically powerful position. Compared to Serenius, Alexander was barely getting started. Indeed, Serenius would be a good role model, someone Alexander could watch and try to emulate. He felt certain his father would agree that he should try to cultivate a friendship with the *epistrategos*.

Later, after washing up himself, Alexander found his way to the house were Serenius said he would be staying. With Serenius was a young tribune -- a *tribunus angusticlavius* – he was called, one of the special tribunes in the legions who came from the equestrian order. The dining table had not been set up for a long, leisurely meal. Alexander saw that they would not be dining in the Roman fashion reclining on couches. Rather, they sat in actual chairs arranged around a table nearly waist high. Neither of his two companions spoke much as they fell onto their meals. Alexander supposed that riding through desert must generate quite an appetite.

Finally, Serenius waved for the servants to remove the dishes. Then he pushed his chair back raising his boots onto the table and crossed them at the ankles. He folded his arms across his chest as well and gave Alexander a direct look.

"Now then, Alexander, I got your letter while I was in Crocodilopolis. It was enough to get me here to Tebtunis, but I need to hear more. It sounds like these Kronos priests were the instigators, but that ... could be a problem. Those priests were appointed directly by the *idios logos*. Many of them have Roman sponsors."

Where Serenius was going with this train of thought, Alexander didn't know. He said nothing.

"Oh, I *can act* on this," Serenius continued and waved a negligent hand. "I certainly have the authority. Still, as always, politics and influence do matter. I need to be sure of the facts before I intervene with these quarreling priests."

Alexander shook his head. "Things may be even worse than you know, Serenius. One of the Kronos priests was found dead yesterday. It looked like murder. ... And I think you may want to have a talk with a Roman named Sabinus if you don't want him taking matters into his own hands."

Serenius lowered his boots from the table and leaned forward. "Sabinus? How is *he* involved?"

"*Oh*, You know who Sabinus is then?" Alexander asked.

The *epistrategos* and the tribune looked at each other for a moment before Serenius replied. "Oh yeah, a lot of people know Sabinus. He is excellent company. 'Can't really ask for a better companion over a flask of wine."

Serenius held up his palms. "...but, you may have noticed it, too. There is something about Sabinus that just feels a little ... *off*. I can't quite define what it is. Still, he *is* a Roman and as far as anyone knows he is very loyal to Rome."

Alexander shrugged. "I know what you mean. Sabinus accompanied me from Crocodilopolis to Philadelphia and he was excellent company, although he could be ... I guess you could call it sarcastic? Cynical, maybe? Still there was no question in my mind that Sabinus is very partial to the imperial family in Rome. When he found out that I knew Lady Antonia, the widow of Drusus,

Sabinus wanted to know all about her and her son Germanicus, too. He even asked about her other son Claudius who, *well*, is not active in politics in Rome."

Once again the *epistrategos* and tribune exchanged a look. Then Serenius turned back to Alexander. "That is all interesting, but it is not *why I am here*. Can you tell me what has been happening with these crocodile priests? Start with this fight you witnessed between the priests at the temple. Why were you even there, anyway? And how did Sabinus get involved?"

Alexander readily agreed to speak. "Yes, I will tell you as much I can, but you should know that Antonia's land agent Hierax might be involved, too – maybe even with the murder. At least, Dionysodoros the *strategos* seems to think he might be. *You* are here about the crocodile priests, but *I am* here searching for that wretched freedman Hierax. However, it seems that my goal may overlap with yours, at least somewhat. Let me explain."

Alexander recounted his tale as well as he could, starting with why he had decided to approach the Kronos priests to look for Hierax. He spoke of the melee fight of the crocodile priests, finding the land agent's secret warehouse with the missing animals and goods, and then of the trip to see young Kronion's body that had been found less than a mile from the secret warehouse.

Alexander thought he had organized his thoughts well and had done a good job of conveying the details. Thus, he was more than a little surprised when the *epistrategos* chose immediately to criticize his actions.

Serenius gave Alexander a disappointed look. "So that was *all* you did, Alexander? You did *nothing* more useful than that? You have managed to stay here in Tebtunis for how many days without accomplishing *anything* further?"

Holding up a hand, Serenius began to tick off points with his fingers. "You did *not* investigate who started this *melee* or why.

You did *not* bother to inquire about any casualties. You did *not* even try to determine if there was any damage to any public buildings. ...

"Really, Alexander, *could you have done any less?*"

Alexander's mouth fell open. The *epistrategos* had asked for a report of anything he chanced to see and Alexander had given him one. There was no just cause for *criticizing him*. It certainly was *not* Alexander's responsibility to deal with the problems of priests. The *epistrategos* had not even asked him to do more than simply observe.

A bad feeling began to emerge. Maybe, just maybe, this was some sort of set up. Maybe the *epistrategos* was nothing more than a bully, someone who liked belittling people so he could feel superior. It was odd. Serenius certainly hadn't acted that way when they had first met back in Alexandria. Why was he acting differently now?

Well, no matter. The fact was, Alexander really, really hated bullies and he had learned that you must never back down to one. Besides, he really didn't have to because he was an *eques* now.

With a shove on the table, Alexander pushed his chair back and stood at his full height. Ignoring the young tribune, he glared at the *epistrategos*.

"My *name* is Gaius Julius Alexander. My *patron* is *Augustus*. I am here at the behest of *his niece*, the Lady Antonia and I am *her procurator*. I am *not your subordinate*. You asked for a report; I gave it to you *as a courtesy*. Our business here is done."

With that Alexander spun around and headed for the door.

Serenius remained seated, but waved a hand at him. "Wait, wait Alexander. So I gave you a hard time. How was I to know that you have such a childish temper?"

Alexander kept walking.

Serenius stood. "Alexander, wait."

Alexander did not wait. He opened the door and left without looking back.

Childish temper? Why would Serenius treat him as if he were some common man? The family name of Julius Alexander meant something in Alexandria, especially now that Augustus himself had decided to keep the alabarchy in the family. Why would the *epistrategos* want to make an enemy of him?

On the other hand, Alexander was forced to admit to himself that *he* should not make an enemy of the *epistrategos* – especially the *epistrategos* responsible for the nome where both his family and Antonia owned so much property. He had allowed that initial flare of anger to take over. Maybe … maybe he should have handled that better.

Alexander blew out a long breath, then walked over to a low wall surrounding someone's courtyard and pulled himself up to sit on it. He was still fuming as he swung his legs, the heels of his boots hitting back against the wall. This caused him to recall a similar scene from several days ago. Then it was young Leah sitting on a low wall, banging her heels and announcing "I am very intelligent, you know." He smiled at the memory of the little one. That made his thoughts drift to the lovely Indike. Thinking of the young ladies seemed to cause his temper to cool.

The crunch of gravel broke into his thoughts as someone walked toward him. A low voice called out, "Alexander."

Looking up, he saw Serenius striding towards him. Anger flared inside him again. Had this man followed him just so he could berate him some more? Alexander stood, thinking that perhaps he should leave before his temper caused irreparable harm to his relationship with the *epistrategos*.

Before he could walk away, Serenius held out both hands

with palms forward. Then he switched to Latin.

"*Pax*, Alexander, *pax*. *Mea culpa*. Stay and hear me out. I was wrong to challenge you so, but I have been so angry about the Alabarch."

Huh? Alabarch? That gave Alexander pause. He spun around to face Serenius. "You are saying you were rude to me because you are *angry with my father*?"

Serenius shook his head. "No, no, not at *your father*. *At you*, I guess." He stopped, looked at the ground and then took a deep breath. "When you came to see me in Alexandria a few weeks ago, I had not heard yet that you are to be the next Alabarch."

Alexander crossed his arms. "So? I only learned of this myself a few weeks ago from Augustus. What is that to you?"

Serenius rubbed his chin. "Everyone has known that your father was ill and probably wasn't going to remain in the position much longer. I recommended a friend of mine to become the next Alabarch. The Prefect agreed that he was the best candidate and sent a letter to Rome endorsing him as well. We thought his appointment would be a sure thing.

"Then ... *you showed up*. Nobody has ever heard of you. What could you possibly know about Egypt's gold mines? ... Look, you seem like a good enough man, Alexander, but why? Why should you become the Alabarch and not my friend?"

Alexander was momentarily without words. The *epistrategos* was angry because Alexander had received preferment from Augustus. He supposed that made some sense. It was well known how much certain people in Rome would vie for the First Citizen's attention. Serenius's disappointment for his friend would explain his sudden rudeness.

Then Alexander pressed his lips together as his anger returned. He was sorry that Serenius's friend was unsuccessful in his politicking, but that was *not his fault*. Alexander pondered how he could explain his position to the *epistrategos* -- that appointing him Alabarch was something that his father and Augustus had decided without consulting him. Alexander had not asked for the alabarchy; he did not even *want* it.

Then he decided that there was no point in trying to make explanations to Serenius. That would only make Alexander look weak. If Serenius had a problem with him, then he should have just come and talked to Alexander like a man. This sniping had been beneath him.

No, Alexander decided that he owed Serenius *nothing* – no explanation, no apology. …but, he stopped himself before he could turn his back and walk away. He should *not* make an enemy of the *epistrategos* of the Arsinoite Nome. Serenius did seem to be apologizing -- sort of -- for attacking him verbally earlier. And, actually, what Serenius had said to him was not that bad. The words were not enough to make the man an enemy.

Taking control of his temper, Alexander turned to Serenius, "I am sorry that your friend did not get the preferment that you both desired. The matter was *never* in my hands."

Serenius stared at the ground for several moments, then looked up, "We should not be enemies, Alexander."

"No, we should not."

The *epistrategos* pointed a finger at Alexander and then at himself. "*Pax, mea culpa.* I started this, so it is up to me to make the peace. …. You told me what you knew about the crocodile priests including the death of this Kronion. How about if in return I help you with your missing land agent problem?"

Alexander's face lit up. "*That* would be most appreciated. Finding Hierax would be good – very good. Also, importantly, I need to find all of the documents about Antonia's estates. Plus there are missing coins from the rent money, tax money, too. The records were not at his secret warehouse. I'm guessing they may be at his house here in Tebtunis. Unfortunately, the house really is legally his and not part of Antonia's properties. If it was hers, I could force my way in, but since it is not..."

He broke off and held his hands up in a helpless gesture.

The *epistrategos* returned a sly grin. "Maybe *you cannot,* Alexander, but *I can.* This is one of *my nomes* and I have full judicial and military authority here. The only man who would outrank me is the Prefect, and I can't believe he would care about the Lady Antonia's freedman when she clearly does not."

Alexander's face shifted into an equally sly grin. "I cannot tell you how much I have been wishing that I could kick that *mentula*'s door down."

Serenius nodded. "Yeah, there is nothing like a good search and seizure to get the blood rushing is there? Come with me while I gather the cavalry, then we will pay a visit to the house of Hierax."

While they were talking, Alexander had seen his servant ride by on a donkey, likely headed to the stable to return it. Amarantus must have seen him, too, because now he walked up and stood near his master. After ascertaining that all was in hand at the secret storehouse, Alexander explained to Serenius about how he had left servants to keep a watch on Hierax's house here in Tebtunis.

"Ranti," he said. "Go check with my father's servants who are watching the land agent's house. I want to know who is inside the house right now. Be discreet. I don't want him to have any warning that we are coming."

In the meantime, Serenius did just as he had offered. He spoke to the tribune who quickly gathered the legionaries and they set about donning their armor and grabbing their shields and weapons. Alexander thought in unlikely that a cavalryman's full kit would be needed to secure the land agent, but he supposed it was just as well to be prepared.

As they headed down the street, Amarantus rejoined him.

"Master, there are two of your father's servants watching the house now. They say that no one has come or gone for days except for the house steward. Apparently, he comes and goes a great deal. They also say the steward left a short while ago, so the house should be empty. ... *No, wait.* They are pointing at someone. *Huh,* look, master, they say that man there is the annoying servant, the house steward. He is the one who won't tell us where his master is."

Alexander, Serenius, and the legionaries all paused and watched as a man approached and entered the front door to the house that belonged to Hierax.

Serenius frowned. "Alexander, did you look for Hierax in his home before this?"

Alexander returned a confused look. "Well, yes, I did. Of course I did, before I even arrived back in Egypt. I sent a letter ahead to Hierax and arranged for a messenger to place that letter directly into the land agent's hands. My messenger returned to Alexandria and said that this house steward insisted that Hierax was not available and he would not say where his master was. I have been having the house watched ever since."

Serenius bit his lower lip and continued. "And, did either your messenger, or you, ever got a physical description of Hierax?"

Alexander shuffled his feet and frowned. What was this about?

"Again, Serenius, we did. Of course we did. That's how I almost caught him in Karanis, I think. But the description was a bit too vague. Everyone said he was medium sized, middle aged, dark curly hair, and always wears a fancy embroidered tunic."

The *epistrategos* took Alexander by the arm and turned him until he was looking directly into his eyes. "That was *no house steward*. Alexander, that man who just entered the house *was Hierax* – the land agent, the man you have been trying to find."

Alexander's eyes grew wide. "What? That was *him*? Are you sure?"

"Yes, I am sure. I've known the man for years. Until you came, Hierax was the land agent for Antonia's properties here in my own nome. You can be sure I am familiar with all of those in charge of the estates of Augustus and his family. That includes Augustus, Livia, Tiberius, Antonia, and their children."

Serenius gestured at the tribune. "Have someone go knock on that door. Tell Hierax that *I* am here and want to talk to him."

Alexander stood back with Serenius as the tribune waved one of his legionaries forward. The man knocked once, twice. Then he beat on the door and yelled for it to be opened in the name of the *epistrategos*. There was a moment of silence as the legionary placed his ear on the door to listen to what was happening inside the house.

He turned back to his tribune and Serenius. "There's a lot of thumping and bumping. I can't be sure, but he may be trying to make a run for it."

The tribune turned to the *epistrategos* and raised his eyebrows.

Serenius answered. "I've had enough of him. Kick that door in."

Apparently there had been a board placed across the door to lock it from the inside, but that wasn't enough to stop some determined legionaries. With a few kicks and shoulder shoves, the door finally crashed in. Alexander did not wait, but pushed his way past the legionaries.

Thud. The noise was soft, but enough to cause him to look up. The sound had come from the top of an inside staircase, the sound of a door closing.

Oh no. Not the roof again!

Alexander ran up the stairs as fast as he could. At the top was a trap door that had been closed. He shoved on it and it budged a little, but it remained closed. There must have been some sort of latch holding it shut. Well, Alexander wasn't going to let that stop him. He *wanted* that land agent and he was going have him.

A legionary ran up the stairs to help, but nearly knocked Alexander over with his round cavalry shield which he was holding in front of him. It took precious moments for the legionary to extricate his forearm and pass the shield back down the stairs and out of the way. Once finally free of his shield, the legionary moved onto the same step as Alexander.

"I think the two of us can get it open," he said. "Put your shoulder up against the door next to mine. When I say go, push as hard as you can."

It worked. When they both gave a big push, the latch broke and the trap door flew open. Alexander raced onto the roof and turned a full circle, but Hierax was not there. Immediately, he cast his eyes further. The land agent could not have gone that far. But where?

Most of the houses here were not as close together as the ones in Karanis. It would not be as easy to leap from roof to roof. But that wasn't quite true, was it? The very next house to the west *was* close enough, and so was the house on the other side of that. – and, look, that far house had an outdoor staircase that went down to the street.

Alexander didn't hesitate. He backed up and took a running leap onto the next roof. An older couple were there taking the air. "Did you see Hierax? Was he just here?" Alexander asked in Greek. Based on their blank looks, he guessed that they probably only spoke Egyptian. There was no one on the closest roof so he walked a circuit studying the roof of every nearby house looking for any sign of the land agent. He saw nothing.

There was no sign of Hierax, *but* ... wait was that a jingling sound near that next house? -- jingle, like the clinking of coins? Once again, Alexander backed up and took a racing leap across to the next roof. There was no one on the roof, but there was an outdoor staircase leading down to the street. He hurried to the edge and looked over, trying to slow his breathing so he could listen. At first, he heard nothing. Then there was the clinking of metal again. Could that be Hierax? Alexander spun around trying to see in all directions.

There. There was another external staircase on a distant house and a man was ascending it. Alexander squinted in the bright sunlight. Was that him? Could it be that the land agent had jumped to this roof, descended the stairs, run down the street, and now was ascending another set of stairs?

Alexander couldn't be sure what to think. That might be that man's own house and have nothing to do with an escaping Hierax. ... Then, in the distance the man climbing onto the roof turned, saw Alexander looking at him and visibly started. Alexander watched as the man seemed to cast a panicked look around him and then headed towards another rooftop. A *guilty look*, indeed.

What to do? There were not enough houses built close enough together to allow Alexander to leap from roof to roof in pursuit. But, if he ran down the stairs and headed in that direction, the land agent would have plenty of time to move across roofs or roads and hide. Alexander felt sure that if he took his eyes off

Hierax for even a moment, he would lose him. He bunched his fist. If only there was someone there to tackle the man, to knock him down.

Wait. To knock him down. Alexander glanced down at the throwing stick attached to his belt – the one hunters used for knocking down fowl. *Hunh.* That couldn't work, could it? Well, he might as well try.

Alexander pulled the throwing stick free from the belt strap, then he moved to the edge of the rooftop. The land agent was now four roofs over. Trying to remember everything he had been taught, Alexander placed his feet, eyed his target, swiveled his hips and flung the throwing stick at the man. ... and missed.

At least he missed the man Hierax, *but* the throwing stick did hit something. A large satchel that had been draped over the land agent's shoulder fell to the ground with the clink of coins, the same clink that Alexander thought he had heard earlier.

Hierax reached down and grabbed a box that had fallen from the satchel, a box filled with things that clinked. He spared time for a quick glance back at Alexander and then took off at a run probably headed for some stairs that Alexander couldn't see from where he stood. There was no way that Alexander could follow him, now without running down to the street and by that time it would be too late. Alexander could only clench his fists muttering imprecations as he watched the land agent slip away.

****

"It is not as bad as you think, Alexander," Serenius gave him a rough pat on the shoulder. "I know Hierax got away, but look at what we have found."

While Alexander had chased the land agent across the roofs, the *epistrategos* and his legionaries had been searching the house -- well, *ransacking* the house if the mess was any explanation for their actions.

The legionaries had not been able to follow Alexander across the roofs. Since they had donned their armor, they were just too bulky to make the leap. But fortunately his servant Amarantus had tracked the sound of him running and had appeared on the street below. Alexander directed him to the distant house to retrieve his throwing stick and whatever was in the satchel that Hierax had dropped. The land agent had escaped with that box and whatever had been clinking in it. Alexander assumed it was probably full of coins. The satchel Amarantus brought back, however, had been full of papyrus scrolls.

Back at the house of Hierax, Alexander and Ranti joined Serenius at a table where they were unsealing and sorting a number of papyrus scrolls.

Serenius continued. "These scrolls that the tribune and his men found here in the house appear to be the ones for the Lady Antonia's property. It will take awhile to sort through them, but I think this is what you said you needed most. Now these here..." Serenius waved a hand over a different pile, "...are the ones that your servant brought back with the satchel that Hierax had dropped on the rooftop. Again, it will take some time to study them, but I suspect these are a record of his shadier dealings, at least some of them."

Alexander grimaced. "Documents are good, very good, but there were no coins? Your men didn't find any coins? There should have been quite a lot since Hierax has been collecting both rents and taxes."

Serenius smiled and shook his head. "No, no coins were found here. I think Hierax got away with them. It's a good thing your family is rich so you'll be able to make up for all the lost tax money."

"Uh, uh," Alexander shook his head back at the *epistrategos*. "Don't even think about it. I will make up any rent money that he has stolen from the Lady Antonia, but..." he held up a finger,

"Neither Antonia nor I ever committed, in any way, to collecting taxes. Someone else will have to take that responsibility."

He cut in as the *epistrategos* started to object. "If you press this, Serenius, I will write to Antonia and suggest that she ask Augustus why his Prefect is holding *her personally* responsible for collecting *his* taxes. I can pretty well guess how that will end."

Serenius didn't seem too upset by this. He just smiled and held up a hand. "Well played, Alexander. I suppose it is too early to worry about that anyway. We don't know how much tax money is actually missing. Plus there is always the good chance that my legionaries will catch up with the *nothus*."

"What about Sabinus?" Alexander asked. "It's pretty likely that Hierax killed his bastard son Kronion. The *strategos* Dionysodoros seemed to imply that Sabinus would go after Hierax because of the boy. I wonder if Sabinus knows something that will help us find Hierax."

Serenius shook his head and shrugged. "Yeah, I thought the same thing, but Sabinus seems have disappeared, too. Well, maybe not *disappeared* exactly, but he is definitely not around. I don't know if he has any idea where Hierax may have gone, but … I suspect Antonia's freedman will be better off if *we* find him before Sabinus does."

****

"Master, it is strange. Our first great mystery in Egypt turned out not to be much of a mystery at all. We searched many villages and the Great Labyrinth for the missing land agent and it turned out that he was never actually missing at all. … He was just tricky and a liar."

Alexander was preparing to leave Tebtunis at last. It had taken several days to review the scrolls that Hierax had left behind, plus arrange for the inventory and disposition of the goods they had found in the secret warehouse. It would take time to figure out how much of Antonia's property had actually been lost and how much had been recovered. Honestly, Alexander found the whole business depressing.

He sighed and rubbed his face. "That man made a fool out of me several times over, Ranti. I suppose that is what can happen to a stranger in a strange land. I may have been born in Alexandria, but I am really an outsider here. That made it easy for Hierax to lay a false trail. ... At least it isn't just me that he has fooled. The *epistrategos's* legionaries still haven't found that pile of *stercus*."

Amarantus thought for a moment then said, "Master, you have recovered the papyrus records, and the goods in the secret warehouse, and chased away the corrupt land agent ... but you did not solve the greatest mystery of all."

Alexander tilted his head and frowned. "And what is that, Ranti?"

"Master, why would anyone steal that evil goat?"

18. The New Alabarch

To Ti. Claudius Nero in Rome from G. Julius Alexander in Alexandria

Be glad that I write this letter in Latin and the Roman style and not in the Greek Egyptian fashion. Otherwise, it would be so cryptic that you would surely have no idea what I am saying.

If you were here with me, you would be resting on a barge or sitting on a donkey. Yes, my friend, I have spent much time bouncing up and down on a donkey. Amarantus has assured me that I look ridiculous, but I defy any Roman to maintain a mien of dignitas while riding on a donkey.

Truly, you will accuse me of weaving a fanciful tale, but I can tell you with all honesty that in the past twenty days I have been in a boat attacked by a herd of hippopotami, chased a villain by leaping across roof tops, forced into a melee fight on the side of a crocodile god, and been tied up in a small shack with an evil goat.

Preposterous you may say? Since papyrus is not costly in Egypt, I have the luxury to write everything down and tell you things as if we were sitting in a Forum tavern sipping wine.

Alexander paused in his writing and flexed his wrist that had become stiff. This was turning out to be a very long letter. Claudius, he felt sure, would be amused by every word of it. Also, Alexander had to admit that it felt good to be able to share with a friend all that had happened to him -- even if it was just in writing.

He had no friend in Alexandria to whom he could talk, at least not yet. Titus Serenius the *epistrategos*? No, he had already said that he resented Alexander for becoming the next Alabarch. Sabinus? No. He was certainly an interesting character, but Alexander just didn't know him well enough to entrust him with his personal thoughts. Besides Sabinus and the *strategos* Dion were both back in the Arsinoite Nome and Alexander had not interest in returning there anytime soon.

Could he confide in his brother, Philo? *Ummm*, not... yet. They hardly knew each other since Alexander had spent most of his life living in Rome. He hoped that would change. It would be good to have a friend and ally in his brother.

He returned to his letter.

> *I will write to your lady mother Antonia separately to tell her of the disappearance of her freedman, Hierax, the former land agent. It was my intent to bind the fool and place him on the first ship for Rome. However, so far he has managed to evade me, the legionaries that have tracked him, and all the port authorities as well.*
>
> *Write to me as soon as you can and tell me all that you are doing. Give my many greetings to your brother Germanicus and also to our friend Agrippa. I think it is safe for me to write to him now that I am so far away. Surely, not even Agrippa would take a ship all the way to Alexandria just to ask for a loan.*
>
> *We must still hold out hope that someday you will be able to come to Alexandria to visit me. Or, that my father can spare me and I can return to Rome for a visit.*

"Alexander, it is time."

Alexander looked up from his letter, and stood when he saw

his father gesturing towards the door.

Amarantus approached and carefully adjusted every fold of Alexander's long linen toga. Of course, he had to wear a toga for his formal meeting with the Prefect. Alexander would be expected to make a stately procession while keeping the voluminous folds carefully in place.

His father checked him over, then reached out and gently touched the side of Alexander's face. "I believe you are ready, my son. You are ready for anything."

Then slowly with the greatest of *gravitas*, Alexander's father gathered his own toga and led the way to the office of the new Prefect named Marcus Magius Maximus. Their house in Alexandria was not far for the administrative offices of the prefect. As they walked Alexander took his father's arm.

"Father, what do you know about this new Prefect?"

"Not much other than the fact that he possesses the rather astonishing cognomen of *Maximus*. Marcus Magius Maximus. The first two names, the praenomen and nomen, come from the family. You can't really help those, but who chooses to call himself *"the Greatest?"*

His father quirked an eyebrow at Alexander that elicited a smile in return. Alexander suspected that his father was simply using humor to stop him from feeling too nervous. Certainly, being called to swear the oath for the Alabarch would have been a nerve racking proposition anyway. But now Alexander had to do it before a new Prefect of Egypt. Magius Maximus had only been installed a few weeks earlier and so far was receiving mixed reports from those who had met him.

Alexander and his father had not been sure what to expect before they entered Magius's office. They quickly learned that the new Prefect was not one to waste time on hospitality – or even courtesy.

"Gaius Julius Alexander, the Elder," Magius stated as

Alexander's father gave the new Prefect a courteous bow of his head. The Prefect looked past him. "...And the Younger. -- Augustus's own choice to handle his gold."

That did not appear to be a question, so Alexander simply said "Your Excellency," and bowed his head. There wasn't much else one could do while wearing a toga except a dignified nod.

The Prefect gave Alexander a quick once over and then said, "I understand that you took some time to deal with the Lady Antonia's estates." His voice went up slightly at the end so Alexander assumed this was meant as a question for him, so he answered.

"Yes. I have spent the last nearly three weeks on this. Before I left Rome, the Lady Antonia appointed me as the procurator for her estates here. In Egypt, this is known as an *epitropos*. The responsibilities of the *epitropos* are vast and Antonia's properties are also vast and required a personal visit. It seemed best to do this first since the Lady is waiting for a report from me."

The Prefect responded, "I understand that you encountered some problems, particularly with her former land agent, who I understand was also her freedman. Do you have this all resolved now?"

Alexander tried not to grimace when he replied. "It is mostly resolved, but not completely, your Excellency. I was able to expose that this Hierax, the land agent, had been stealing from the Lady Antonia, and also from many of the farmers around Lake Moeris. I have been able to recover most of the records and physical goods, but Hierax has successfully disappeared along with a box of silver and gold coins that did not belong to him."

"*Hunh*," the Prefect said, "The only viable port to return to Rome is here. If he comes north to Alexandria to try to take ship, we should be able to put our hands on him without too much trouble. I'll notify the legions and port authorities to keep an eye out for him."

He gave a dismissive wave of his hand. "For now, I need

you to put all of that aside. The Alabarch is going to have bigger issues to address."

The Prefect turned to Alexander's father, who was the current Alabarch. "Have you told him about the problem he will be facing now?"

"I have *not,* your Excellency. My son has mostly been away since his return in August and I could not be sure what plans or changes you would wish to make as the new Prefect."

The Prefect nodded. "It is just as well, because I *will* be making changes to the duties of the Alabarch. So, Alexander, neither of us has been in Egypt for long. Let's begin with what I know.

"Rome's *only* gold mines are located here in Egypt. No doubt, the First Citizen has his legions out looking for new sources of gold and silver, but right now this is it. *All* of Rome's new gold comes from Egypt. Augustus *needs* these mines to provide a steady stream of income to him in Rome. Currently, *they do not.* Part of the gold being mined is disappearing somehow. Exposing and resolving that will now be *your* responsibility."

Huh? Alexander looked at his father who gave him a small nod in return. He supposed his father may have hinted at this, but this was Alexander's first confirmation that he was being brought in to resolve a problem – apparently, a big problem. He turned to Magius Maximus.

"Your Excellency, are things really so bad?"

"They *were* not that bad," the Prefect replied, "at least not originally, but the problem has been growing steadily. -- And by problem I am talking about gold shipments that have gone completely missing as well as ones that are short of what appears on the manifest. Since I have arrived in Alexandria, I have made inquiries. No one seems to be able to tell me where or how the gold is disappearing. Instead of getting answers, I have been getting crazy stories about curses and magicians casting spells to make the gold disappear."

The prefect raised his eyes toward the roof and shook his head. "This last batch of gold we received from the mines was unexpectedly small. Augustus is *not happy*. We need to find out why this is happening. ... or rather, *you, Alexander, you* need to go to the mines and find out why."

Alexander's father frowned and said, "That is not really the traditional role of the Alabarch. We weigh, measure, and test the purity of gold. The Alabarch does not manage the mining or transport."

"That is correct," Magius Maximus replied, "Or at least, that *was* correct. I have enough to do as a new Prefect that I need to delegate this problem to someone else. Being new, it is difficult for me to know who will be trustworthy and capable. I have read Augustus's commendation of young Alexander here. *He* thinks that Alexander is reliable and therefore *I* shall think that, too."

The prefect turned his attention from the father to the son.

"So Alexander, before you take the oath I need you to understand that I am granting new plenipotentiary powers, at least for the short term. The function of the Alabarchy will no longer be just about staying here in Alexandria weighing and assaying Rome's gold. I need you to get out to the mines; get on site. Find out what or who is delaying Rome's gold shipments ... and *Fix it*. Are you prepared to do this?"

This was *unexpected*. Alexander lowered his eyes to the floor and thought. He had *not* wanted to be the Alabarch when it was just assaying gold. Why would he want it now when it required riding around in the desert looking for gold thieves? ... but, he could hardly refuse when it was Augustus himself who appointed him to this position. ... and he did sort of think it might be interesting to investigate the problem of the missing gold.

Alexander looked for guidance from his father who appeared to be bemused. But then his father slowly nodded his approval. Alexander paused, took a deep breath, and looked the new Prefect directly in the eye. "Yes, your Excellency, I am prepared to do what needs to be done to get the gold flowing again."

The Prefect let out an audible breath. Suddenly, Alexander realized that Magius Maximus had been nervous as well. Augustus always *personally* chose the Prefect of Egypt. The Roman Senate did not have a say in this one appointment the way they did in the naming of procurators for Rome's other provinces. For Magius Maximus, this made him one of the most influential men from Rome. It also meant, however, that the actions of the Prefect were closely observed. There was no room for incompetence, and missing gold shipments would not be tolerated for long.

Magius Maximus gave Alexander another appraising look. Who could tell if he liked what he saw? The Prefect gave a quick nod of his head and said, "Are you ready now to swear the oath of the Alabarch?"

"Yes," Alexander replied glancing again at his father for moral support. "I am ready."

After that, things proceeded swiftly. The mantle of the Alabarch was passed from his father's shoulders to his own. Magius Maximus provided some specific information to help him to pursue the missing gold shipments. Alexander noted that there was a coolness to the prefect's manner, or, at least a decided aloofness. It was clear that, for whatever reason, the Prefect was being careful to maintain some distance from his new Alabarch. Why? At the moment Alexander found he didn't really care.

He had enough to do. There were still many loose ends with managing the Lady Antonia's estates. There were his family's own properties that he would need to learn to manage as well. His father was ill and Alexander could not guess how much longer his father would be there to guide him.

Now, as quickly as he could Alexander would need to learn the traditional duties of the Alabarch, those that revolved around the weighing and assaying of Rome's gold. Besides all that, he now had to discover who was *stealing* Augustus's gold. That was … *a lot* for one young man who had only been in Egypt a few weeks.

Alexander's mind felt a little overwhelmed as he exited the palace of the Prefect. His father was tired and had his servants take him home in a carry chair, but Alexander had too much nervous energy to stay still for more than a moment. Instead, he walked towards the harbor enjoying the sharp breeze that rustled his hair and clothing.

Then Alexander's thoughts narrowed onto the last thing the Prefect had said -- the most curious thing. Apparently, the incoming reports, even those from Romans of rank, all said the same thing. They all blamed an Egyptian magician for the lost gold shipments. –And not just any magician, they attributed the missing gold to *magic -- Egyptian dark magic -- spells, curses and the evil eye.*

Some of the reports came with suggestions for how Alexander could track down the magician. None of the reports, however, seemed to have any advice on what to do once he came face to face with an evil magician. Magic, curses, spells. Alexander ran a hand through his hair and told himself that the Lord would protect him from this dark Egyptian magic. At least he hoped so.

Hunh. Dark Magic. Alexander shuddered as a chill ran through him. A gust of wind blew in from the harbor, caught at his robe, and billowed out the voluminous folds of linen … then whipped them back with the ominous snap of a toga in the wind.

Epilogue

Running. Running. Panting. Rope sandals slapping against the bare soles of his feet.

How had it come to this? He had been so clever, hadn't he? Every year, he had taken just a little off the top. Always, always he made sure the records looked right. No one should have suspected a thing – not a thing at all.

He was her own freedman, part of her *familia*. Her loyalty should have been *to him*. Why had she sent that *boy* to Egypt?

Curse that *nothus*. He should have hit him harder when he had the chance.

That noise. Getting louder. There were more behind the one chasing him now. *Run faster.* His feet splashed into a mud puddle. Ahead was a small irrigation channel; he leapt over it. The pounding behind him was drawing closer. He needed to concentrate on escape, but his mind kept wandering back to the *why* of it all.

Why? Why? It couldn't be that he had gone too far, could it? Maybe he had gotten a little greedy – but only just a little. And he supposed Kronion might have been a mistake. It had been risky to mess with the priest; something like that could offend the crocodile god. Still, Kronion had gotten indiscreet so he had to go.

His legs were tiring and he stumbled and fell, knees sinking into the mud. Then he staggered back to his feet as quickly as could. The herd of hippopotami was still running behind him.

What had set them off? It must have been that noise. *Someone* must have made that loud crashing noise that had startled them. But that made no sense.

This place should have been safe. After the warehouse had been discovered, everyone had expected him to go north – to Alexandria. So he had come *south*. No one knew about *this* secret place. Well, Kronion had known, but Kronion was gone now. Who would Kronion have told anyway?

Time. He just needed a little more time and then he would be able to sneak onto a ship. A bribe should take care of everything. But bribe with what? He had dropped his box back there behind him -- the one with all the silver and gold coins he had been collecting. He needed to go back and retrieve that box. Just as soon he outran this hippopotamus.

Look, over there. Not far ahead was the Nile. If he could just make it that far, then perhaps he could hide in the reeds. Surely, the hippopotamus wouldn't find him there.

The stomping of the creatures behind was loud – so very loud. He tried to run faster, but he was panting too hard. Maybe, maybe he should … *Aghhh*, pushed hard from behind, he fell forward.

No! No, this can't be happening.

He pressed his palms into the mud trying to push himself up. A massive four-toed foot came down on his back. He felt shock and disbelief. But he knew he could get out of this; he was good at getting out of things. He was sure he could. … There was an audible crack as his spine snapped and then there was only darkness.

A hippopotamus stretched open its massive jaw and let out a resounding roar.

Up near the fields, not too far away, stood the big curly-haired man with the Roman nose. He had done what he had come here to do. Now, he was just waiting ... watching as the great beasts continued their run for the Nile and the body of the former land agent was pressed deeper and deeper into the mud.

In his hand, he held a box that he had just found. When he picked it up, it had made clinking, metallic sounds. Ahead, the last hippopotamus ran past the fallen land agent and submerged into the river Nile. The big, curly-haired man nodded his satisfaction, shook the clinking box ... *and then he smiled.*

... and not too far away on the banks of the Nile, two unblinking yellow eyes had watched the stampeding beasts ... and the man who fell. That fool had thought he could take that which belonged to a god and survive. No, he would not be rising again, not now, not ever.

The large crocodile seemed to nod its head. Then it slipped down the bank into the Nile and began swimming north in the direction of the large temple, the one that was south of the lake.

HISTORICAL NOTE

This novel has been built around a number of actual papyrus documents and artifacts that date to Egypt's Roman period (30 B.C. to the Muslim conquest in 639 A.D.) Papyri, Karanis glass, mummy portraits and more have been excavated from what was the Arsinoite Nome and is now called the Fayuum. The papyri are a mish-mash of genres, events, and dates that rarely tell a coherent story, but are useful for inspiring a sense of the people, place, and time.

The Author's Note at the beginning of the book reviews the two mysteries from the village of Tebtunis including the petition from the *"legitimate priests"* against the *"bastards from the temple"* (P. Tebt. II.302). There was also the petition from another crocodile priest about men who invaded his home and beat his brother with *xulons*, or sticks (P.Tebt. II.304).

Horse thieves and cattle rustlers did exist in ancient Egypt and so petitions regarding missing animals were not uncommon. There really were complaints of a missing red calf and a wheat-colored mare from Karanis (P.Karanis 523 and 527 respectively). However, there was no record of a missing evil goat.

The ululating castanet dancers from Chapter 14 were inspired by a papyrus contract to hire Isidora and two other castanet dancers to perform at a festival in Philadelphia. (P.Corn. inv. II 26 at Cornell University).

Poor Nemesion from the village of Philadelphia did have his brother make a petition claiming that some official was *"making him disturbed"* and *"wearing him down"* (P.Mich.inv. 1638). In that case, the official was *"Papei, on account of the chief of the armed guards,"* but

Papei became Hierax the land agent for this book and the missing cattle were added.

Drawing on a limestone ostracon of the crocodile god Sobek, from the artisan village of Deir el-Medina. The picture was originally created using the pigments of red-orange, yellow, blue, and black

Source: Jacques Vandier d'Abbadie. *Catalogue Des Ostraca Figurés de Deir el Médineh*, 2 (1937), no. 2650, Plate LXXVI

--Kronos and the Crocodile God--

The Egyptian deity that took the form of a crocodile, or a man with a crocodile head, was known in the Egyptian language as Sobk or Sobek, and in Greek as Souchos. Some villages had variations on the name such as Petesouchos in Karanis or Soknebtunis in Tebtunis. These were considered to be different incarnations of the one god.

By the first century B.C., virtually all Egyptian gods had a Greek god equivalent: Horus = Apollo, Thoth = Hermes, Hathor = Aphrodite, Taweret = Athena, etc. One notable exception was the crocodile god Sobek/Souchos who for some unknown reason was not equated with any Greek or Roman god even though Souchos was the official god for the entire Arsinoite Nome.

Except!! *In one place, at one time, Souchos was equated with the Greek god Kronos.* In the village of Tebtunis, in the first and second centuries A.D., Kronos became a separate manifestation of the crocodile god Soknebtunis and was represented as a crocodile or as a man with a crocodile head. Kronos had his own priests and his own *stolistes* who were the attendants who dressed the statue of the god.

> **when certain bastards from the temple asked for leave to cultivate the land before** . . . , late epistrategus of the Heptanomis and Arsinoite nome, ... he reserved the land for **us, the legitimate priests**, according to the report of the trial in our possession. (P. Tebt. II.302 - dated 71-72 A.D.)

Tebtunis papyrus, no. II.302 (dated 71-72 A.D.) was a petition against the *"bastards from the temple"* who were trying to muscle in on the land profits of the *legitimate priests*. In Roman Egypt, a *legitimate* priest had to prove he had inherited an Egyptian priestly blood line, and then had to petition to be granted permission for the two physical signs of a legitimate Egyptian priest which were circumcision and having his head completely shaved.

The suggestion that the *"bastards from the temple"* in P.Tebt. II.302 could be identified with the priests of Kronos is completely fictional.

There is no evidence for an Egyptian priest, legitimate or otherwise, having a partially shaved head such as a *tonsure*. The practice of shaving a circle on top of the head was later widespread among Catholic monks, but there is no historical record of where or how the practice began.

The tonsure of the priests of Kronos is the author's imagination of how to explain the identity of the *"bastards from the temple."* Perhaps these were priests who were considered to be illegitimate because they could not prove a hereditary priestly bloodline and therefore could not legally fully shave their heads.

[The evidence for Kronos being a crocodile god comes from nine papyri, all excavated from Tebtunis (P.Tebt. 294, 295, 298, 299, 302, 309, 311, 598, 599). These papyri are in the public domain and available online at: https://archive.org/details/tebtunispapyri02univuoft]

--The Arsinoite Nome--

In both the Greek Ptolemaic and the Roman periods, the area around Lake Moeris was an administrative division designated the Arsinoite nome. In the first century, the nome was particularly important for two reasons. First, it was the source of much of the wheat that was shipped to Rome to feed its million-plus residents.

Second, it was an area where Greek and, later, Roman soldiers were given land and settled after they retired. Agriculture and settlement were made possible because of an elaborate canal and irrigation system that was carefully constructed and maintained.

By the third and fourth centuries, the Roman central government of Egypt had stopped the expensive process of maintaining the canals. Most of the villages had to be abandoned as the once productive farmland quickly reverted back to desert.

There is no surviving map of the Arsinoite nome as it would have existed in the first century A.D. It has been speculated that there were over a hundred villages in the nome, but only a handful of these have been positively located through archeological digs including the villages: Philadelphia, Karanis, Theadelphia, and Tebtunis.

--Antonia Minor and Egypt--

Antonia Minor, (36 B.C. – 37 A.D.) was the daughter of Marcus Antonius (Mark Anthony) and Octavia Minor who was the sister of Octavian (later known as Augustus). Her older sister was Antonia Major, or Antonia the Elder. Neither girl ever knew their father who was already having an affair with Queen Cleopatra VII in Egypt by the time Antonia Minor was born.

Alexander (the Alabarch) was the *epitropos* for Antonia Minor in Egypt (Josephus, *Jewish Antiquities*, 19.276). This was a type of procurator, or administrator of her *ousia*, or her combined estates. The scope of Alexander's responsibilities as *epitropos* is unknown, but almost certainly it was a position of importance because Antonia herself was politically important in Rome. She was also one the largest landholders in Egypt in the early first century.

Antonia Minor had a strong personal relationship with her uncle Augustus and her brother-in-law the Emperor Tiberius. She was the mother of the future emperor Claudius and grandmother of the emperors Gaius (Caligula) and of Nero through the latter's adoption.

Numerous extant papyri from contracts to tax and census lists indicate that Antonia Minor (also called Antonia the wife of Drusus) owned extensive properties in Egypt. There is no comprehensive list of all of Antonia Minor's properties. The map at the front of the book shows Antonia's properties that can be documented with extant evidence *with one caveat*. Some of the papyri refer to *Antonia* and do not specify whether they refer to Antonia *Major* or Antonia *Minor*.

There is no evidence that Antonia Minor herself ever visited Egypt. However, when her oldest son Germanicus visited Egypt in 19 A.D. he was received with a startling degree of adoration and acclamations (*Select Papyri, II.211*).

Drawing on a limestone ostracon of two men stick fighting, Deir el-Medina. This is an outline but the picture originally was done in the pigments of red-orange, yellow and black.

This appears to be *the last extant piece of historical evidence* for Egyptian stick fighting and dates to ca. 1300-1200 B.C.

Source: Jacques Vandier d'Abbadie. *Catalogue Des Ostraca Figurés de Deir el Médineh*, 2 (1937), no. 2448, Plate LXII

--Ancient Egyptian Stick Fighting--

In the second century A.D., a priest of the temple of the crocodile god Soknebtunis, filed an official complaint that his brother had been *assaulted by men using sticks*. In the papyrus, the Greek word used for stick was ξύλον, transliterated as *ksulon* or *xulon*. The Greek could mean wooden stick, stave, or cudgel. (Tebtunis Papyri, II.304, 167-8 A.D.)

During the time of the pharaohs, Egyptians employed stick fighting both in the military and apparently for athletic competitions. The evidence for stick fighting comes from a handful of illustrations that have been carved into the walls of various tombs or painted on ostraca (broken pottery shards). The earliest known image of Egyptian stick fighting dates back to the fifth dynasty of the Old Kingdom, ca. 2500 B.C. Other images date to the Middle and New Kingdom (up to 1200 B.C.)

- Pyramid relief carving of Sahure (Old Kingdom, V dynasty, c. 2500 BC) (near modern Cairo)
- Three tombs in the necropolis of Beni Hasan (Middle Kingdom, 1900 -1700 B.C.) 12 miles south of modern city Minya)
- Tomb of Merire II at El Amarna, c. 1350 (ca 200 miles south of Cairo)
- Tomb of Kheruef, no. 192 at Thebes (New Kingdom, c. 1350 B.C.) (near modern city of Luxor)
- Drawing on ostracon from Deir el Medineh (no. 2448) (New Kingdom, ca. 1300-1200 B.C.) (near modern city of Luxor)

The word that the Egyptians used for the stick or for stick fighting during the time of the pharaohs is unknown. There is also no clear line of evidence that the art of stick fighting continued into the Greek and Roman period (332 B.C. to 6th century A.D.). In fact, the author has found no conclusive evidence for any type of formalized stick fighting at all after about 1200 B.C. However, it seems unlikely that the Egyptians would suddenly forget or deny two thousand years of cultural traditions. So I think there was probably some type of continuity and stick fighting was still practiced into the Greek and Roman periods.

In *modern* Egypt, stick fighting exists as both a sport and a ritualized dance for men. The stick is called by the Arabic word *tahtib* and is a term that would *not* have been in use in Egypt before the Muslim conquest in the 600s A.D. There is a gap of literally two to three thousand years between the last evidence for Egyptian stick fighting and the later evidence for Arabic *tahtib* fighting.

Since it is unknown if Egyptian stick fighting existed in the Roman period, I have used my author imagination to recreate it.

--Terms of Address--

In petitions to officials and in private letters, one may occasionally find terms of rank and address used such as is indicated below.

Most illustrious (Greek: *lamprotate*) is used to address the Egyptian **prefect**. [Source: P. Karanis 529, petition to a prefect, dated 232-236 A.D.)

Most excellent, or **Excellency** (Greek: *kratistos*) is used to address an ***epistrategos*** [Source: P. Karanis 531, official letter to an epistrategos, dated 174 A.D.]

Kurie (Greek: vocative case of *kurios*) – The Greek word *kurios* (lord) was used frequently and in different contexts in Roman Egypt. For example, Jews used *ho kurios* to refer *The Lord*, their god. Husbands and wives of no great social standing referred to each other as *kurios, kuria* meaning that they are master or mistress of the household.

In the papyri, the term *kurie* is used as a polite form address to a man of higher rank. *Kurie* should *not* be equated with the medieval *My Lord* which was used to address nobility. Some papyri translate *kurie* as *'sir.'* Neither *'Lord'* nor *'Sir'* convey what the original Greek probably meant. It was intended as an address showing respect. I have decided not to translate *kurie* as *Lord* because the expression could be too easily misinterpreted.

- When Alexander refers to his god using *kurios*, I will use **The Lord**.

- When persons of lower rank refer to Alexander using *kurios*, or lord, I will use the Greek form **kurie**. It is intended as an address showing respect.

Master (Greek: *despotes*, and especially in the vocative case *despota*). I have found no evidence in the papyri that slaves addressed their owner as *Despota*, or *Master*. It appears a slave simply called his/her owner by their given name. For Alexander's fictional world, slaves will call their owner Master and address anyone else who outranks them with the respectful *kurie*.

Note that some terms such as *'your honor'* as a form of address may appear in English translations of papyri, but these words are not actually in the original Greek text. They are not authentic to the period.

--About the Images--

Works of fiction are not usually accompanied by images – but perhaps they should be. Everything from photography to the Web has made the world much more visually oriented.

None of the portraits in this book are actual mummy portraits from Egypt. All of them, however, were created (by the author) to be similar to real mummy portraits from Roman Egypt.

Most of the other images are from Library of Congress, or, from early twentieth century books that are now out of copyright. Two images, the hippo mosaic and bust of Antonia Minor, are digital photos taken by the author during a trip to the Roman Forum. Others images such as the olive press, the flat roofed house, or Philadelphia are the product of the author's imagination and very limited artistic ability.

All of the images in the paperback version of this book are in black & white because the cost for publishing in color was prohibitive. The ebook version has color pictures.

--Alexander the Alabarch--

Alexander of Alexandria, also known as Alexander the Alabarch, was an historical person who lived during the first half of the first century A.D. He is known through several ancient sources including the first century historian Flavius Josephus (The *Jewish War* and *Jewish Antiquities*), one book by Alexander's famous philosopher brother Philo of Alexandria (*On Animals*), and several papyrus scrolls found in Egypt. One papyrus was written by Alexander's real-life freedman named Amarantus.

Alabarch: When Augustus conquered Queen Cleopatra VII, Egypt became Rome's first and only source of new gold. Since it was easier to transport small gold bars, than large bags of bronze and silver coins, gold became essential for supporting the legions throughout the growing Roman Empire.

There are eleven surviving historical references to Alabarchs in Egypt. Five are literary references in Josephus's *Jewish Antiquities,* one is from a list of names on a Greek papyrus, three are from Greek inscriptions, and two are from Latin legal texts.

Two Alabarchs, Alexander and Demetrius, were Jews from Alexandria. The Alabarch Mausōlos prayed to the Greek god Poseidon, and Alabarch Anastasios was a Christian.

Only one of the eleven ancient sources explains the duties of the Alabarch. In his *Edict XI,* Emperor Justinian describes the historical role of the Alabarch in order to explain why he has decided to eliminate the function of the Alabarch and switch the duties to his Treasury Department.

> 2. 2. ... But it was wholly necessary to have an overseer of gold, at that time it was the prefect of Alexandria and who also at the time was given a magistracy as was customary, at that time it was the alabarchy, but who now and in the future time will be our dedicated treasury, so that no one assaying gold (literally: testing gold by fire) will receive profit or gain.
>
> 3. Thus, moreover, the justness of this law will be applied with careful diligence, which our magistracy is undertaking, in case that **the assaying of gold is a sacred duty of our alabarchy** of the prefect, or a sacred duty of himself to bestow freely.... [Justinian, *Edict* XI]

See more at: http://kassevans.com/Alexander/Alabarch.html

The Alabarch was responsible for *obrussa* which was Latin for testing metal by fire, or assaying the purity of gold. After testing, the gold was shaped into a bar and then stamped with the assayer's name. It is possible that the Alabarch had additional related duties beyond assaying and stamping gold.

Relationship to Imperials: According to the historian Josephus, Alexander was *old friends* with the Emperor Claudius and the *epitropos* (procurator) for Antonia Minor. Through his acquaintance with them, Alexander was likely familiar with other members of the imperial family, such as Claudius's older brother Germanicus.

Some of the Roman administrative positions in Egypt were direct appointments by Augustus and subsequent emperors. This included the Prefect, several members of his cabinet, and possibly each *epistrategos* who was required to have the rank of *eques*. Given the importance of Egypt's gold supply, it is possible that the Alabarch was appointed by the Emperor directly, too.

Alexander's Brothers: In his book *On Animals*, Philo describes a dialogue he had with his brother Lysimachus which also mentioned their other brother Alexander the Alabarch. Philo and Lysimachus are discussing their nephew, Tiberius Julius Alexander, who was the son of Alexander the Alabarch.

In that context Lysimachus makes the rather startling observation that:

> (2) he [Ti. Jul. Alexander] is my uncle (mother's brother), and my father-in-law as well. As you are not unaware, his daughter is engaged to be my wife. [Philo, *On Animals*, 2]

Some scholars have assumed that Philo, Lysimachus, and Alexander (the Alabarch) are full brothers by blood. If all three men had the same mother and father, then the quote from (2) above is ridiculous since a full blood relationship would preclude Lysimachus from being the nephew and son-in-law of Ti. Jul. Alexander.

This relationship was *entirely possible* through both Roman and Jewish law, if Philo, Lysimachus, and Alexander the Alabarch were *not blood brothers* with the same mother and father. Alexander and Philo may have been, but Lysimachus was probably adopted, a step-sibling, or an in-law sibling equivalent.

<u>Relationship to Judea:</u> Alexander the Alabarch had the gates of the Jerusalem temple gold and silver plated. He married his oldest son Marcus to the oldest daughter of King Agrippa I of Judea named Berenike.

The historical sources indicate that Alexander was a very wealthy and important man in the first century. His influence spanned the Alexandrian, Roman, and Judean worlds.

For readers interested in learning more about Alexander, or in viewing images from this book, I invite you to visit the Web site at http://kassevans.com/Alexander.

Kass Evans | Toga in the Wind 299

Some of the characters in this book will be returning in *A Toga in Time* (Alexander the Alabarch, 4)

 Alexander the Alabarch	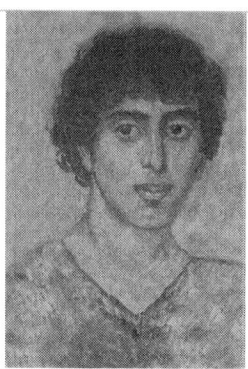 Amarantus, slave	 Leah of Judea

 Sabinus, Roman citizen	 Indike of Crocodilopolis	 Titus Serenius, *epistrategos*

From the Author

Thank you for reading my second novel.

Your time is precious and I appreciate you spending it with Alexander the Alabarch.

If you have any comments, questions, or suggestions about Alexander, please leave a few words on Amazon or Goodreads.

I am particularly interested to know what you thought of the images.

Kass Evans
mail@KassEvans.com

****

Other books In the Series
Alexander the Alabarch

1. *A Toga of a Different Color* (2018)
2. *A Toga in the Forum: Two Short Stories* (2018)
3. *A Toga in the Wind* (2021)
4. *A Toga in Time* – After assuming his role as Alabarch, Alexander's first duty will be to face off with a magician who is causing gold to mysteriously disappear.

Made in the USA
Columbia, SC
01 December 2021